MORNINGSIDE HEIGHTS

NEW YORK STORIES

Joe Tsujimoto

Bamboo Ridge Press

ISBN 978-0-910043-78-6

This is issue #92 (Fall 2007) of *Bamboo Ridge, Journal of Hawai'i Literature and Arts* (ISSN 0733-0308).

Published by Bamboo Ridge Press
Printed in the United States of America
Indexed in the Humanities International Complete
Bamboo Ridge Press is a member of the Council of Literary Magazines and Presses (CLMP).

Cover: "Blue Makua" by Hal Lum; acrylic on paper, 18" x 24", 2005
Page 171: Excerpt from "Anger" reprinted by permission of Miki Yazawa Bunn

Typesetting and design: Wayne Kawamoto

Bamboo Ridge Press is a nonprofit, tax-exempt corporation formed in 1978 to foster the appreciation, understanding, and creation of literary, visual, or performing arts by, for, or about Hawai'i's people. This project was supported in part by the National Endowment for the Arts (NEA).

NATIONAL
ENDOWMENT
FOR THE ARTS

bamboo ridge press
Celebrating 30 years
of local literature

Bamboo Ridge is published twice a year. For subscription information, back issues, or a catalog, please contact:

Bamboo Ridge Press
P.O. Box 61781
Honolulu, HI 96839-1781
(808) 626-1481
brinfo@bambooridge.com
www.bambooridge.com

5 4 3 2 1   08 09 10 11 12

For Joe, Sully, and Monk,
and especially the Boss

ACKNOWLEDGEMENTS

First, I would like to thank the staff of Bamboo Ridge Press for their dedicated work, especially its very special editors, Darrell Lum and Eric Chock, who have done more for local literature than anyone else in island history, who have supported me and my work immeasurably, as have Joy Kobayashi-Cintrón, Wing Tek Lum, and Milton Kimura. I also want to thank Cathy Kawano-Ching, Carlyn Tani, Evelyn Kam, Ian McMillan, Sheryl Dare, and Steve Wagenseller for reading my work with a critical eye, and Hugh Mosher for his New York sketches. Further, I want to thank Joe Calnan for his practical advice. Finally, I would like to thank my wife Sharon, who had little choice but to read my work while in progress, enduring my grumpiness, and finally approving my finished drafts. I'm indebted to her patience and boundless support.

NIGHTWALK

When you come back, as you always do, even if to return
is to walk down one of the streets of your mind, you see
the street, as you feel the snow crush beneath your soles,
as you formerly did, and the sense of home, no longer your own,
yet changeless, is repossessed. New storefronts, new faces
are haunted by the old, and those that are old are too old
to recall yours, though there is a familiarity in your gesture
as you sweep with bare hands the inch-thick snow off the hood
of the car at the curb in front of Adolph's Deli, owned
by a Greek for the past ten years. The feel is unmistakable,
the light frosty crust on top of loose moist snow that clings
with the slightest of packing into an irregular ball of finger-
grooves. You see it speckled with soot under the lamplight and
drop it into the gutter, unused to the cold.

Up the side street you feel a different ache, at once giddy
desperate, and numb, and you know you wouldn't be here if
it weren't for the Boss's funeral, the promise to meet old
friends, who, like yourself, are blessed and cursed with the
same past. As you descend the stairs to the basement bar and
grill you are twenty-four years old again. Your mother,
in the second-story apartment across the street, still in
her fifties, can wait. Michael is tending bar, his liver,

like Tommy's, still intact. Fernando is drinking beer; he
won't drown in Sheepshead Bay for several years, next to Dondi
who will drink himself to death, his dog asleep, curled around
the pole of Dondi's bar stool. On leave, bent over the jukebox,
Manny and Young, the Chinese guy, play Dylan before shipping
out to Nam and tripwires. In come Florelle and Christine, their
cheeks bright with cold, still untouched by electrical fire.
The Boss, who will die of AIDS in California, is behind the
counter smoking a panatela, listening with his one good ear
to the basketball scores on the radio propped on top of the
register. "Well, how ya doin'?" he says, waddling round the
pillar, wiping his hand across the bib of his soiled apron.
Except for two white tufts above his ears he is bald and pink
like Santa Claus. They are all here. Inscribed in snow.
This is how you exorcise the living, those rude, cheerless
strangers who bump into you in the daylight.

MORNINGSIDE

The first time I ever saw my mother really cry was in the kitchen. I mean, she was sobbing, sitting on a chair, her winter coat still on, my younger sister stroking her lightly across the shoulders, saying, "C'mon, Mom. It'll be okay, Mom," neither of them looking at me. Two women. One in her late forties, the other twelve. I had just come in from the hallway and was standing by the refrigerator. Fascinated, really. The sounds she made were a little bit eerie. Funny. She never cried like that before. Not even when the old man died.

I suppose it was the way the vice principal spoke to my mother and the Methodist minister she brought along (to act as translator and intermediary). Hair the color of lead, no bigger than my mom, a fierce nose, lipstick painted wider than the corners of her pinched mouth. Her voice loud, harsh, even violent, as though avenging some patriotic wrong—smacking her puppy across the room having practiced his new-found hump on her knee—hell, it was anybody's guess. All I recall was the anger and spite hurled across the desk at the two innocent, ashen-faced adults—without motive: that's what impressed me the most. Dumbfounded, half believing, how could they respond to such offended conviction? It's like five black dudes struttin' down the street, stopping and saying, "What did you say about my mother?" There's no out. Your words mean shit. You're gonna get your ass kicked. Period.

So, big deal. I got kicked out of school. My mom cried. My sister stroked her hair. Big deal. And I walked out of the apartment and into the street where I belonged.

We lived on 119th Street between Morningside Drive and Amsterdam Avenue, on the edge of Harlem, across the street from Columbia University, which would later buy up the apartment buildings in the neighborhood, virtually wiping it clean of families, middle class or otherwise. While children were anathema, whatever their color, unless strapped in carriages. We were too noisy, too raucous, too unseemly, too swift, the campus guards could never catch us, not on the University grounds, nor the adjacent ones at Julliard, the Union Theological Seminary, the Jewish Theological Seminary, Riverside Church, Barnard College, Teachers College, St. Luke's Hospital, the Cathedral of St. John the Divine. It would not do to disrupt the patrician pursuit of absolute truth, even if the absolute truth was a white history professor found hanging from the limb of an oak in Morningside Park, still clutching his briefcase. Besides, the University had the authority, status, history, power, money; heck, at the time, they owned Rockefeller Center and half of midtown Manhattan.

"Yo! Sullivan!" I called, sidestepping some dog crap as I walked between the parked cars to cross the street. He was just turning the corner with a hand truck stacked with boxes of groceries, delivering for the A & P on 120th Street. The whole stretch of street across the avenue to Columbia used to be a pig farm in colonial times.

"So, what happened?" he said, pushing the truck slowly up the incline past Laureate Hall. "They bounce you?" Beano, the black, one-armed elevator operator, tipped us with his cigarette.

"Yeah. I'll tell you about it later," I said. Walter, the gimpy superintendent of 419, was limping down the street. "What time you getting off?" I asked.

"Half hour."

"How you boys doing?" said Walter as he limped past us.

"Hi, Walter," Sully said. "Just fine, and you?" Walter's limp seemed more pronounced these days. He stopped at the steps of Laureate Hall to shoot the breeze with Beano. Two years later Walter would drop dead in the middle of the street, of a heart attack, with a monkey wrench in his hand. His wife Vera, who worked the lobby switchboard, always gave us heat for using the building's back alley catwalk as a shortcut to 120th Street, where we'd play stickball. She was a bitch and would die with the neighborhood foot up her ass.

I told Sully I'd meet him in front of Hartley's, the drug store, and left him under the blue awning of the Campus Dining Room, a basement bar and grill, which, much later, would become a famous watering hole for several years along the upper West Side, until booze and bad livers, heroin, the Vietnam war, gambling, prison, unemployment, AIDS, violence, the general fatality of adulthood, would cut us down one by one, coitus interruptus, so much wasted seed. While others would grow up, conform during the day.

The concrete gray sky was already dark near 5:30, didn't even know when the street lights went on, and it was getting colder. The dry cleaners on the corner, which would later become a flower shop owned by a Greek, used to be a shoe repair store run by two old Jews, who even shined shoes; everything, then, smelled of leather and was made out of wood. When I was small, I used to watch the tinier one, in his apron, place my shoe upside down on this brass leg with a little foot and pound little nails into the new soles and heels, making the workbench tremble. Then he'd draw his hands over the new leather and smile at me, his glasses barely clinging to his nose.

Next to the cleaners was Adolph's, a deli, but not owned by Adolph, a middle-aged Jew, who, after work, always went home in a taxi. He shared the work with Angel, a handsome Puerto Rican, who cut the bologna, which he'd pretend was his cock, on the slicing machine. Angel's brother Casey worked for Jack, another Jew, in the stationery store next door, which was also very woody, with candy and magazines, papers and pens, manila folders and notebooks, and a toy section in the back where we got the pink Spalding balls for stickball. Jack was a pretty good guy: sold us cigarettes when we were twelve, hired the kids in the neighborhood to deliver the Sunday *Times*, liked sports, always talked about seeing Tom Gola and Cousy play basketball. He worked hard, came early and, also in a taxi, left late; always, it seemed, in the same flannel shirt.

Come to think of it, all the stores on the block were owned by Jews: another cleaners, Okum's grocery store, the jewelry shop, and Hartley Chemist (which had a soda fountain). But what did Mr. Hartley do? When the old man was sick I'd run to Hartley's to fill the prescription, where he'd take the doctor's slip, disappear to the back, and reappear again some five minutes later with a vial of pills, a box of tablets, or a flask of syrup. The old jeweler, on the other hand, worked his craft in front of you on the glass counter, fitting that small, funnel-like eyepiece into his socket, probing the back of the watch with miniature tools, all those intricate circuits of springs, fulcrums, and gears, with the softest, whitest, cleanest hands. He was bald, too. When he bent over the felt padding on the counter to examine my father's pocket watch, which I eventually sold to him, I wanted to touch his head, round as an observatory.

All the stores were generally busy now, people coming home from work, pick up the evening news, a quart of milk, Teachers College and Columbia students at the deli or the soda fountain, beautiful girls, you could tell, even under winter jackets; Red the Cop talking to Polly, the fattest girl in the neighborhood, the traffic thick and noisy, the Amsterdam bus coughing, grinding up the avenue; and the television man who lived in my building pulled by his mutt, brushing past an old woman with groceries, dragging his game leg sideways; the man never smiled, not even when he came to our house to fix the TV, don't know his name, he never talked, a drugstore Indian. And there was Joe. He nodded toward Adolph's.

"What's up?" I said, as I followed him into the deli. The place was crowded.

"Where you off to?" he said.

"So, can I help you, gentlemen?" said Adolph.

"Yeah," said Joe. "Give me four slices of bologna, two pieces of white bread, and a quart of milk." I knew that was Joe's dinner. Like me, he didn't have an old man either. Think he was an alky or something and left after Joe was born. Joe lived with a bedridden grandmother and a mother afflicted with arthritis so bad she could barely get around in a walker.

"How come you work so slow?" I said to Angel.

"Yeah, don't you Puerto Ricans know how to cut meat?" said Joe, ribbing Angel.

"Come, gentlemen," said Adolph, "there are people waiting."

"Yeah, why don't you juvenile delinquents take a hike?" said Angel. "Chops," (Sullivan's nickname, he had just come in the door), "could you escort your ugly friends to the street?"

"Hey, Angel," Sully said, smiling.

"Wait a minute," I said, "I'm a paying customer, you know."

"Gentlemen, gentlemen."

As we crossed the street, past the water pump house on the corner, a real throwback in architecture, a short squat building made of cobblestones, pitched roof and all, among six story apartment buildings, Sullivan told Joe I got the boot.

"You're kiddin' me?"

I laughed. Who was kidding who?

"You dumb shit."

Joe had been kicked out of Archbishop Malloy just after Kennedy was shot, though he would graduate from my old school. A long-distance runner, a mick who couldn't hold his liquor. The Brothers and the high priest called in a pair of Irish cops who hauled him into the trainer's room adjacent to the gym where the dance was held and whacked him three or four times across the back with their billy clubs (to teach that miscreant a lesson). He showed us the long, thick, purple welts (at four in the morning while we smoked cigarettes and played bridge at Johnny's house): he took off his shirt, "Look. Look what those fuckers did!" We never let him live it down. Years later, even during a stickball game on 120th Street (we played the game into our mid-twenties), someone would take his shirt off while Joe was at bat and yell in mock anger, shedding mock tears, "O look what they did to my back! Those bad policemans!"

"Yeah, you dumb shit," said Sullivan, who himself wouldn't last the semester at St. Joseph's. We waved past Mr. Vincennes, Ruben's old man, a union rep for the carpenters, a Marxist, and a lover of Caruso and the Brooklyn Dodgers.

"So what're you gonna do?" Joe said.

I shrugged. "I don't know." I was working part time at Columbia's business library as a page, where Joe and Johnny worked. "Maybe I can ask Mr. Draper for full time." What else could I do?

"Wouldn't hurt to ask," said Joe. "Where ya goin' now? Poolroom?"

"Yeah," said Sullivan. "Wanna come?" Joe said he had homework and left us on the corner of 118th Street.

Boy, was it cold.

But it was pretty. The street lights on Amsterdam swept down to the ravine of 125th Street, then rose steeply uphill for ten city blocks. It was like the first drop on a roller coaster. Nothing would ever be like it again. Like the first snowfall, the first kiss (Christine on the lips as soft as salamanders), the first time you walked across the Washington Bridge, or 10-year-old DeMoralis chasing a twenty-five-cent, balsa wood glider run down by a car on Morningside Drive, or the death of a father, and every time you fell in love. I mean, there had to be more.

HOMER • SOCRATES • PLATO • ARISTOTLE • HERODOTUS • DEMOSTHENES • VIRGIL • CICERO, in yard-high letters, were inscribed on the frieze of mighty Butler Library, Doric columns and all. To our right, up two flights of sweeping, low-angled steps, sat the dome of Low Library. We were walking across the 116th Street promenade of Columbia's quad, the largest open space in the city barring Central Park, toward Broadway to catch the subway.

"Besides," said Sullivan, "school's a drag. It's the most boring thing ever invented by man. Whoever thought it up must have been a faggot. I don't remember half the times I've been slapped around by a Brother at St. Joseph's." Sully walked with a hitch to his gait. Had a metal pin in his thigh from jumping off an alley wall.

"You know what that bitch said to my mother?"

"What bitch?"

"The vice principal. It was like she was yelling at her: 'Your son's attendance record is a disgrace! And his grades are abysmal!' Abysmal. Who gives a rip. Plus, she said I got into fights and I threatened a teacher, this skinny math dude who said something to me and I said I would kick his ass or something. I don't even remember. Then a couple days later, after school, Perry the Cop snatches my books and says, 'Follow me' and leads me down the hall to where the math teacher is standing, and the teacher says, 'That's him.' Perry gives me a warning then adds, 'You better be careful. Mr. So-and-so has a black belt in judo.'"

"Judo?"

"Yeah, bullshit. I feel like kicking his—"

"Chops!" We stopped and turned around. It was Pops, a wiry Negro kid a little older than us, who grew up playing and fighting with Sullivan since they were in first grade. Pops had the best left jab in the neighborhood and had been nickel-and-diming us to death. We gave him money, first out of fear, and then, just because he was Pops.

"Two-to-one," I said, "he hits you up for some bread. What's happening, Pops?"

"How ya doin', Kenj." Pops had gleaming white teeth. "Say, Chops, look, man, I need a little favor." Pops's voice was soft and confiding, sad and intimate. "I need fifty cents. My sister got sick and, you know, I'm a little short."

Sullivan was an easy touch. With his lips pursed, one side curled up, he dug into the front pocket of his jeans and pulled out a half dollar. "Thanks a lot," Pops said, turning. "I'll pay you back later, man. Promise."

He was always a dapper dresser, Pops was, like Miles Davis the trumpet player, not flashy, and no one ever knew where he lived or what kind of work he later made a living by; he just showed up, played ball with us; first a Negro, then a Black, then an African American. Last I heard (from Sully) was that he turned gay. Hard to believe. I'd like to shoot the bull with him. Where are you now, Pops?

As we turned to go, Sully said, "He's full of shit."

"I heard that," Pops said, half turned, smiling broadly. I just cracked up.

So we headed up to the Puerto Rican-Cuban poolroom on 137th Street. That was the night Sully's old man—a good six-foot-two, burly, beer guzzling, bulging man—barged into the poolroom, cracking Sullivan a couple of times to the back of the skull, all the time cursing him, yelling imprecations, swearing what he'd do once he got him home.

ALL HALLOWS' EVE

Sometimes it is difficult to say with any conviction that, like a dream or wish or reverie, something actually happened; that your recollection had substance, like a bruise or a burn; that your memory, at times as elusive and deceptive and fleeting as sleep, was genuine witness to a physical past, like the film in a bank or a courtroom camera . . . the whole truth and nothing but the truth, so help you, God.

    I was with Adrien in his 11th floor apartment in Butler Hall on Morningside Drive overlooking the dissolving white rooftops of Harlem. Fog. Thickening fog. Curling and shifting and expanding in all directions like ouzo or milk softly immersed into a glass of water that was the sky. It was dusk, the rooftops steaming with gauze, silent as a city recently sacked, like Rome, like Carthage, the streets smoking, and I knew, soon, the demons and ghouls and fairy tale princesses, Snow White and the Mummy and Frankenstein, would populate the streets, and the long fog, palpable as wool, would seep into the nostrils and the mouths and ears and eyes, diminishing distance and sounds and smells and proximity, and the one color would be the vague orange of jack o' lanterns and lamplights and flashlights and headlights aglow in a halo of watery tomato soup, swirling, rising, like damp steam from gratings and gutters and sewer covers and the wet streets cracked open like blood-red pomegranates.

    Fittingly, Adrien had lit dozens of red candles and propped them here and there throughout the living room, on coffee and side tables, on the bookshelves and the radiator, on the floor and window sills, as though it were a wake, his living room a chapel.

"It's a sign," Adrien said, almost in a whisper, as we watched the rising, wispy trails of fog and the frayed edges of cloud wrap themselves around antennas and chimney pots.

"A sign?"

He was full-blooded American Indian, or at least his mom was. She was a single mother, a cripple, her left arm rounded off half way down her forearm, her hair thick and black as licorice, always remonstrating, reminding Adrien of something or other in a scolding voice. His mother was always aloof with us; we never saw her smile. While all the boys craved Adrien's sister. In my dreams she always appeared in braids and moccasins, otherwise naked, but in silhouette, dancing in front of a fire. Her eyes, like Adrien's, were black as night, and just as intimidating. It was like she dared you to speak. Bruce and Donny and the other big boys in the neighborhood would always fight with Adrien, who always seemed to instigate the fights, who seemed desperate to prove something to someone, who, though a good boxer, always seemed to fare the worst. Secretly, I always rooted for Adrien to win. He was different like me, only he was more different.

"An omen."

"An omen of what? What're you talking about?"

"It's Halloween."

"So?"

The fog was creeping through Morningside Park, rising, climbing the stone walls with wooly feet, crawling over the black iron fencing between the pillars, soon meandering across the Drive, scaling the sides of the buildings as if climbing the fire 'scapes. Adrien was staring through the window at the darkening fog, his eyes cold, colorless, fixed on nothing. He seemed to recite from memory something that, perhaps, was drilled into him, becoming a mouthpiece, for the voice was not Adrien's. He never spoke like this before, not with this voice, not with these words, some I never even heard before. I mean, he was just sixteen, only a year and a half older than me; he could have been a shaman or witch doctor.

"The dead rise to visit the living. Curious as wolves. Late tonight, swear to god, pray to god, you will hear them howl, blaspheme, and screech, venting their succubus souls, pent like nuns and priests in the basement of churches, hungry for chocolate and viscera."

"C'mon, cut the crap," I said with mild trepidation.

"Once a year, in the safety of pumpkins, we choose, like candy, our own aberrations, play out our secret perversions in the sweetest of grave clothes—"

"You're sick, Adrien."

"Chalking our faces, we rise, like violet gas, from crypts and sepulchers and parade as spiders and walking trees, hoisting illuminated baskets of marzipan skulls."

"Where'd you learn this stuff?" I said, my voice rising. But he wouldn't turn his face from the window. "*Hey,* you hear me?"

"Under a hunchback moon, we chirp and gambol in cartoon fright, paying reverence to the dark, to the neighbor, Mr. Kenji"—he said, turning his head to me upon a swivel—"ignorant of his guests, that Mr. Kenji, too, is among the dead, that we are his escorts. For starters," he said, gesturing flamboyantly, as if ripping off a mask, "I open my face and show him my brain!" Then he laughed hysterically, then coughed uncontrollably, as the fog appeared at the window like ectoplasm.

"You're crazy, Adrien," I said, anxiously.

He laughed, eyes watery, saliva collecting at the corners of his mouth, trying to catch his breath.

"And damn stupid."

"Look at the moon," he said; it was hidden behind a shroud, barely glowing, like an orange-yellow hall light in an old, musty, dilapidated apartment smelling of old people and decrepitude. The glow seemed more frightful than the darkness. "Tell me *that's* not weird," he added.

"You're weird."

Then he turned to look at me; he seemed to have regained his self possession. But, odd, this Adrien was different from the Adrien I knew, even the Adrien that just chanted about Halloween. Though usually serious, this Adrien was a stranger, someone remote from me, peering at me darkly from a distance as if trying to figure me out, trying to place me; his face and eyes, void of any intimacy, any familiarity even, told me that I was not his friend, that I had never been his friend, that he had no friends, that he was both puzzled and suspicious of my unaccountable presence, that in fact he was annoyed with me but would suffer my company in his living room out of spite. It was as though he had wakened from some hypnotic state and things had gone awry, and he had changed personalities. This was no joke; he wasn't given to joking. Nor was he an actor. This was more than spooky, I wanted to go home. But there was no graceful way to take my leave, and I didn't want to rile him. I kept hoping that Sully would show up as he had promised. There seemed something ferocious just below the taut, tawny skin of Adrien's face that frightened me, that threatened me, that any untoward movement, any hasty glance, any unexpected look or intake of breath would unleash, in a flash, savagery.

I sat tensely in an overstuffed chair, measuring Adrien's profile, the sharp, high cheekbone of his Indian face. Then suddenly it didn't matter if I was there at all, here in this suddenly foreign, suddenly crowded room. And I knew my nerves could not endure very long at the edge of his indifference; I wanted to slap him hard across his face, cut his cheek and bloody his nose, growing in savagery myself. *Hey, remember me?* Make him assume that familiar boxer's pose, jab me in the arm, in the chest. Whatever, but I just couldn't sit any longer, I had to move, had to get to my feet, as Adrien stared at the window—when he said, in a whisper, "It's dark now—"

When the doorbell rang.

Hope it's Sully. "I'll get it," I said, suddenly relieved.

"Wait, take that basket of candy with you," he said matter-of-factly. He seemed to be himself again, though bloodshot and tired. "Probably some trick o' treaters. Little kids."

When I walked into the kitchen, I said to Adrien, "Some big kids, too," Sully and Joe at my elbow, Sully sucking on an orange lollipop, Joe lifting from a paper bag a bottle of Chartreuse, a green liqueur of cloying sweetness. Before the long night would end—or was it the next night?—all four of us would get sick-to-our-stomach drunk, retching and heaving ourselves dry.

"This should clear the fog from your head," said Joe. Adrien was by the counter beneath the glass shelves, filling the floppy foot of a long, black sock with all-purpose flour. You'd whip the loaded sock around like a sling and, whap, you'd thump people on the head, on the shoulders, across the back, and the poor victim, smarting from the blow, would be covered by a cloud of white flour, humiliated at the same time. We were hoping to ambush some Harlem Baldies or Sinners from 104th Street, the Puerto Ricans from whom we learned the trick the hard way.

"Where's mine?" Sully asked, peeking over Adrien's shoulder.

"This is it. The rest are on the kitchen table," he said, motioning with his head.

We nestled our weapons in our sweatshirt pockets, pulled hoods over our heads, and descended in the elevator, Joe and Sully getting off on the first floor. We'd meet them at the corner; we would flash our torches toward them twice. Adrien and I pushed open the elevator door into the dimness of the basement and the damp smell of garbage, masonry, and the stone corridors that, in my mind, led every which way beneath a convolution of various pipes, to the waste room, the humming boiler room, the coal room, mysterious rooms behind black iron doors, Adrien leading the way, trying one door after another like a burglar or grave robber in the underground vaults of an old church. Adrien was moving swiftly now, while I dawdled at the threshold of one door after another, wanting to see for myself the dusty tools and spare parts in the work room, the black cat, the count chained to iron staples in the rough hewn wall—when I opened the door to a room full of cigarette smoke and several old Asian men playing cards, who stopped to stare at me, frozen at the door. *What the hell? Who were these people?*

I closed the door and saw Adrien's leg as he turned the corner at the end of the corridor. "Wait!" I called. I had to hurry.

I could hear the faint sounds of music, rock 'n' roll, growing louder as I rushed down the corridor and turned the corner into a low-ceilinged, darkened room, where two or three shadows slow danced to music from a boxy record player. Bridget? Fernando? The basement air was heavy with musk and perfume and perspiration. And I was thinking, *How come they didn't invite me?* when Adrien waved to me from the opposite door. No one greeted me as I wound my way across the floor; I got the sense that this wasn't a happy gathering.

Along another corridor, I stopped before a door left ajar and peered around it to find myself facing the foot of a brass bed in which an old man was covered up to his chin, his head sunk on several pillows meant to prop it up, his eyes closed. Another man, dressed in a white smock, approached the bed from the right, as if from off screen, and placed a drinking glass upside down over the man's nose. From my position I could not tell if the glass fogged. The man in the white smock said, without turning his head, "If you'd excuse us, please." Whereupon I shut the door quietly, then ran down the hall in my sneakers as fast as I could to tell Adrien and burst out the door into the alley, into the street, into the endless fog. *Adrien.*

But I lost him. I mean, you couldn't see six feet in front of your face, so thick was the fog, while shining the flashlight made visibility even worse, constricting the space before me as though I were in a cocoon, my lungs constrained; it was hard to breathe, like tasting fleece or breathing chaff.

"Adrien!" I half shouted, as though he were close by. "Adrien, Where the hell are you?" I was stumbling about blindly, tangled in the fog, whose density, like damask or corduroy, muffled my floundering. My god, I couldn't see my own hands. I then remembered and flashed twice in the direction I thought was the corner, where Sully and Joe were supposed to meet us. Orienting myself with the hard edge of the building and the faint glow of the streetlights along the Drive, I flashed twice again, but again there was no response, even after calling their names, which the fog seemed to swallow.

I walked toward the end of the building, sidling along the wall, which seemed interminable. And slowly my head was filled with fog, a down counterpane comforting my brain, so that I felt a kind of equilibrium between outside and inside and I felt oddly calm. When a voice within my own skull began whispering to me, as if the speaker and myself were sharing the same dark alcove at the far end of my consciousness, someone whispering to me in Japanese, I thought. And the idea rose in my mind, like a ghost, that the speaker was my father, who had been dead now for nearly three years. But the voice remained an incoherent whisper, though it grew in its insistence, and as it grew, I grew in my fear that I was growing mad, going crazy, until another voice intervened. It was my maternal grandmother, who was also dead, only more recently, and she was speaking to me in Japanese, and somehow I understood that my father loved me very deeply, that I was the most important thing in his life, that my father, not one given to words or talk, wanted to tell me that he always believed that I would thrive in this world and would be worthy of this life given to me and that I no longer needed his assurance; that, also, I would not feel saddened when, in the pursuit of my own life, with her blessing, through the years we would be apart, my mother and I would grow estranged, an idea that frightened me and I could feel myself shaking. Then I could hear Adrien.

"I told you to keep up," he said. I was fending off the light with my right hand.

"What happened?" Sully asked, switching off his torch.

"I guess he tripped," Adrien said.

Joe and Sully got me to my feet. "You okay?" asked Joe.

"Yeah, yeah. Just got this splitting headache," I said, roughly pushing his arms away. "Just give me some room, already."

"Wo, hold on, Kenj," Sully said, about to put a hand on my shoulder, then thought better of it.

Then I stared into the night, watched as the fog, from moment to moment, receded down the Drive, then retreated around the corner, and I caught myself. "Hey, look. I'm sorry. It's just this head, man."

"Forget it," said Adrien. "Pick up your sock. The night's not over."

"It is for me," I said. "Look, I better go home."

"C'mon, Kenj," said Sully.

"Seriously, I gotta go lie down."

And I did. And for the longest time before falling asleep, I replayed that voice in my head, remembering what my father wanted me to know and would replay it again and again throughout my youth. There was nothing I could not do.

Forgetting my mother would come years later.

SULLY

He was a gregarious, fun-loving bartender, Sully's old man, known for his legendary strength. Once on a bet over at Donovan's he lifted the bar right out of its stanchions and dragged it into the street, then, with another guy, hauled it over to Riverside Drive. After several busted heads, it took five cops to wrestle him into the paddy wagon. He took crap from no one, especially Irish cops. Bulls, we used to call them.

By comparison, Sully had a much longer fuse. Though, when lit, he was equally as mindless and ferocious as the old man, becoming the personification of anger—so selfless and pure it was almost holy. The difference was that Sully knew the consequences, his legs shaking from fright. Until he was struck. Then the whole world went red. Where the old man felt no man on two legs could best him head on, Sully, out of pride, refused to back down no matter how big (like DeVaney) or skillful (like Pops) his opponent was, something he learned early in his career as a roly-poly kid (called Porkchops) growing up in the neighborhood which gave no quarter to deficiencies of any kind, imagined or otherwise, especially of the physical kind. So he had no choice. Always the underdog, he occupied the moral ground and won even when he was beaten. He had heart, a kind of courage that overflowed into every aspect of his life, a courage that allowed him to be genuinely open with people—of all kinds—having grown up with all kinds, unlike the old man stalled in Irish ghettos and gin mills, hostile or, on his good days, merely tolerant of "those spicks and niggers, wops and kikes," though the ones he knew, who came into the bar, he took to his heart.

Sully's generosity of spirit was simply greater. Our nightly jaunts to poolrooms, bowling alleys, bars throughout the city brought him in touch with a whole host of people, most of them taken by his politeness, his affability, his humility and humor. People would flock to the bars he eventually worked. And he became the best bartender on the Upper West Side, displacing the old man even in the neighborhood.

Anyway, two months after the old man dragged Sully home from the poolroom, the old man left the fifth-floor walk-up on 123rd Street and never returned. Sully's mother, an Italian, started tending bar in the downstairs pub.

Sully once said, "You know, Kenj, my old man said he used to work for yours."

"When?" I wondered, since my old man had died four years earlier. "Doing what? . . . At my father's restaurant?" which seemed odd, since, back then, all the restaurant workers were Japanese immigrants, barely able to speak English.

"I don't know," he said, blind to the pedestrian traffic passing between us and Adolph's Deli. It was just after five and cold, and folks were returning home from work or shopping for groceries; Columbia, Barnard, and Teachers College students were returning to the dorms or going out to eat. Pretty girls, you could tell. And, normally, Sully would be the first to point them out, staring sidelong at anything with a skirt. We were leaning against the hood of a car at the curb, two sixteen-year-olds, two dropouts, Sully smoking a cigarette, his empty hand truck standing at his side. He'd be off work in half an hour. It was already growing dark. "I wonder if he's still alive."

"Who?" I said, thinking about the dinner that night.

"My old man." We waved to Red the cop and grumpy Mr. Chavez, the superintendent of 420, as they sauntered by. "Dig this," he said, changing the subject. "On my second delivery this morning, I go to Butler Hall, 10th floor, the Ruggieris, people I never delivered to before. So I ring the doorbell and hear this shouting. I ring again. More shouting. I mean, this goes on for a couple of minutes, and I'm thinking I should split, groceries and all. Then the door opens and this raven-haired woman is standing there in a thin, blue nightgown with a drink in her hand, a cigarette pointing from the fingers holding the drink, lipstick on the glass. I mean, its 10:30 in the morning, for Christ sake; even my old man waited till lunch. Anyway, she must've been good looking when she was younger 'cause, I'm tellin' ya, her body wasn't bad at all, what with the light streaming through the nightgown. But her face was creased and her teeth were yellow. Then down the hall behind her comes this voice, like someone from England: 'I mean it, Maggie, I've made up my mind. I *won't* do it.' Then over her shoulder she says, imitating his accent, "That's *Lady Marg'ret*, to you, Professor." Then more quietly she says, 'Professor, my *arse*.' I almost cracked up. Then like some old-time actress, she eyes me up and down, steps back and holds the door wide open, and motions me in like I was royalty or something and says, 'Down the hall, young sir. The pantry's to your right.'

"The apartment is huge, the parquet hallway wide as my bedroom, with an Oriental runner all the way down. At the far end, this man is standing in socks, wearing only his drawers and undershirt— no kidding—his eyeglasses dangling from his hand. Then he says, 'I'll simply inform them that we've changed our minds.' I push the hand truck past these dark side tables and big mirrors, and then past this dim room with the door half open, smelling of medicine. And I see this bed and this old man's bony face propped on pillows. And I could see the old man's eyes. I swear to god, Kenj, it was weird. They were looking dead into mine. I mean, passing the doorway didn't take a second . . ."

"So?"

"Well, I can't describe it. Those eyes were kind of wet, it looked like the old man was in pain . . . Can't get them outta my head . . .

"Anyway, in the kitchen I say to the woman, 'Where do you want I should put these boxes?'

"'How quaint,' the raven-haired woman says, leaning against the doorway, where she sips her drink and says, her voice raised, talking to the man in the other room, 'Poor, poor, Malcolm. I wonder: is that really the name your parents gave you? Honestly, love, how *could* your parents imagine such a name paired with *Ruggieri*? Mal-colm. That's a WASP name, *doncha think?*" she says to me. '*Whatsamatta, Antonio* not good enough for *ya?*' Now I just want to get outta there. But she's blocking the doorway and I'm afraid to interrupt.

"'That's enough, Maggie,' says the man from somewhere in the living room. 'And I mean the gin. Haven't you had enough this morning?'

"Then she says, 'You adopted that name yourself, didn't you, love? To impress your colleagues. You know, Antonio, you are more English than any Italian I have ever met. Especially in bed.' She said this nasty-like, and then said, 'In fact, you are more English than I am, and I *am* English.'

"Then the man said, happy like, 'No you're not, Mag. You're really Italian. You never had much sense of real drama, Mag. But, alas, few of us are endowed with the talent we imagine ourselves to possess.'

"I say 'Excuse me—' but she cuts me off and says—'You bastard!'—and I gently push past her, dragging the hand truck.

"'Now, now, Mag. It's best we face the truth, like proper Englishmen. Excuses aside, you were simply not very good. Yet you insist on playing your life as the tragic heroine. But honestly, Mag, you should rehearse.'

"Then outside the front door, I hear, 'Fuck you, Malcolm!'

"Then he says, 'See what I mean, love?' and the door shuts."

"You got stiffed," I said. We were standing in front of the grocery store.

Sully just shrugged. "All day I kept thinking of that old man in the bed. The guy must be dying."

The image of my own father arose in my head.

"We all gotta go," I said, as I made room for an old lady coming out of the store. *He is lying in the bed, which was mine. My mother is kneeling on the floor, leaning over Father's body.*

"Yeah," he said, about to go inside.

"Look"—*Holding an empty water glass over his nose. The glass doesn't fog*—"I forgot to tell you. Mr. Draper is having a dinner tonight for some of the library guys. Joe and Mike are going," I said, lying about Mike. "And Mr. Draper asked me to ask you to come," I lied again. But I knew that old Draper wouldn't mind.

"That fag?"

"He ain't a fag. Well?"

My boss, Mr. Benjamin Draper, head of the Columbia Business Library, where I worked as a page, was a three-martini man (on the rocks with a twist), the third usually ushering him to bed. Unless he had guests. Then he'd nurse them, maybe five or six, before he slurred his words, grew silent, and drooped in the easy chair next to a very bright lamp on a side table, which held, as did the clean pine wood shelves behind him, an array of Southwest American Indian pottery. He lived in a large seventh-floor apartment on Claremont Avenue across from Barnard College, sharing it with another Columbia librarian, a Mr. Ferry, whose collection of leather-bound books impressed Sully ("He read all these?"); there were so many, some in pairs or sets, of the richest colors, classics, so clean and neat and new-looking—who made it known to me and Sully that, yes, the books, all of them, were his—as Draper, from the kitchen, sardonically made claim to the pottery, the sofa, and the burgundy love seat.

"Well, you can divide up the rest among yourselves. I've got a theatre engagement. Ben, please try to remember to leave the door chain undone," he said as he passed the dining room down the spacious hall.

"My best to Thelma," Mr. Draper said, as he came in from the kitchen with a small jar of basil. He handed it to Sully, whose job was to prepare the dressing for the salad. I had to set the table.

"Who's Thelma?" I asked.

"Oh, that's his sister. But he's probably off to the baths."

"Baths?" Sully said.

"Oh, you know what I'm talking about," said Mr. Draper, dressed as usual in a white shirt, though without a tie. Sully turned to me and mouthed *Baths?* When the doorbell rang.

"That must be Joe," I said.

"Oh, I forgot to tell you. Joe couldn't make it. Something or other about his mother feeling weakly," Mr. Draper said, as he left the dining room.

"Mike?" said Sully.

"I forgot to tell you. Mike couldn't make it either."

When Mr. Draper ushered in his guest: "This is Mr. Malcolm Ruggieri. He teaches at the University. This is Kenji, who works in the library, and this is Sully, a former employee."

"*Malcolm*," said Mr. Ruggieri, shaking our hands. His was large, soft, and clammy, even though it was cold outside. He had a pale complexion, shiny, slicked-back hair, and a thick, peppery mustache he would stroke all evening with his thumb and forefinger. He was old, but it was hard to say how old. As he was taking off his coat I eyed Sully who nodded imperceptibly, but it was obvious that Mr. Ruggieri had not remembered Sully, the delivery boy. I wanted to ask Sully what color old Malcolm's drawers were.

He reeked of gin.

"Let me take that for you," Mr. Draper said, relieving Mr. Ruggieri of his coat and the bottle of wine snug in a paper sack.

"That's kind of you, Benjamin," he said, without any trace of an English accent. "That's an old Barolo from the old country. I think you'll enjoy the bite."

"Martini?"

"Yes, love one. Warm the heart," he said, rubbing his thick hands. "What about the boys, Ben?" Mr. Draper looked at us with a deadpan face. Like his voice, it rarely changed. Like everything else about him, it was absent of any trace of drama. He was hard to read.

"No thanks," Sully said, answering for both us.

Mr. Ruggieri wore a maroon sweater over a dark brown, flannel shirt buttoned to the throat. He didn't have much of a neck. He wore dark brown pants and cordovan wing tips. Maybe because of the movies, he reminded me of a Mafia don. "Maybe because of the movies, he chose to dress that way," Sully would say later. But he did not talk with his hands, though he talked a lot over the salad. Sully seemed uncomfortable with the talk; he kept rubbing his right thigh beneath the table, the thigh with the steel pin in the bone, something he tended to do when he felt anxious.

"Your mother is Italian? Does she speak the language?"

"A little, I think," said Sully. "My grandmother does."

"She's sick in bed," I added, suddenly remembering the old man Sully had seen in Ruggieri's apartment. *Just like the old man*, I thought.

"I'm sorry to hear that," Mr. Ruggieri said.

"Do you speak Italian?" I asked.

"Not very well, I'm sorry to say. Just French and some German," he said, fingering his mustache. "And your father's Irish? What does he do?"

"He's a bartender."

"I see . . . What, by the way, do they speak in Texas, Ben?"

"Steak," Mr. Draper said, winking at me and Sully, and we all laughed. There was a growing redness round the rims of Mr. Draper's eyes.

"I first met Ben a few years ago in Athens at this dinner party. It seems we both shared the same acquaintances, *lit-trary* types, if you know what I mean. Young snobs, really, all burning with the gem-like flame of inspiration. Art for art's sake, that sort of stuff."

"*Writers* he means," said Mr. Draper.

"Both Ben and I were decades older than these chaps but were, nonetheless, warmed by their enthusiasm. Their spirit. Which is why, I suppose, old Ben here returns each year to the cradle of civilization. To renew himself in the fountain of youth. Is it not so, Ben?"

"Now, now," Mr. Draper said, raising his eyeballs to the ceiling.

"At first, after they learned that Ben, in his misguided youth, had studied medicine, the young philosophers lunged upon this as the reason that Ben was such a cold fish. But, of course, none of this ultimately mattered to them, since, of course, Ben was a Beckman. However tenuous the association."

What a bunch of bullshit, I thought. And wished that Sully had said yes to the martinis.

"Anyway, I was thinking of you, Ben, when I was reading Maugham. Are you acquainted," he said, turning to me and Sully, "with Somerset Maugham? *Of Human Bondage* or any of his plays?"

"Not recently," I said.

"No matter. Well—"

"Malcolm teaches British literature," Mr. Draper said. "He has fire."

"—I was reading Maugham and came across some lines that made me think of you. Maugham, you see, was studying medicine for a while, too, though he was in truth a writer. His artsy friends, however, did not know this. In fact, he was halfway through writing his second book but was too shy to tell them. Then he says—now let me get this right; I memorized this for you, Ben—then he says: *it was with great mortification to me, burning as I was too with a hard, gem-like flame, to be treated as a Philistine who cared for nothing but dissecting dead bodies and would seize an unguarded moment to give his best friend an enema.*"

We cracked up.

"I liked that last part," Sully said.

"Why thank you, young sir," he said.

"Why don't you help me put on the steaks, Malcolm?" Mr. Draper said, rising unsteadily from his place. "You can open that Barolo."

"*Bene,*" said Mr. Ruggieri, following Mr. Draper into the kitchen.

"Man, that guy is *weird,*" I said.

"He didn't recognize me. Not only that, I'm hungrier'n hell. I'll give you three-to-one he's Draper's boyfriend."

"I told you," I said, "Draper isn't a fag. He's just . . . he's just a little prissy, that's what he is."

"You mean *sissy*. And he's half in the bag."

"And you told me yourself that Ruggieri has a wife."

"Maybe he's AC/DC."

"Well, he seems to like you and your Italian nose. You better watch out. He didn't ask me about *my* parents."

"You? If I had face like yours I'd kill myself. Besides, you know those Greeks."

"What'd ya mean, he's Italian."

"Let me tell you, he's at least part-Greek. Gotta be. He and Draper always visit Greece, don't they?"

"You're nuts. You've been watchin' too many Fellini flicks."

"And you been watchin' too many American ones. Look," he said, "wanna play some pool at Hess's after we eat?"

We heard them murmuring in the kitchen.

"Shh," I said.

After Mr. Ruggieri poured the wine, he made a toast to everyone's health.

Then Sully got up, which surprised hell out of me, and lifted his glass and said, "Happy birthday to James Sullivan. Happy birthday, Pop, wherever you are."

I was stunned. "Today's your old man's birthday?"

"That was very touching," the professor said. A month later they would find Sully's father in the men's room of the Broadway

Bar & Grill, dead from a busted liver. The next day Ruggieri's father would die from his long bout with cancer. "Fathers die," Sully said later. "We're all destined to be orphans. Wonder what old Malcolm and Maggie will argue about now."

After dinner, we left Mr. Draper and Professor Ruggieri with their coffee, and I could hear Mr. Draper hooking on the chain after the door closed, thinking of poor Mr. Ferry returning from the *baths*.

As we walked up the hill to Broadway, to the 116th Street subway station, I said, "I gotta tell you the truth. Mike was never invited. Joe was. I just included Mike to make you want to come more."

"That's all right," he said.

"Something else. When I said that Mr. Draper wanted you to come, too? Well, that wasn't true either"—and I knew, soon as I said it, the truth wasn't called for. *The stupid*.

But Sully never changed his stride or looked at me.

"You know," I said, "you looked a little down, and I knew Mr. Draper wouldn't mind."

"Yeah, he's a good man. So's that Ruggieri guy, I guess."

"What do you mean?" I said, "I thought you said they were fags."

"Could be. Doesn't matter. Not really."

We walked a little ways in silence. And I caught myself repeating his words, *Doesn't matter. Not really. Doesn't matter. Not really,* when he broke the round:

"You know, Kenj, that story I told you?"

"What story?"

"You know, about delivering groceries to the Ruggieris at Butler Hall?"

"Yeah. So?"

"Well, there was no Mrs. I just made her up."

"You just made her up? You turkey!" I said, stopping in my tracks. (It wasn't till years later that it dawned on me that the Margaret he had invented was a composite of his mother and grandmother and that witch who worked the switchboard in 419. I mean, fictions don't come from nowhere.)

"And Ruggieri wasn't standing around in his drawers," he said, turning around to me, "though he *was* drinking. But that old man in the bed who looked me in the eye as I was passing his room in the hall? Well, that was real, Kenj. That was true. C'mon, let's shoot some pool. Gotta work off this steak."

It was cold. My hands deep in my pockets, I followed him up the hill.

THE OLD MAN

According to my mother, my father came to America sometime between the two world wars as a stowaway on a Russian trawler, emigrating from Wakayama-ken to the borough of Brooklyn. I figured this must have been before 1924, since that was the year the immigration laws were changed, prohibiting the entry of Asian nationals. Whether or not he intended to stay in the States permanently, we housed his urn in a vast cemetery in Queens in 1957, the first time I ever rode in a limousine. Of his childhood, I have no idea. He probably came from a family of farmers. Meat eaters mostly.

He was a proud, handsome man, dignified, elegant even, looking taller than he really was because of his slender build, always dressed in a suit and hat when he left the house. I remember a photograph of him in a straw hat in a sea of straw hats in a city street, one of the few times he was ever photographed smiling. The oldest picture I recall is him standing, almost at attention, in what looks to be a study, dressed in a tailored servant's suit, a German shepherd at his heel. Among his papers, I later found a letter of reference signed by a lawyer named Brandt, recommending my father's exemplary service.

I guess just before or during the Second World War he saved or raised enough capital to own a dry goods store. In the picture, he is standing behind a counter in an apron, a complexity of cans and packages and jars rising around him, stacked on the shelves on three walls to the very ceiling, and he was allowed to prosper. I wondered where in the city his store was located. I wondered what he felt when the Japanese bombed Pearl Harbor. *Where was he when the news came? Did he fear for his own safety, the safety of his friends? Of his family in Japan? Did he ever write letters? I see your hand nowhere.*

How did he feel when—under the urging of the Hearst press, farm and labor groups, local and national magazines, California Attorney General Earl Warren, Walter Lippmann, civil rights fighter Carey McWilliams—the government evacuated the entire Japanese population along the West Coast, stripping them of their land and houses and businesses, their personal property, and scattered them in ten relocation camps, incarcerating them behind barbed wire in the hinterlands of California, Arizona, Idaho, Wyoming, Colorado, Utah, and Arkansas? I mean, did he feel anger? Outrage? Or did he simply say *shikata ga nai?* It can't be helped. He must have felt at least fortunate, having by accident taken root on the East Coast, where, like the few others of his kind, he was generally ignored.

More than 9,000 casualties, over 600 killed in action, the 442nd Regimental Combat Team and the 100th Battalion of second-generation Japanese Americans, the most decorated unit in American military history—with wives, children, mothers and fathers, relatives and friends still penned in hovels—Were he not old, would he have fought for America?

Could he?

After we dropped two atomic bombs, within two working days, on Hiroshima and Nagasaki? Disintegrating whole populations like a modern movie. What could he say?

Shikata ga nai?

Shortly after Pearl Harbor, my grandmother (a picture bride who came to America to marry an unknown tailor) was transferred into a relocation camp somewhere in Arizona, followed by another widow, my mother, who had been teaching Japanese language out of an abandoned freight car in New Mexico when she heard the news about my grandmother. Fearing that Grandmother wouldn't survive the relocation by herself, my mother dropped her work, took up my half-sister, and joined Grandmother inside the camp. Years later, across a kitchen table, my mother would say that she had "fun" in the camp, despite her nervous breakdown. But Grandmother took care of her, just as she'd take care of us kids when my father would die. She was one of the hardiest, most enduring, most devout women I've ever met. Humble, gentle, she once smacked my mother across the meaty part of her arm for some maternal impropriety. I was sitting on the rug playing at the time, and surely I must have smiled.

My mother is known as a *kibei,* someone who was born in the States and educated in Japan. Part of that education, I suppose, was marrying a Methodist minister, who, after sharing in the birth of my half-sister, promptly died. Whereupon my mother returned to the States, reuniting herself with my grandmother. After the war, through another Methodist minister, this one acting as a go-between, my Christian mother was encouraged to meet my atheist father in the equally godless New York City. But he was as handsome as she was beautiful, and besides, he was a good storyteller. Which makes me doubt some of my mother's knowledge of my father's past, like that business of his being a stowaway. But that's romance. And so I was born with a host of other baby boomers in 1946, in Bellevue Hospital, infamous for its mental ward.

On hot summer nights, my father and his friend Uncle Bill would sit on the first step of the stoop talking in the language of the old country, knees in the air like refugees, or my father squatting in front of the old TV set watching his horse run out of the money. "Somnabitch!" My younger sister and I would play under the lamplight, floating matchstick covers, ice cream sticks, and bottle caps along the canal of the gutter, round gates of refuse, down the slope of 124th Street, making a left at the corner, then down the hill of Amsterdam Avenue to 125th Street, another left, then beneath the viaduct to the Hudson

River, thence to the Atlantic. The *Niña*, the *Pinta*, the *Santa Maria* going the other way. All to the sounds of mambo music descending from the upstairs apartments across the street. One by one the lights going out as the night grew late.

The only sounds were a truck or two echoing in the night and Uncle Bill's low, gravelly voice. He was grizzly too, smelling of the Ballantine beer he drank from a paper sack. He never came upstairs. Nor did I ever learn the kind of work he did. Maybe, like my father, he owned a restaurant (which he bought after the dry goods store), since he too only showed up after ten at night.

Occasionally, Uncle Bill, who owned a car, would drive us into the countryside, where my sister and I would run about under a moonless sky in the tall grass of some nameless meadow, chasing fireflies, to my father's murmurings, the crickets, the locusts, the cicadas, or whatever was spawned beyond the Washington Bridge. Uncle Bill always brought along a thermos of cool water to quench our thirst. And inevitably we'd be fast asleep by the time the car slid quietly to a stop in front of our building.

On one rare summer day, Uncle Bill took the whole family to the countryside, my mother taking along a lavish lunch, which we ate on a picnic table beneath the green limbs of a towering shade tree near a railroad track. Toward late afternoon, the sky still yellow bright, a freight train chugged past us, slowly, endlessly, freight car after freight car, rock-rumble-rock, the weathered sidings of the drabbest colors, rock-rumble-rock, the orange light of the setting sun flashing between the cars, glinting off my mother's glasses, my mother who simply stared. *Where, from what distance had the train come?* My mother would often fall into these prolonged reveries, almost like a trance. Like at the cutting board or frozen over her knitting as though listening to some distant music. I supposed like myself she was daydreaming of another life, creating perhaps a more interesting world, or maybe she was remembering a former life when she was younger and the times more exciting and full of hope.

The only thing my father ever created that I could call artistic was a three-dimensional sketch of a train engine on my notebook paper, of one of those old type trains that look like they have teeth in the front. For some reason, he liked trains. Every Christmas, before he got sick, he would unfold this large plywood platform across the dining room table. Triple-rail, Lionel tracks were nailed into the platform in an elongated circle. He would stand at the controls with an engineer's cap on his head and watch, like a kid, the train go round and round in its endless circle, whistling white smoke from its chimney, through tunnels, over trestles, into the countryside, perhaps to pick up a load of coal or fir trees for city families like ours, for fathers who required big trees and lots of light and loved you beyond the dimness of your memory. Later, when my younger brother broke one of the passenger cars, the old man spanked him in a fury.

One December, about two weeks before Christmas, Father told me to follow him into my parents' room, where he lifted the overhanging bed covers, and down on his knees with me, pointed to the long, bright red, hook 'n' ladder truck, still unwrapped, beneath the bed. Other nights, when the front door would close like a refrigerator, he'd come to the threshold of my room, his overcoat still flecked with glistening snow, to hand me a set of bow and arrows, a toy gun, or a rubber sword. One Christmas, from black boots to black hat, I was Hopalong Cassidy.

If Christmas was for children, New Year's Day was for adults. My mother and grandmother would fix up a feast of traditional Japanese New Year's food—of the most peculiar kind, things like taro root, sweet black beans, and other odd vegetables—and all my father's immigrant restaurant workers would come to drink and talk and dine. There was hardly room on the table for the old man's ashtray. He smoked like a gangster, though he didn't like to drink. It made his face red. Like mine.

For the first nine years of my life I grew up in a neighborhood of Puerto Ricans, Negroes, and oddly enough, four or five Japanese families, an unheard percentage of Asian Americans in any neighborhood of the city, excepting, of course, Chinatown. And, of course, whether we were Japanese, Korean, or even Filipino, we were all Chinamen in the eyes of the children in our neighborhood. Ching-chong-Chinaman! You drop silverware on the floor, ping-pong-pang, that's how they name each other, ha, ha, ha. The children knew best. It was all the same. You were a spick whether you came from Puerto Rico, Cuba, Santo Domingo, or Spain. You were a nigger whether you came from Harlem, Mississippi, Jamaica, or Haiti. Whites were honkies, even the Jews, except among the whites.

I remember walking down the street one afternoon, hearing the taunts from across the street. Ordinarily I would have felt humiliated, self-pitying, even believing the deficiency implied by the tint of my skin or the angle of my eyes. But because my father was with me, I shook with rage, wanting only to kill, to rise up like the god of death, an eclipse shedding darkness, disease, destruction over the entire city, obliterating even myself and my father. Looking at him from the corner of my eye, I wondered what he would do. Of course, he remained unruffled, permitting nothing to perturb that distant, manly, even stately exterior of his that housed the secret of his dignity. No doubt, given his years in America, expressions of ignorance, blatant or subtle, through word or gesture, were common experiences of his, where he learned to rise above the pettiness and the pain. Oblivious to commonness he led me across the cobblestone avenue of Broadway, past Julliard, the Union Theological Seminary, Riverside Church, across the granite promenade of Grant's Tomb, to Riverside Drive overlooking the choppy, slate-gray Hudson River rushing from the north and the promise of the countryside. This is what old Henry Hudson must have seen and felt as he sailed upriver against the current toward India.

During the long slow days of August, quiet and still as Sundays, when the University closed and the business was slow, my father would close the restaurant for two weeks, and we'd take taxi rides everywhere: to Macy's, the Empire State Building, the Bronx Zoo, Orchard Beach. Or we'd ride the 125th Street ferry across the Hudson to Palisades Park to ride the motorboats in the man-made canals, or ferry up the River to Bear Mountain. Often, we rode the subway to Coney Island, in Brooklyn, my hands and face pressed against the window watching the on-rushing express, the shifting of levels, the weaving of tracks through the narrowest of tunnels, growing intimate with the city's underbelly where the noise and power and speed really lay, perpetually seething like dragon dreams, like my horrific childhood nightmares. Again and again, I am moving down a terrifying city street, everything red, fiercely red, under a fire-engine sky deepening to blood and darkening anger, toward a monstrously red book, big as a building, which looms threatening over me as though it were shouting at me, and I'd awake with a terrifying scream. "It's okay now," my father would say, hoisting me atop his shoulders, "Papa's here," and he would walk us up the hallway into the living room light, which quieted my crying.

As an adult, I would walk that street again, read the title of the book, open its pages, finally become a man.

"You know what America means?" Arthur would say to me after my father's death, taking over his restaurant, overseeing the marginal well-being of my family. "Money. You follow me? Money, that's all it means. Without it you're less than nothing. Weak. You follow me? And if you're weak and poor, they'll throw you away like garbage." At the time, he was the superintendent of our building. Ralph's father, a small bitter man, a bottle scar below his right cheek and chin. He could never forgive his country's confiscating his trucking business, expropriating his house and property, stealing, through a political con, his hard-earned wealth. Fuck 'em. He would be forevermore a spy, a saboteur in the enemy's country, vowing to wreak his revenge through economic leverage, exploiting the labor of the poor to outwit and rob the well-to-do, to rise by stealth and obsessive hard work into the upper reaches of the middle class—where the established, professional Japanese scorned his crass ambition and material appetite. Fuck 'em. Bringing shame upon the community; scorning his janitor's dress, the flannel shirt, the ball of keys hanging from his belt loop. He practiced a personal frugality, which his more docile children would adopt, hating any sense of showiness or fanciness or refinement that did not accrue in a profit. Fuck 'em.

With the 5,000 dollars he had borrowed from my father, no mean sum during the early Fifties, he parlayed the loan in crafty, cut-throat real estate deals, buying and selling brownstones and apartment buildings. Like the heady playing of the market, like smart fishing, he came to love the process of making money. I mean, this was what America was about.

My father, on the other hand, though he prayed at the same altar as Arthur, working just as hard as he, was not the devotee that Arthur was, for the precepts that governed his life made room for generosity. This was true even after his luck in choosing horses soured, his business falling off precipitously, evermore just this side of bankruptcy, his health in decline, while my mother stood behind the half-open door, shaking her head vigorously, as my father agreed to loan money to yet another young man just off the boat or staving off imminent poverty. According to my mother, we simply couldn't afford it. *What foolish dream, what delusive pride did he live by?* But she had little say in the matter. He was a Japanese man and she, American in name only, was his wife and therefore must defer to him, must accept his imperfections as he had accepted hers, whether or not the money and bread he brought home were sufficient to clothe and feed the family, however much the cultural balance of power privileged the male. And she was a Japanese woman. For—beyond his charm and tenderness, his humor, industry, or sex—it was that stubbornness of pride, that imperiousness, that god-like anger, that insanity to risk everything for an idea that was, from the very beginning, my mother's ideal of a man.

Several images mingle in my mind when I think of them as a couple. First is his coming home one winter night to tell us of a stabbing he had witnessed in front of the corner bodega, Mother scolding him for telling such tales to little children. Then he is walking jauntily down the hospital corridor, his robe open like a sail, a Chesterfield smoking from his fingers, greeting us, his visitors, with a triumphant smile on his face in a room filled with windows. Then it is Saturday morning. He enters the room in pajamas as we eat our breakfast. He bends over Mother, pressing his cheek against Mother's. She squirms away in pleased irritation, for he hadn't shaved, the first and only time we had seen them touch in any way. Then the old man is dead. I am sitting in an armchair opposite the foot of the bed. Mother is kneeling on the floor next to his chest, holding a water glass upside down over his nose. It does not fog. "That's peculiar," she says in Japanese, shaking her head as if mystified. "His legs are still warm."

Had my father been present, he would have ridiculed her logic and scoffed at her hope. Like others, my father was least patient with and expected the most from those he held closest. He would suddenly scold my mother in the same way he would chew out a cabbie who had betrayed his trust, both making mistakes of judgment, though the latter felt the full force of my father's American invective. "Somnabitch!"

I don't know how many times I disappointed him, giving him good reason to slap me across the head. I was the brattiest, most spoiled, most insufferable kid that was ever spawned on 124th Street. Once we were walking down the street, going somewhere not to my liking, perhaps to cut my hair, a process which I feared and loathed, or to the doctor's, which wasn't much better, or to keep an appointment with the nursery school director at Riverside Church, a responsibility usually reserved for my mother; causing the school no end of trouble, teasing, harassing, fighting my peers. Anyway, I threw a tantrum in the street; whereupon my father turned me around and dragged me into a nearby lobby and cuffed me a good one to the side of my skull behind the left ear. *I was never to display such behavior again in public. Ever. Did I understand?*

Another time, after we moved to 119th Street, I faked illness to stay home from school; then in the afternoon, I lit out with friends to use the school's basement pool, later stashing the wet bathing suit in the empty bottom drawer of my bureau, which, uncannily, my mother discovered and, unbeknownst to me, reported to my father upon his return from work. He simply walked into my room, turned on the light, turned me over, pulled down my nightclothes, and without a word, whacked me on the butt, repeatedly, with the heel of my school shoe. Another time, after taking his afternoon nap, he asked me, as was reported to him, whether it was true that I had been riffling the penny drawer of the large secretary in the back of the restaurant. I had no choice but to admit the crime, at which point, he turned his face from me.

My older half-sister disappointed him too, as he no doubt had disappointed her. Neither could give to, nor want from the other what both would have desired had they been flesh and blood. It was a no-win situation. Especially for Reiko. There was no way my father could treat us equally. I was his first born, his first son. I got the attention and things she could never have. And if she teased me meanly in the presence of my father, he would explode, as he once did when she pinched me, probably in retaliation. Caught in the act, she ran to her room. Too slow. By the time I stood at the threshold, she was sitting on the floor, legs askew, crying her face off. It surprised me to find her crying at the old man's funeral.

My younger sister Mimi knew the score, too, though the bias shown to me was more subtle. She simply grew up feeling a general resentment toward me. We got along for all that, though I sometimes bullied her as I bullied my classmates.

Things didn't fare much better for Reiko once we moved to 119th Street, next door to my father's restaurant. The doctors discovered tuberculosis. *Shikata ga nai.* She was sent away to some clinic, got an operation, and returned to us after a year, showing me the half-moon scar on her back. Which, I judged, was pretty clean. Nothing like the half-ass job they did on her leg, when as a kid, it was run over by a truck on Broadway. And what did she get? A few lousy thousand. I remember my mother encouraging her to use part of it, when the restaurant was dying, to help pay off one of the old man's debts.

Nor did things fare much better after my father died, for then Grandmother ran the household, while my mother worked long hours for Arthur in the newly renovated restaurant. Grandma simply perpetuated the bias, especially at dinnertime, giving me the best and biggest cuts of meat, the biggest portions of her homemade apple pie. By this time, even my younger sister would complain.

The summer of 1955, about a year after we moved to 119th Street, was the start of my short-lived baseball career, though I would love the game like a religion all my life. All its gods. It began on the first day of Cathedral Day Camp in the green field adjacent to the length of St. John the Divine, whose transept, after so many decades, was yet to be built. Excepting Columbia's old Foreign Student Center on campus, once an asylum for the insane, the Cathedral was the oldest architectural structure in upper Manhattan, and still the transept was incomplete.

The program was run by a white-haired old man we all called Chief, who mostly confined himself to the Cathedral's vaults, supervising the little kids in arts and crafts, board games, ping pong, in the granite coolness, shrill voices echoing off walls, in niches, down stone corridors, off limits, receding into darkness. Ghosts.

The action for the rest of us—Michael, Johnny, Blume, the two Frame boys, and kids from the other neighborhoods—was upstairs in the sunlight beneath the stained glass windows of the towering nave walls, where pigeons roosted in the flute work. And there you could hear the crack of the bat—Raphael, the counselor, smacking a softball over the short right field fence, bouncing between two cars into the courtyard of St. Luke's Hospital. He could kill the ball.

Against all advice, more or less the story of my life, I would walk up to the plate dragging the biggest, heaviest bat on the field. I was going to hit the ball clear to Amsterdam Avenue, a good 500 feet away. No clever, practical little singles through the hole for me. I wanted the whole thing. The big one. And so, like Ted Kluszewski, I took huge, mighty swings at the ball, in the strike zone or not, and of course I'd miss, striking out more times, within two weeks, than Mantle during the entire season. Let them laugh. My goal was clear. To rap the holy hell out of the ball.

When fourth grade started, I'd run home, drop my books, pick up my mitt, and run back to the school's concrete playground to play as many innings as I could, every day until the skies darkened, until the winter snows came. Often under the lamplight of our street, we'd play flies up throwing a pink ball off the wall. My arm grew strong. And fairly accurate. I could heave a snowball from halfway up the block and hit the Amsterdam bus across the avenue. With practice, I could hit the driver's narrow side window, which was usually cocked half-open for air. Then we'd run like hell.

I loved to run. Every game we ever played included running. Then I'd run just for the hell of it. To Adolph's for bread or milk. To Jack's for a pack of Chesterfields for the old man, who began to nap more and more in the afternoons, between three and five, when the restaurant business was slow, playing knock rummy less and less with the restaurant workers who lived next door, which was just as well. Every time I came to visit, I noticed that the stack of chips in front him was always smaller than everyone else's. They'd bribe me to go away, tossing me a quarter.

The following year I was the best ballplayer in the fifth grade, and everyone knew it. I was the first chosen in every pickup game. I might have told my folks, but they seemed too absorbed with work and other mundane things. Besides, they didn't speak much English. Sometime in the fall, my father took over my bedroom, so I had to sleep in the back with my brother on a Castro Convertible. And Mom began helping out at night when the restaurant was busy.

By sixth grade I was the best ballplayer in the school, at the peak of my physical powers. I could whack a softball to the left field fence and let the old man know it, too, who was laid up in a sick bed, my bed, the cowboy bed, caramel as the Rawlings I pounded as I strutted the linoleum hallway in the pear light, head bobbing like a cork in the mustard-plaster air, a jitterbug, the first boy in class with hair on his balls, shouting as I passed the bedroom, "Willy Mays is going to the park!"

I was enamored of strength—the long rifles—the black haft of Newcomb's right arm, Snider gunning 'em down from the crevasse of right center, or Colavito humming Verdi to the catcher, like radio, smacking Kate Smith on her ass.

In early December it snowed all night long. The first snow of the year. Packing snow! Fourteen inches! If I had a long enough arm I could lift the window and scrape a handful off the window ledge and drop it down the back of Bonnie Broom's dress, who always made fun of the holes in my pants. But look at it! The park across the street was blanketed with the stuff. The wrought iron fence, the bare limbs and branches of the giant maples and oaks, their top sides frosted, the mountainous boulders that rose up the hill to Morningside Drive, where the buildings stood like cakes beneath a thick white sky, and the stuff kept on softly falling, falling, falling, while Mr. Bellay droned on about Algonquins and other boring, prehistoric stuff, when we should've been out there running in the brisk air, the clean snow, instead of nodding to sleep like Robert in this stuffy room to the hiss of the radiator, the smell of damp boots, raincoats, and galoshes, the triangle of a brown overcoat sleeve sticking out of the closet.

When the bell rang, waking us from our slumber. Three times!
"Fire drill!"
"Fire drill!"

"Hot dog! We're goin' out!"

"All right!"

"Fire drill!"

"Settle down, boys and girls. Row 1, beginning with Suzanne, please get your things from the closet and line up in size places outside the room. You know what to do. Quietly, I said."

So there we were, on the sidewalk across the street from school, right next to the virgin park, standing at attention knee-deep in the stuff. It drove every kid in every class in every line in every size place crazy. So Harold Ford, the biggest and blackest kid in class, slid down and grabbed a gloveful, squeezing it into a crude ball; then very craftily, he flicked it with his wrist, whence it rose in a beautiful three-yard arc to land perfectly on Gladys's head; Gladys who took guff from no one, girl or boy—

"Shit! Who did that?" She stomped out of line and came toward Harold with a waving finger. "Nigger, I'm going to—"

"It wasn't me," Harold said innocently. "It was Kenji."

"Not me," I said, pointing to the guy in front of me. "It was Dilday." Without discrimination she bent and shoved both arms deep into the snow as if to hoist a log and threw snow on all of us. So the lines broke and suddenly the whole school was screaming and running into the park, where the teachers and the old principal allowed us to play for a short half-hour, while they huddled along the fence, smoked cigarettes, coughed, and stamped their feet to keep warm.

It seemed we were sweating from the moment we first tackled each other, trying to put snow down one another's back. Wap! I got Bonnie Broom square in the ass. Steve then shoved me into Suzanne, and we both fell. Rolling, tumbling, chasing each other, our wool gloves all wet, ear muffs lost, striking at Gladys from a distance—it all seemed to end too quickly with the principal's metallic whistle.

Trudging out the gate, back to my place in line, I felt a hand on my shoulder. Mr. Bellay's. He bent over me and said, pointing, "You see that squad car in front of the entrance to school?" It was idling smoke, and a burly policeman was removing himself from the front seat. "Go," he said, pushing me gently in the direction. "He wants to talk to you."

But I didn't do anything, I said to myself. It was Harold. He started the whole thing. It wasn't me. They gotta believe that. No, I ain't gonna squeal. It'll be useless anyway. One thing though. If they try to handcuff me they'll have to use force. Without a word, the officer opened the back door for me. I sat on the ripped back seat of the squad car as we drove up the block to Amsterdam Avenue to the static of the police radio. It was cold and my stomach didn't feel right. I had no idea where they were taking me.

On 122nd Street, we took a left and followed the curve up Morningside Drive, then turned right on 119th Street and came to a stop in front of my apartment building—when the officer turned without wrinkling his neck and peered at me with electronic eyes and told me my father just died.

LOOKING FOR WORK

We were standing behind the Circulation Desk of the Columbia Business Library, in front of Closed Reserve—Friedman, Galbraith, Keynes, E.G. Liberman, etc.; Ricardo, Schumpeter, a whole row of Samuelson, Adam Smith, etc.; like the Army-Navy discount stores on Delancey, if you want it, we got it—overlooking the spacious rotunda of desks and chairs and shelves and books, graduate students dressed in business suits, even the women, moving briskly, leather satchels, briefcases, portfolios, the *Times,* the *Wall Street Journal* pinched under their arms; their pale, dour faces lit by the cloudy, late afternoon light that streamed, like laundry, through the semicircle of tall, two-story windows.

Phantoms, really.

"Continuation School? What the hell's that?" Joe asked. He was working Circulation while I was emptying the bin of books, ordering them by Library of Congress number on the book truck, to shelve in the upstairs stacks.

"I don't know," I said, feeling harassed. "I just got the notice this morning in the mail. Said I had to attend this school once a week every Monday morning until I'm sixteen. Some goddamn law or something. First, they kick me out of school; now, they want me back. —For what? Mondays?"

"You're kiddin' me," said Joe, looking up from the overdue cards, like a teller losing count over a fistful of money. I swear, you could show home movies on his forehead it was so big.

"Yeah. It's somewhere around the Bowery." Joe just shook his head. I sidled next to him to look at the desk calendar. "Today is February 2. March 12 is my birthday." I counted. "That means I gotta go six damn Mondays."

"Could be worse. Did you ask Draper for full time?" he asked.

"Not yet," I said. I just couldn't feature myself working in a business library for the next hundred years. Not that I thought very much about the future. It was Friday, payday. I'd be meeting Sully after work to head down to Hess's poolroom on 96th Street.

Joe walked me to the book lift and said, "Why don't you talk to Draper now?"

"Yeah, why not," I said, walking into the workroom. Draper's office was on my way to the card catalog, my last shift for the afternoon. I stuck my head in the door. "Got a minute, Mr. Draper?" Miss Rayburn, the reference librarian, second in command, was leaning over Draper looking at some papers. She wouldn't have put up with us if it weren't for Draper. A bit effeminate, he liked the company of young men.

He lifted his eyes over his half-glasses, then lowered them again to the papers on his desk. "So," he said, in his Texas accent, handing a catalog card to Miss Rayburn, who left the air thick with her perfume, "heard you encountered some misfortune at school."

"Who told you? Joe? Yeah, they gave me the boot."

"Well, Mr. Mori, what will we do with you now?" he asked, placing a fountain pen in the pocket of his white shirt. In his youth he had studied to be a doctor. Wonder what happened? He was a soft-spoken man, never got excited over anything.

"I don't know. Thought you, well . . . you could hire me full time," I said.

"Well, I don't know if I can," he said softly. "But, oh my, let me see what I can do." What I liked about Draper was that, though he had misgivings over some of the decisions we made, he never lectured us. If he gave us advice, it was voiced almost under his breath. He seemed to have enormous faith in youth, that everything would turn out all right, which I believed half the time, or he didn't give a crap, which I believed the other half of the time. In any case, he knew we would do what we wanted whether he liked it or not. "I'm having a little dinner tomorrow night. Joe's coming over. Why don't you come along?"

It was through Draper's quiet ways that Joe and Johnny, after graduating from City College, would earn their MBAs from Columbia, as several of the other fellows would do, like Nachman, the photography nut, and Sweeney, who would eventually sell used cars in Queens.

One good way to be schooled by New York is to ride the subway when you're feeling depressed. Or even when you're not. Were the City ever to replace the cars with rubber wheels, as in Montreal or Paris, it would not for a lick diminish the fleeting desire I had, for six straight Monday mornings, to throw myself off the platform before an oncoming train. Had a crowd exhorted me—as I had once seen them yelling encouragement to a madman threatening to jump from the roof above a Broadway theatre on 44th Street, a spotlight on his frozen body—I might have taken the leap. Into the lion of empty air. It was not so much the thunderous, hellish roar of the trains as it was the silent scream of an insane painting hung on the wall of my bedroom: the grimy steps that descend into the black maw, the seediness of the station, its basement smell, the forlorn benches against greasy, white-tiled walls recalling the neglect of public restrooms, the poverty of advertisements; the ghostly faces, all in a row, seated across the train aisle opposite my own ghostly face, averted, expert strangers, seeing without being seen, no raised eye, ever, touching another's; the flickering of the train light as phantoms pass before a stop action camera, the brown, black, navy blue overcoats, jackets, the shiny red handbag, shoes, boots made cheap and shabby by the cold, reflected the dread of my going. The process of going, which, by law, left little alternative. Take your pick: Continuation School or Sing Sing. Purgatory or Hell. The subway moving. Or forever stalled.

Rising up the stairs out of the Bowery station, beneath a gray strip of sky, I zipped my jacket and raised my collar against the Lower Manhattan wind. But the cold was relentless. The point of my nose, the corners of my ears, my fingers grew instantly numb. I quickly moved south, blowing into my hands, accompanied by my reflection in the windows of soup kitchens, a closed barber shop; passing a faceless man, a wraith dressed in soiled fatigues, broken sneakers, a crushed hat, rags wrapped around his knuckles; passing a darkened heap asleep on the exhaust grating in front of the corner diner, whose window was smeared, it seemed, with unrinsed soap. Across the street, across the expanse of gratuitous gray earth (about a block in width), across another street, the school stood on the corner among darkened tenements. Like most public schools everywhere, it looked like a warehouse.

To Room 202, a seat in the middle, among black, brown, gray faces of kids fourteen-fifteen years old, deadpan faces, vacant eyes, to hear a distant, desultory, disembodied voice speaking perhaps about traffic safety, dental hygiene, fire prevention, library use to a roomful of defeated bodies empty of spirit, absent of mind. For three straight hours, gone from the world. Thinking, in a rare moment of consciousness, about The Great American Lie: the lawyer, the gangster, the broker, the politician, the successful entrepreneur, the successful everywhere, watching their daughters bleed, lying to themselves, sobbing—"Everything I've done I've done for my children!"

Or the lie that the middle class suburban housewife swears to herself that All children are Our children.

Children . . .

I am scurrying like a mouse under the chairs and tables of the darkened dining room of my father's restaurant, playing hide and seek with my younger sister, while my father counts the receipts under the tiny register light, his horn-rimmed glasses at the tip of his nose. Then I am sitting on a yellow blanket on the summer grass of Morningside Park eating a picnic lunch with Mother, in a loose flowery dress, and Ronald, a black kid who lives down the block on 124th Street, who has a funny mustache of milk above his lips. Then the scoutmaster, a small German man, pulls me aside at the end of a Friday night meeting, held in the basement of a small Catholic church on 68th Street, to tell me that some of the parents (mostly of Japanese and Italian scouts) are troubled with the new kids I have recruited for the Troop: Paul, a black boy, and Steve and Danny, Puerto Ricans, kids who have been in my class for three years, playing flute and recorder with me at school performances, playing ball with me every day after school until dark.

It was dark outside. The wall clock read 10:35. When Mr. Broder, the gaunt program director, opened the classroom door, raised his transparent eyebrows at the instructor, then looking at me said, "Kenji," waving at me to follow him into the hall.

Seated opposite me, he fit his spectacles on a sharp nose and bent his head over a manila folder, wisps of reddish hair barely covering his speckled skull. "Well." he said with a slight lisp, lifting his head, removing his glasses, a dot of saliva in the corner of his lips, "I guess we won't be seeing you after today. Your sixteenth birthday falls on Thursday. What do you think of that?" I shrugged, keeping myself from staring at the spit. Bending to the folder again, he said, "It says here that you're employed by Columbia . . . in the Business Library. That right?" He lifted his head, eyes watery. My suspicion rising.

"Yeah," I said. Like a cop pulling a gun from his back pocket, he removed a neatly folded brown handkerchief, the color of his paisley tie, and wiped the corner of his mouth; brushed twice beneath his nose, across his reddish mustache.

"Just a little cold. You like working there? The people? Like shelving books?"

"It's okay." He stuffed the handkerchief back in his pocket.

"Think you'll work there a while? I mean down the road? Is there other work that you'd like to do?"

I shrugged.

He leaned back in his swivel chair, elbows on the arm rests, his long thin fingers intertwined against his tie. His fingernails immaculate.

"You like books, Kenji?"

"Kenj."

"Kenj. Kenj, do you like books?" *Now what?* "I don't mean business books. Schoolbooks. I mean stories, novels. It's amazing what happens to your mind," he said, tapping his left temple with the tip of his index finger. "And, frankly, I've never met anyone *un*interested in the quality of his mind. Ever read any?"

"A few. For school." *Eleven o'clock.*

"H. G. Wells? *The Time Machine*?" I shook my head. "Orwell's *1984*?"

"No."

He got up, scanned, at a distance, the neat pile of books stacked on top of the file cabinet next to the hat stand, where hung his plaid top coat and red scarf; he plucked from the pile two worn paperbacks and placed them on the desk in front of me. "Try 'em out. It'll give you something to do the next time you ride the subway. Another thing," he said, taking his seat, pulling open the desk drawer, "here." He handed me a card. "Call this woman up when you decide to go back to school." *Go back to school?* "She'll help you. She's helped a number of kids like you get back in." *You had to be kidding. Go back to school?* "*Miss Bernice Klinger*"? I stuck her card in *The Time Machine* and, unknown to me then, I would look her up a few years later, when she would get me into City College. When Broder would be dead, stabbed to death on the steps of his West Village brownstone by some teenage punks.

"Should I go back to class?" I asked.

"No," he said, shaking his head, "you've done your time. Go ahead. Take off." He put on his glasses and bent over another file. "Give me a call sometime. I'm in the book."

"Thanks," I said, turning at the door. But he didn't look up, simply wiped at the saliva at the corner of his lips.

Riding uptown in the subway I flipped absentmindedly through *The Time Machine*, lights flickering intermittently through each subway car. I guess there were a few administrators who did give a crap. I mean, why else would they work with kids? Unless they were perverts. Could become a scoutmaster or, like the Chief, the head of Cathedral Day Camp. The Chief had white hair. Mr. Broder's was red. Mr. Broder reminded me of Mr. Draper, only there was no question that Mr. Broder was in the guidance business. It was the directness of his talk and his habit of offering advice and tossing you an aphorism that made him different from Mr. Draper. Draper was much more restrained in showing his concern. Mr. Broder kind of challenged you through the questions he asked. He was like a teacher, always trying to make you think. *Yeah, I'll look him up in the book*, I joked.

Just then the subway shot out of the tunnel onto the elevated tracks—into the shocking sunlight. I had missed my stop. But that didn't matter. The light was like summer.

So, in the spring, Draper got me this full time job at the Medical Center on 168th Street on Broadway, in the medical library, moving and shelving books, like bones, in the catacombs of the basement stacks, working with a thin, cadaverous, black kid named Darwin, who did more reading under the bare ass forty-watt bulbs than he did shelving, while I had no truck with any of it. Hard to believe, but the books were even duller and dustier than those in the business library. If I read anything it was the sports section of the *New York Post*. Interviews with sports figures, the joke page, the cartoons in

Playboy—now those were the kind of women they could've used in those stupid anatomy books or the books on skin disease and obesity, instead of those pasty-looking ones with freckles between their boobs and droopy butts, what, I imagined, English teachers looked like if they ever took off their clothes. Two of them had a penchant for "accidentally" sitting on my hand.

I mean, reading wasn't my thing. It had never been. But that's not to say I never read at all. Besides a bunch of Classic Comic Books (*Jekyll and Hyde, The Bottle Imp, Prince Valiant*), I recall an autobiography by Ted Williams, *The Sea Wolf*, and other sea adventures about boys who helped the cook and brought coffee in a tin cup to the captain on deck, "Aye-aye, Captain," storms and shipwrecks and deserted islands. Basil Blume and I would borrow books from the public library on 125th Street, but it was hard finding something worthwhile to read, so I often ended up with old, thick books, the kind that Basil checked out, at least giving the other kids the impression that I was smart. I envied Basil's Jewish holidays and his 165 IQ and wished that I could read his collection of Poe stories, but Poe's words were as long and as hard to pronounce as those in the physiology books I had to shelve.

I remembered my mother reading (it must have been in broken English) children's stories to me. Golden Books. And Bible stories, of course—Joseph in Egypt sitting forlornly at the end of a bench at a long dining table, an Oriental-looking boy among adults. But I especially remember Uncle Remus stories with pictures of Brer Rabbit skittering deftly over, under, and through the briar patch or, more poignantly, his leaning dangerously over a dark, choppy lake under a stormy night sky, his hand to his mouth, calling futilely out to the opposite shore. As for reading to myself, I was never much good.

Once (it must have been in third grade) on a warm, very bright sunny morning, the windows open, we were all sitting quietly at our desks reading, waiting our turn to read aloud to our teacher, a pretty blonde lady. When it was my turn, after I read to her, she became so upset with me that she grabbed the book from my hands and flung it to the floor. *Crash.* Where it skittered like a dead bird across the front of the room. The kids in class, I remember, were more startled and shocked than I was, thinking, *What in the world could be so bad?* This happened so long ago that I'm not even sure it actually happened. It would be several years later, while stationed on Guam, a rock if ever there was one, that I would read for pleasure—anything to kill the boredom, and the library was cool—reading Dumas, Dickens, all of Sherlock Holmes, and most of F. Scott Fitzgerald, while sampling the famous names mentioned by my high school teachers. A few years later I would think of Darwin perusing medical books, as I read about Ralph Ellison's invisible man playing with lights in a basement, while I read about Malcolm X's voluminous reading in prison, while I read about Richard Wright's black boy pretending to borrow books for a white friend from a public library he was prohibited, by law, to use for himself.

The book that held my imagination the most, one I tried to read on my own in fifth grade, was *Great Expectations.* For the longest time, secretly, I was the boy-hero Pip, who in time would realize, as the world would, the singular and true dignity of my person. Different from Pip, however, in *my* grand design (never so much tainted by words), I was under the protection of divine providence, however forgetful divine providence proved to be. Moreover, there was an unmined ore of genius within me that begged smelting, that required, on the whole, patience, really, since it would not do, considering one's station, to soil oneself like a common prospector. All one need really do was outwait a lazy god.

Most like Pip, I, too, was in love with the heroine Estella. Only her name was Suzanne, the haughtiest girl in New England. Distant, cold, dark-haired, without breasts, she was the penitence I owed for my sins, a protracted, unrequited love that would ravage my heart, cause me no end of humiliation, distract me from baseball, TV (Funicello was shit), breakfast, homework, the very continents in my geography book or the last of my corn flakes taking on her face, her portrait, her profile everywhere. And—as I would later, throughout junior high school with a Puerto Rican flower named Luz—I would follow Suzanne everywhere.

It was a mad chase, Darwin reading about heart disease under a naked bulb and me the mad taxi driver racing down Broadway, catching, by a whisker, the green light on 110th Street, 96th Street, 72nd Street, 59th Street, 42nd Street, 34th Street, 14th Street, through the canyons of Broad and Wall, past Battery Park, to the empty pier of the Staten Island Ferry, and, like Brer Rabbit, one hand on the piling, calling out over the dark sea, "Suzanne! Suzanne! Suzanne!"

Work in the medical library was forlorn. Tedious at best. At its worst, it bred a sense of dread that fed the creeping guilt I was feeling since getting kicked out of school and making my mother cry and wishing, years earlier, that my father would die. I knew these things without words. The image of my mother's quaking shoulders and her eerie sobbing like moaning; the terrible words I yelled at my father ("Weak old man!") laid up in his sick bed, would come to me whenever I edged toward the margin of despair—a check against self-pity—oddly, making me sane again.

So, at the beginning of summer, I quit. Never to see Darwin again.

Sully and I, under a lamplight of snow, caught the Broadway bus on 116th Street. We always rode the bus to Hess's poolroom and always sat at the right rear, one in back of the other, next to the windows nearest the sidewalk, to watch the girls walk by. Besides, it was the warmest place on the bus.

"Sully. The bookstore." They were standing in front of the show window. The light behind them, outlining the fall of their hair, their cheeks, the bulge of their breasts, their legs, as they talked.

"O, momma," Sully said. Another joined them just as our bus was edging away from the curb. She was pulling on her jacket. "Damn," he said, nearly breaking his neck, "they must be 42s."

"She's got a face like a melon," I said.

"Who gives a shit? What're *you*, a bargain?" Sully was so randy he would have done it with a tree if it moved or made noise. Not that I was much different. But, hey, it was the time of life when our brains depended from our groins like ducks hung in the window of a Chinese deli. There was nothing to do but rub it with salt.

And there they all were, walking up and down the avenue, mothers with their school children, professors, girls from Nigeria, Indiana, girls with dots on their heads, teenagers in private school pleats, Virginia and her sisters—hey, there's Mr. Draper—walking by the West End Bar. As we pulled to a halt at the 110th Street stoplight, next to the subway trough, where people coming home from work were rising up, like the dead, from the ground, the complexion of the neighborhood gradually changed from the predominantly white, Ivy League internationalism of the university crowd to the gray, brown, and black overcoats of the ethnic working class. From 110th Street to 96th, dotted with Irish bars and Jewish stores, Broadway and its environs became predominantly Hispanic, with Puerto Ricans, Cubans, and a few Dominicans, one of whom, with enormous mammary glands, Sully would marry.

Pure romance. That's what drew us away from school and up the flight of stairs into the poolroom. And, mark you, yeah, the stairs creak and the air smells of gymnasium, and upon occasion you'll see men selling each other all manner of contraband, like Duffy, a desiccated vaudevillian throwback, buying a package of cold cuts; a quick dice game; deals, bargains; wily conspirators whispering to each other at the top of the stairs—Pizza and Eddie the Face. Pushing through the double doors, we followed them in. The place thick with villains and twisted victims.

"Hiya doin', Manny," said Sully. Manny Hess was standing behind the register, mumbling out of his bulldog face. He had, as usual, a glossy tan, always running off to Miami with his profits.

"Hello, boys."

"Here's the fin I owe ya," said Sully.

"Boy, it's really packed tonight," I said. "Hiya doin', Brady." He was leaning against the windowsill looking out over Broadway, dressed in a black sweater over a blue plaid shirt buttoned to the throat, still wearing his trench coat. He was the best shooter in the house, a hawk eying the pigeons below. Always watching, waiting for some action, some quick hustle. At 29, without family, working for the Transit Authority, he hardly ate and barely slept—"For what? Life's too short."

"Hey, Kenj," Brady said grinning. "If I knew you were coming I would've baked a kike."

"Aww, don't say that," Hess admonished in a loud whisper, shaking his head in disappointment, then nodding to Table 1 where Dave the Refugee was playing one pocket with another Jew who looked like he had palsy, his cue stick shaking over the bridge of his left hand, who nevertheless, at the last moment, struck and pocketed the balls; who, like several others sitting along the wall, had blue numbers on his arm.

Amon then came up to the desk. "I'd like to make a formal complaint," he said, deadpan as ever. He worked as a doorman during the day and loved action, gambling with anyone on almost anything, pool, pinball, cards, ping pong at Reisman's joint across the street, even shooting dice with kids in the schoolyard on his way home, giving them the wrong odds, then losing. And he lost a lot at pool, sometimes losing his entire paycheck, and we'd laugh, not maliciously, but it was comical the way he'd act afterwards, pacing the poolhall, pulling at his hair with both hands or gently banging his head against one of the pillars, saying softly, "Schmuck, schmuck." He was a polite, gentle man with a lot of heart, which is why we rooted for him; he was a hell of a shot maker and had a Jewish mother who wouldn't leave him alone, calling him up every two hours; he was the only one who ever answered the public phone.

"What?" said Hess.

"What kind of establishment are you running here?" Amon said.

"What? What do you mean?" mumbled Hess.

"Table 11 isn't level and there are cockroaches inside the table."

"What're you talking about?"

"You know, I could report you to the Board of Health."

"Stop busting my chops, will ya, Amon?"

"I'm serious. You can take a look yourself."

"Christ," Hess mumbled as he followed Amon past the tables, past Pizza and Face leaning against the pillar with the telephone, past the cue stick racks.

"You know," said Brady, "we come in here a lot, spend a lot of dough, and you'd think Hess would once in a while say, 'You guys want some coffee or something?' The cheap bastard."

I walked over to Pizza and Face and asked them how many balls Dave the Refugee was spotting the old guy with the shaky hands. Both were dapper dressers, con men, gamblers, and sometime-thieves. And very rough customers.

Pizza, a wiry Puerto Rican lover, who worked the pizzeria on 104th Street, was signaling to Momo, who was sitting against the wall between Sully and a junkie, that he wanted to bet a fin on the Refugee. Momo nodded, then mimicked the shaky old man as though he were on a roller coaster, then pointed to himself smiling, showing his teeth, raising and lowering his thick eyebrows like Groucho Marx, as though the bet were a lock and Pizza was giving him money for free. Momo was a card. It was almost more fun watching Momo's antics in response to the game than the game itself. Momo would elbow Sully then whisper something, and Sully would crack up, and Dave would turn around and say, in a German Jewish accent, "Is it all right with you if I make some money?" and Sully would apologize. Momo then would point to the junkie sitting next to him, screwing up his face as though he had smelled some terrible odor, then would mimic the junkie's nodding toward the floor, then would quickly turn away when the junkie woke up, pretending to study the old man's shaky stroke, again and again, cracking us up, Sully in convulsions, his hands over his mouth, Dave raising both arms to the ceiling in self-righteous indignation, saying to Hess, "How can we play the game in peace? Do something!" and Hess saying, "C'mon, fellas, let them play." To think that raunchy Momo, who always dressed like he just woke up in a boxcar, was an English teacher in a posh girls' private school teaching Shakespeare to 10th grade virgins. "—C'mon, you fuckin' refugee," Momo said, "shoot the ball."

To think that, in 1985 at the age of fifty, afflicted with disease, he'd put a .32 in his mouth and blow himself away, outwitting Mr. Cancer.

"That Momo," Face said. "What a nut. They oughta lock him up somewhere." But Face, of all people, should talk. The first time we ever saw a *part* of him was at Aqueduct raceway, just after the officials had put on the overhead monitor the photo finish of the eighth race. It looked like someone had touched up the photo, for the winning horse seemed to have an elongated neck—when suddenly before us this huge man leaps in the air in front of the TV and puts his fist through the screen. Face, no doubt, had the same tip we did.

Horses, they'll break your heart every time. Face, by the way, is named Face because his is long, like a horse's, long and blank, and if you've ever looked into Face's when he was angry, looming down in front of yours, and looked into his eyes, search as you might, there was no one home. When he lost his temper over a pool game, he'd go berserk, smashing his pool cue over the edge of the table, pulling out coat hooks from the wall paneling, which finally forced Hess to bar him from playing, permanently. Face was frighteningly articulate too. "Fuck you, you little fuck! And fuck your poolroom!"

The second time we ever saw him was at Reisman's basement ping pong parlor, where Reisman, in another one of his failed money-making schemes, arranged a one-man karate exhibition, charging a dollar a pop for admission. Less than half the hundred folding chairs he rented from a nearby Catholic church were filled. We were sitting in the front row watching this Korean guy go through these machinations, punching and kicking the air, sweating and yelling with each blow, breaking boards and bricks with the side of his hands, his feet, then his head. It all seemed very silly to me, especially in the era of knives and guns. Then he stood before us, securing his black belt, and asked members of the audience to come onto the mat and hit him as hard as they could in the stomach. I mean, the guy was built like a Coke machine. No one took up his offer. So he pointed to the rear and said, "You. Come." We turned around and saw this pair of shoulders and a head at least a yard above the others'. It was Face.

"Come," the Korean said very amiably. "Try." Face just shook his head. "You no hurt me." And the few others in the audience egged Face on. So he had no choice. He got up, walked over to the mat, and, standing with his back to us, his simian arms dangling at his side, said, "What do you want me to do?" "Just hit," said the Korean, pointing to his stomach.

Face turned his head around and laughed. "*Just hit.*"

"Here," said the Korean, pulling open his *gi*, clenching his fists, tightening his stomach so that it bulged like an anvil, losing all expression in his face as he focused his concentration on the point of impact—as Face reared back, twisting his torso like a pitcher, like a discus thrower, his fist like a canned ham, and, rising from his heels, broke the Korean's fucking jaw.

It was dumb Irish luck that the Korean didn't die. It was dumb Irish luck that, a number of years later, Face would survive a brawl and shootout in a bar on East 57th Street, catching two slugs in his left thigh and one in his knee for his big mouth and his vile loathing of Negroes.

And here was Dave the Refugee swaggering smugly after winning his third game in a row, the taxi driver smelling sweetly of Canoe after-shave. But let the whore of fortune turn, as she would in the next eight games, and you'll see a grown man cry, "What is this? He aims for this ball and these two go in," talking to himself, to nobody, to everyone, bewailing the betrayal of the gods; and his game would collapse, miscuing here, snookering himself there, scratching in the funniest, most unpredictable ways, about to break the stick by bending it over his own balding head. Pizza and Face berating him. It was tragedy at its comic best, for Dave would keep raising the stakes, keep losing, damned if he lost again to a guy with palsy, to another Jew on top of that.

Sully and I got an open table at the rear, vacated by two college guys, and started playing straight pool, the game for purists. To practice the craft, the art of making impossible shots, impossible position, to run as many balls as you could in a single turn under the three bright lamps over a green felt sea, where the numbered balls were like islands, like planets; to suddenly fall into a mysterious, unconscious rhythm where you can do no wrong, where nothing is forced, nothing is strained, a time when everything you've learned is forgotten, all your tricks, all your technique, all your knowledge, all becoming a part of your body, as if the cue stick were an extension of your arm, and it's as though you were watching yourself play as you leaned over the table, calling your shots in an inevitable sequence of supreme logic, too involved to be in awe of yourself as you reduced the game to its divine simplicity, its divine beauty, which all athletes and artists of any talent have felt at least once in their lives. All you know is that you are moving around the table and the balls are dropping as they should be. That you are hot. That for ten minutes, an hour, maybe two if you're blessed, you are a hero. That you have been allowed for a fleeting moment a peek over the wall, a glimpse of the wide, endless vista of greatness.

That there was hope.

GONE

After my father died, Arthur, like a general, took over my father's restaurant and renovated the place, gutting the kitchen, the pantry, the storeroom; firing most of the old-timers who worked for Father, old family friends (now all dead). Arthur claimed that a few of them were taking kickbacks from the meat man, the vegetable man, the beverage man, and claimed he paid off my father's debts. I don't know.

Anyway, for the next several months I worked at the new restaurant off and on (mostly off) washing teacups and glasses and bussing tables. While my mother worked thirteen-hour days, six days a week, making sushi and cooking tempura with sixteen-inch chopsticks over a giant wok filled with simmering oil, smudging her glasses, splatter burns on her arms; returning Mondays, her day off, to launder the napkins, tablecloths, aprons. How she could stand it, I don't know.

Though at first it was a fun challenge for me to keep ahead of the dinner rush—cups, glasses, ashtrays, tables, clean and set with fierce economy—the game quickly grew old. The sameness, the tedium, the repetition was relentless, my fingers and palms always wrinkled, my arms always wet and soapy up to the elbows, my apron forever damp from thigh to waist string to breast, and perspiring (it was summer), my feet sore standing over the salt boards, and worst of all, there was no one to speak to in my native tongue, were there people my age to speak to. Nor could I speak Japanese. My soul screaming with every lipstick smudge, caked rice bowl, the cigarette butt crushed in a bed of pickles, the garbage heap of dishes, thinking myself the lowliest grunt in the universe. One eye always on the clock.

And there was Sully. I could see him from the back door of the kitchen across the alley, across the street, pushing his hand truck of groceries up the hill in the sunlight, stopping to talk to big black Ernie (his hand truck empty) beneath the blue awning of the Campus Dining Room, turning to laugh at me as I helped Arthur's son lift a giant, headless tuna up into the first floor window of the storeroom.

"Hey, Kenj, that fish looks like you!" yelled Ernie, Sully cracking up.

They'd be off in an hour to play stickball on 120th Street. The lucky punks.

In six months Ernie would be working for St. Luke's Hospital as a maintenance man. Then one month into his job, on the very day he got his draft notice, a box of spare electrical parts, from a high shelf in the utility closet, would fall on Ernie's head, ruining cartilage in his neck. Like Sully and the steel pin in his thigh, Ernie became instantly 4-F. And instantly wealthy because of the lawsuit he filed against the hospital. The lucky punk.

In October, at the behest of my mother (restaurant work driving me crazy), Arthur got me a job as a stock and delivery boy at a Japanese dry goods store on Columbus Avenue run by a sad old man who rarely talked. And again, like working the stacks in the Medical Library or, later, working at the Sherry, Wine, & Liquor warehouse during the Christmas rush, I was stuck in a dusty basement storing things in the half-light. Sad and lonely as the old man, who had lost his only son during the Korean War. Once in a while, he would stand in the doorway, a silhouette at the top of the steps that led to the basement, still as his shadow, as though listening to someone speaking to him. Trying to hear something. Perhaps remembering. Or having forgotten something. Which way he was going. Why he was standing there. A silhouette.

I'd come home grumpy and grunt in response to my older sister's questions. *Christ sake, leave me alone, Reiko.* The same old questions: *How was work? Why are your eyes red? Did you read the book I gave you?* Or she'd tell me what to do with my life. My younger sister Mimi, who was two years my junior and smarter than I was, would simply ignore her. Reiko was studying to be a doctor, but she would mysteriously drop out a few years later. I never asked why. Curious. For someone who liked to talk, she never talked about her past.

Anyway, she told me I should stop smoking. She told me I should go back to school. She told me I looked depressed, that my complexion was pale, that I should change my diet. She even told me what drugs to avoid to preserve my health. How ironic. She and her pre-med friends had experimented with pharmaceuticals long before they became popular among the hippies in the late 60s and 70s. But she was thoughtful. Later, by way of birthday gifts, she'd make appointments for me to have my palm read, to see a homeopath, to have my soul charted by an astrologer, to see a Chinese herbalist who did acupuncture on the side. Later she became adept in Tarot cards and I Ching reading and picked up reflexology and worked me over with shiatsu. And throughout, I had to put up with her interminable talk, her ceaseless advice as to what I should think. "For one thing," she said, "this war is wrong." At the time she was dating this Japanese-American army vet who had busted eardrums from a swimming accident at Coney Island. So she also learned how to sign. Nearly talking him blind.

My younger sister Mimi, on the other hand, hardly talked at all, except to say, "Take your feet off the coffee table." She was petite, tiny in fact, and pale and wore her hair pulled severely back in a bun, and she, thrifty as she was, wore the finest of clothes made of the finest materials, tastefully matching her gloomy reserve, whereas Reiko, at times, dressed dangerously like a juggler. Mimi dated now and then but was basically reclusive, and not because she was mugged in the basement of our apartment building (among a half-dozen, coin-operated washing machines), though the harrowing experience confirmed her long-standing disappointment and mistrust of the world, which was "crass, ravenous, ignorant," which treated her as a child, an inferior, and a foreigner, to boot, in her own country.

Instead, Mimi preferred the quiet of my mother's apartment, in the living room, the kitchen, in her bedroom, between the covers of a book. Most of them written by women about women. She especially admired the beautiful Kaiulani, the Hawaiian princess, who died too young, too delicate for this world. But there was also, at fifteen, a stubbornness and impatience to Mimi, the deeply sighing superiority of an aristocratic old lady. Not only did she not like visitors; she felt, sometimes, her own family, like rude peasants, intruded on her privacy. Nor did she like Japanese people very much, particularly Japanese nationals and immigrants, for they gave her the impression that she should behave like them, like a traditional Japanese woman, like her mother, apologetic and deferential to a fault. Otherwise, she was enamored of the crafts and artifacts made by Japanese artisans and artists and went to every showing in the City announced in the Sunday *Times*.

She simply said, "If you're dumb enough to go into the military, don't go into the Army. They'll train you to be a killer. We've got enough in the City already."

But in November, the draft notices fell upon the young men of the city like snow.

Snow. Like the day my father died.

That Thanksgiving night we were standing and sitting around the statue of Alma Mater, on the steps, overlooking Columbia University's quad. It was cold and the sky was unusually clear, and you could even see a few distant stars. "And there's the Hope Diamond," Sully said, trying to lighten our mood. On any other night, most of us, taking turns, would sing rock 'n' roll songs in four- or five-part harmony on the corner of 118th Street or in the vestibule of 401, old stuff from the late 50s and early 60s, from the Platters, the Skyliners, Dion and the Belmonts. But not tonight. Besides, Sully, like Joe and Ernie, was tone deaf. He couldn't hold a tune to save his life.

"I can't believe my luck," Andrew said, one of our baritones. He was a handsome Chinese guy a couple years older than the rest of us, who had been working in a bank for over a year now. Unlike the rest of us, he dressed conservatively and neatly. "Number 16. Can you believe that?" He was talking about his lottery number for the draft. For the war in Vietnam was growing like a tumor.

"Sixteen?" I said, stunned. *He's gone.*

"What?!" said Sully.

"Can you believe that?" repeated Andrew. *He's a goner.*

"Yeah," said Mulligan, shivering dramatically, holding his hands to his throat as though a victim of the Boston Strangler. He was the runt of the group, our first tenor. "Numerologically speaking, 16 has little character. Now 69, you dig, has a certain charisma, don't you think?"

"Sixty-nine?! You got 69?" said Joe, as if to say that Mulligan was a likely goner, too. And he was right. Mulligan would catch shrapnel in his head at Khe Sanh, and some of it would have to remain there, like the intermittent pain, for the rest of his life, as he took his government disability checks to Hollywood in pursuit of an acting career, acquiring bit parts. Then Joe added, "They're not getting my ass." He and Theo had recently received their acceptance letters to City College. He could talk.

"You know," Andrew said, "if they'd take money, I'd give the government ten grand right now not to go." *He was gone.*

"You aint got ten grand," said big Ernie.

"Ever heard of a loan?" said Casey, who, at number 104, would be shipped down South, acquire an accent, marry a local, and become a career man. He would never come North again. He had a beautiful, deep, mellow voice. What a loss.

While Andrew, like Vinnie Garcia and Mitchell, would simply be gunned down on night patrol.

"There's always Canada," said Joe.

"Ah, what do you know?" said Lobo, our redheaded bass, who was consistently mistaken for Irish, though he was Cuban. And cruel. He flicked his cigarette butt far down the campus steps. Like a tracer. And at number 52, he would join the Air Force and work as an air traffic controller some place in England and experience multiple breakdowns. After his medical discharge, he'd wear tailored suits and tweed jackets to the high school where he'd work as an art teacher, dapper as an Englishman, to terrorize his students with his blank stare and the odd tic below his left eye.

"I mean, we're already there," said Jankowski. He didn't sing. He hardly talked. "Might as well finish it." And at number 29 , he would end up scouring bunkers and the interminable maze of termite tunnels, here and there, somewhere in the boonies outside of Da Nang. Right after they sprayed. Back home, working for his superintendent father as a handyman, he'd smoke dope all day in his basement apartment, a sixteen gauge cracked on his night stand, his only companion his Doberman Thor. For fifteen silent years he'd suffer one illness after another, affecting one organ after another, swearing it was Agent Orange, losing over 150 pounds. Shriveling to nothing. Then gone.

"You're outta your mind," said Joe.

"Like I said, what do you know?" said Lobo, giving Joe that look.

"What he means," said Ernie, "is that you guys are a bunch of chumps if you do go. Especially you, Andrew. And Kenj here. And even Andrew's cousin Bob. Shit, none of you *have* to go and that's the damn truth."

"Ernie's right," said Theo. "Especially you guys with your ugly Asian faces. It's nuts, man. Who in the world, even in Asia, can tell the difference—Chinese, Japanese, Filipino, Korean—though you're damned Americans and wearing American uniforms. I'm telling you it's nuts. Asians killing Asians."

"Asians killing Americans," added Ernie. "Americans killing Asians. And where you folks are concerned, Americans killing Americans. Friendly fire. Your ass grass," he said, slapping Theo five.

"Picture this," said Theo. "You guys are on night patrol and get caught in a fire fight. And everyone is letting off their M16s. And for a moment only your face shows up between two banana leaves. Now, you're telling me Janko or Casey or old Lobo here wouldn't take you out?"

"In a blink," said Ernie. "Especially Lobo."

"Fuck you, *nigger*."

"Fuck you back, *spick*," Ernie said, rising to his full height, stepping toward Lobo, whose blue eyes glowed, almost with glee.

"Now, now, children," said Joe, stepping between them. "Let's use proper English here."

"O, fuck you, you *mick*," said Mulligan, which cracked us up. "Let 'em kill each other."

"Yeah," I said. "That'll solve everything. To tell the truth, I have no idea why the hell we're over there in the first place."

"Me neither," said Sully.

"Duty," said Jankowski. "We made a promise."

"What do you mean *we*. I didn't make any promise," said Lobo. "None of us did."

"Aren't you American?" said Mulligan.

"So?"

"Know what'll happen if Nam goes?"

"You're nuts. You don't believe that crap. You told me so yourself."

"No, I don't believe it. But, I mean, it could happen," Mulligan said, his index finger at his right temple. "And if it does happen, you know what that means?"

"What?" said Ernie, who took the bait.

"Well, Andrew and Kenj can't eat rice anymore."

Andrew threw his leather glove at Mulligan, while I doubled him over with a fake blow to his groin.

"No kidding," he said. "I think going over there would be kind of fun—"

"Fun?" said Joe.

"Adventure," Mulligan said. "Never been out of the country."

"Shut up for a second," Sully said. Then talking to Andrew, he said, "Remember the time you and Kenj took me and Reuben to a dance at this Buddhist church? You had just broken up with this chick named—what was it?"

"Nalissa," said Andrew. "We got back together again."

"Man, she's a fox," said Casey.

"She got big ones?" asked Lobo, cupping his two hands over his chest.

"Like mangoes," said Casey. We cracked up.

"You guys are really dumb," Andrew said.

"Hold on, hold on," said Sully. "Now isn't her old man a priest or something?"

"Forget it," said Andrew. "I'm neither a Buddhist nor a conscientious objector. Forget it. There's no way I'd even approach her father."

"What about for Kenj, then?" asked Sully.

"Yeah," said Joe. "What about your pal Kenj?"

"No way," I said. "Plus her old man thinks I'm a bum 'cause I don't work in a bank like Andrew here."

"Let's face it. You *do* dress like a bum. Just like Sully and Joe."

"Oh, give me a break," I said, zipping my jacket to the chin and, like the others had, raising my collar. It was late and the wind had picked up and bit at our ears.

We would get the news from Nalissa after Andrew was drafted. Irony of ironies, Andrew would go off to Officer Training School and begin to like the idea of leading a platoon. The next we heard, from his cousin Bob, was that he was dead, caught in a crossfire, taken out instantly. Mulligan was back by then, and I remember him crying his head off so bad we had to get him out of the funeral home.

Andrew's cousin Bob, number 31, would feel he was the most fortunate of us all, stationed in Saigon during the early part of the war. All he'd do, he claimed, as a supply sergeant, was drink, carouse, and smoke giant joints laced with hash. He'd return home with a Vietnamese wife, who forced him to go back to school on the G.I. Bill; where he'd get a degree in special education, teach in an elementary school where the kids would climb on him. Every month or so he'd have the guys over to his house in Queens to sing again the same old songs from the 50s and early 60s. They made it an all-day thing when it was warm, barbecuing some ribs and chicken and flank steak. And if the weather was good, they'd sometimes amble over to the cemetery a couple of blocks away and they'd remember old Andrew, Garcia, Mitchell, and the others, and some still missing in action, like Earl and Lobo's younger brother Franz.

I had number 58.

It started to snow.

"Let's tip," said Sully, standing up, rubbing his thigh, the one with the steel pin in it. "You got school tomorrow?" he said to Joe.

"Damn," said Andrew. "Gotta work tomorrow."

"What are you? Special?" I said.

"Check it out," said Ernie. The snow was pretty, falling softly all around us, slowly powdering our hair and shoulders, filling the night sky, clearest beneath the campus lamplights. Snow everywhere. When Casey started humming "White Christmas" in that deep, beautiful bass of his. Lobo joining in. Then Mulligan. Then me and Andrew.

Jankowski stood up and lit a joint: "One for the road," he said, smiling for the first time that night.

We sang as we walked to Amsterdam Avenue, then down the hill.

On 118th Street, in twos and threes, more or less, we parted company.

VIRGIL

After looking him up in the book, I phoned Mr. Broder ("Fred") and told him I quit my job at the Medical Library where my old boss, Mr. Driver at the Business Library, got me a full-time job. No, they treated me okay; it was just boring as hell. He told me to hop on the IRT Local and get off at Sheridan Square in the Village. Go over my options. Yeah, I had already eaten.

Rising out of the sweltering station, I mopped the perspiration at the back of my neck with an already damp handkerchief. Nor was it much cooler above ground, even at nine in the evening, what with the crowd of people near the mouth of the steps listening to a tall black man, dressed in a mauve dashiki, who, with sweat dripping from his temple into an angry beard, stood atop an apple crate railing against the government, the escalation of the war, and the impending death of hundreds of thousands of young people like ourselves. His voice was a West Indian bellows. As I skirted the edge of the crowd and reached the street, he implored the audience: "This is not America's war! This is not our war! And it's surely, my friend, not your war! But then, whose war might it be? Whose war might it be? That young Americans must bleed and die rotting in a jungle—upon foreign soil! Whose people have done us no wrong! What harm have they done us? In God's name, what did they do? Whose war might it be—that we must kill their young men, their women, their children, their grandparents? Whose war might it be? That many of you young people standing before me shall soon be drafted. Brothers! Boyfriends! Fiancés! Husbands! Fathers! Friends! *Drafted*! To go into the Army! To be trained as killers! To pick up an M16 and spit poison into a headwind! I know! You see this eye? It's made of glass! The government gave it to me. I speak to you with one lung. Could I show you! And many of you will go! Some of you will even volunteer! For what? For what reason? To save America? To save Sheridan Square? To save us from what? From what? Communists? Marxists? Whatever these words mean, we have some in this crowd! More in the Village! More at NYU! More at Columbia! And what have they done to you? To America? To Sheridan Square? As for dominoes, the only dominoes I know are played by old men on the hot sidewalks of Spanish Harlem! That's what I know! Whose war is it? Whose war, really, is it? . . ."

His voice trailed off as I turned the corner and walked down a side street past a few dressy tourists emerging with packages from a downstairs dress shop, past a young couple, both with long hair, he with a leather headband, she with large looped earrings, beads, a long cotton dress, arms about each other, swaying, laughing, stopping to kiss under a street lamp, and I envied the boy; smelled mothballs; suddenly turning to the wailing harmonica that coursed through the open door of a music shop, next to an old book store, books on Zen by Hayakawa, odd books on astrology, tarot, palmistry, macrobiotic diets, Castaneda, Huxley's *The Doors of Perception*, Lao Tzu, Ginsberg's *Howl*, Herrigel, *The Student As Nigger*—and there was *1984*—Herman Hesse, Huysmans, books in Hebrew and Chinese all dusty like the others and, god, in no particular order; I pulled from a crowded shelf, smelling of iodine, a slim book with close print and skimmed a page from a section called "The Treatise on the Steppenwolf," which irritated like ivy, like a rash were growing at the back of my sweaty neck, barely understanding the words:

Now it is between the two, in the middle of the road, that the bourgeois seeks to walk.

He will never surrender himself either to lust
or asceticism. . . . He strives neither for the
saintly nor its opposite. The absolute is his
abhorrence. He may be ready to serve God,
but not by giving up the fleshpots. He is ready
to be virtuous, but likes to be easy and comfortable in this world as well. In short, his aim
is to make a home for himself between two
extremes in a temperate zone without violent
storms and tempests . . . A man cannot live
intensely except at the cost of the self. Now
the bourgeois treasures nothing more highly
than the self (rudimentary as his may be). And
so at the cost of intensity he achieves his own
preservation and security. . . . The bourgeois
is consequently by nature a creature of weak
impulses, anxious, fearful of giving himself
away and easy to rule.

That was enough; I replaced the book and, by habit, straight-
ened the books surrounding it, then walked into the street and the
humid night air, sidestepping strangers, a portly man with mottled
face eating an Italian Ice, smelling incense in front of a head shop
where a couple, leaning against each other, pressed their faces to the
glass, pointing to water pipes and bongs and various colored rolling
papers, tweezers, rolling machines, miniature spoons on chains; passing others who led each other by the hand out of little shops display-
ing dresses, T-shirts, Indonesian wall hangings, the smell of Burma,
refuse, and from somewhere the trace of marijuana.

As I turned the corner onto a narrow cobblestone street, the
shops, the lights, the noise of human traffic grew gradually sparser,
only a guitar, one note at a time, something invented for the moment
by a kid with long blonde hair, girl or boy I couldn't tell, sitting on the

curb next to two others, a bottle of black wine between them, passing a joint that for a second lit up a young girl's face. "You want a hit?" she said, when I asked where Baker Street was. She pointed to the corner. Turn left, I thought, remembering Mr. Broder's directions, when the one in the middle, also a girl, lay back on the sidewalk cupping her eyes, saying, "Where are the fucking stars, man?" then more quietly, "Like I don't ever want to go back home."

On Baker Street I walked beneath the cool leafage of young maples opposite the row of three-story brownstones, "in a bourgeois neighborhood," I thought. I lit a cigarette and sat on the steps of Mr. Broder's house and wondered why I was there. I mean, what did I expect? I didn't even know why I had called. I flicked the butt into the gutter, irritated at myself. I felt like a stray dog.

When the door opened: "Yo, boy." I turned around, my eyes like discs; I mean, the guy was huge. And black as Maxwell House Coffee.

I sprang up, "I was just—"

"You *Kenji*?" (*Who was he?*)

"Yeah," I said. His trapezius muscles were like black wings, like the lats, pinions to the massive knobs of his deltoids, cinched, as with wire, from the triceps, biceps, as though his arms were stuffed with sweet potatoes.

"Well, come on in, boy," he said impatiently, turning sideways, his pectorals like saddlebags, gesturing with his head. "Fred's in the dining room." I followed him into the dimly lit hall, which smelled faintly of turpentine, stopped as he did next to a staircase, where he said, "Take off your sneakers, boy." I looked at my feet. Then he walked down the bare hall in black, felt Chinese shoes embroidered with gold, baggy black sweat pants, and a sleeveless black under-shirt, his arms barely swinging, held naturally apart from his torso, as though he were carrying suitcases. Sitting on the bottom step of the staircase, I pulled off my sneakers, decided to take off my damp socks, too, placed them neatly next to the tall Oriental urn, which sprouted a couple of umbrellas and a wicker cane. I felt a little anxious without my shoes. In my dreams of flight, I was always in the city, in the neighborhood, running away in bare feet. I was sure there was somebody in the house upstairs.

"Well, I see you found your way all right," Mr. Broder said. It was a lofty, dark room, its walls crowded with vague canvases, illumined by the light from the kitchen at Mr. Broder's back and a string of Christmas lights, red hearts, strung above the tall windows to his left. "I guess you already met Mr. Hughes, but you can call him Virgil." They were sitting on either side of a long table in pews painted with brown enamel. Mr. Broder was dressed in a tan polo shirt.

"Have a seat, boy," Virgil said, staring me straight in the eyes.

"Kenji," I said, staring him back. At which point he smiled and lowered his chin, chuckling to himself.

"Okay, Kenji. Have a seat," he said, gesturing me to the place next to Mr. Broder, to a pair of chopsticks laid over a paper napkin and an empty black dish. "Hey, bro, this kid's all right."

"What, didn't you believe me?" said Mr. Broder, lighting up a Chesterfield, refilling his goblet with the magnum at his side.

"New York City. Ha!"

"Help yourself," said Mr. Broder. "Virg, why don't you tell him what you've prepared." The table was thick with ceramic plates and bowls filled with different foods, most of which I couldn't recognize, though they appeared and smelled Oriental.

"No thanks. I've eaten," I said, looking at Virgil; I suddenly realized, in the block of the kitchen light, that Virgil was at least as old as Mr. Broder. He had little coils of gray in his short hair and flecks of it in his mustache that curled around his thick lips into a short beard. "You made all this?" I asked.

"Virgil is a chef, Kenji. At the Polynesian Room. And a poet," Mr. Broder said, wincing a little.

"Want a hit of Darvon?" Virgil said, eating from his chopsticks something that looked like crooked orange wires. "Oooooie, that's a

killer! That fucker is spicy! Korean *taegu*," he said to me, "dried cod-
fish, chili pepper—what ya think, Fred?"

"It'll subside."

"What's wrong?" I asked.

"Gout," Mr. Broder said, lifting his swollen bare foot, resting it
on the pew. Damn, it was big as a pork butt."

"Don't know your foods. Your chemical makeup, bro. Looks
like I gotta carry you home again," said Virgil. Which puzzled me.
Home?

"What's this I hear?" I turned around to meet a slender woman
with large, flattened breasts in a blue halter-top and paint-stained cut-
offs, dark blonde hair wrapped in a towel. "Have you been a naughty
boy again, Fred? A glass of wine, please," she said to Virg—dawning
on me that this was Virgil's house, that, of course, the electric hearts,
the pews, were his. The paintings hers. That the wicker cane was Mr.
Broder's.

"Melanie, meet Kenji," Mr. Broder said through clenched
teeth.

"Hello, Kenji," she said, smiling, sitting next to Virg.
"Continuation School, right?" Her skin was pasty white.

"A former student," said Mr. Broder, easing his foot down.
"How's the work going?" he asked, blotting his forehead with a
napkin.

"Good. Good," she said, sipping her wine with one hand, the
other raised to the back of her head, adjusting the towel; she had hair
under her arms. "Mmmmm." She reached over to Virg's plate for his
chopsticks, plucked from a brown bowl a chunk of something dark
red, wet with seaweed. "When you're better I'll show you."

"Raw tuna," Virg said, "marinated in soy sauce and sesame seed
oil. The green stuff is Atlantic seaweed. Crunchy, makes for good
contrast with the fish. Try some. Melts in your mouth."

"Has a lot of protein, too. Well, gotta go," Melanie said, lightly
rubbing her arms. "Starting to feel it." She rose. "Nice to meet you,

Kenji." Then she did something which seemed totally spontaneous. She leaned down to Virgil, put her right arm around his neck, pressed her cheek into his, and bound the embrace with her left arm, her left hand pressed to his other cheek. And for long seconds their faces and arms, her hand upon his cheek, were momentarily frozen in the square of the kitchen light, oblivious to our presence, perhaps oblivious to each other, though there was a sameness in their faces, his wrinkled dark skin and pug nose, her pale white skin and translucent eyebrows, and their half-closed eyes—a sameness, a wholeness beyond human affairs that leaped out at me, suggesting ancient anguish and greatness, filling the upper reaches of my chest, the back of my neck, my head tingling, my eyes welling, nearly blacking out holding my breath. It was also spooky. I was unable to glance at Mr. Broder. Then picking up her wine glass, her eyes already preoccupied, she vanished from the room.

Virgil looked at me serenely and said, "Try some."

"Melanie," Mr. Broder said in a tired voice, "is sensitive to chemicals in the air. Not only from pollutants but from fabrics, perfumes, that sort of thing. Fifteen minutes in Bloomingdale's and she panics, choking for breath. Sometimes she'll break out in a rash."

"Fred, here, thinks it's mostly in her head," said Virg, smirking, flexing his pectorals, first the left then the right.

"That's not entirely true," said Mr. Broder, almost under his breath, wiping beneath his reddish mustache at the corners of his lips. "Virg can show you her room. A glass door with a speaker in the middle. The windows sealed. Even in the bathroom. Air-conditioned twenty-four hours a day. She comes out—what—for two or three hours at a time?" (Virg nodded) "to work in her third floor studio . . . Virg," he said, almost under his breath, "I think I better call it a night. No, Kenj, you stay awhile. Talk to Virg. He'll be right back. I just live next door."

"Sure," I said, surprising myself.

After hearing the front door close, I sampled some of the Korean *taegu*—man, was it hot! I washed it down with the remains of Mr. Broder's goblet and, glancing around the room, wondered what Melanie was doing. I sidled out from my seat and looked at her paintings in the dim light. They were all large, unframed canvases, and except for the one above the low bookcase, they were all paintings of nude women. One was hard to see; it was a tall canvas hung on the wall between the two double windows beneath the electric hearts. It looked like a stream made up of strings of different colors, until I recognized her form. The woman was almost invisible. Another woman was part of a volcano, while in the one next to it, against a reddish background, lounged a buxom woman on a couch. It was stunning the way the painting drew your eye to the woman's enormous, powerful thigh. In another, a woman, presumably the mother, sat with a scrawny child on a stone bench, the mother's arm around the child's shoulder; both were bald; a muted, sad, grayish painting. But my favorite was the one hanging above the bookcase: it was of a naked child jumping rope in what looked to be the bottom of a stone well, its face strained with the wrinkles of an old man, its knees up in midjump, beneath the arch of the rope. I wished I had painted that.

"Like it?" Virg walked by into the kitchen. I hadn't heard the front door.

"Yeah. Yeah. She's some painter," I said. "Does she sell 'em?"

"Why?" he said, sticking his head out the doorway. "You want to buy something?"

"Man, if I had any bread, I'd buy this one," I said over my shoulder, my face feeling warm from the wine. I sat back down. He soon joined me, placing a clean goblet in front of me as he took his seat across the table. I shook my head and pushed the glass toward him. He filled it halfway and pushed it back toward me.

"I know you drink," he said.

"I was thirsty. The *taegu* was hot as hell," I said, pushing it back toward him. "Really, man, I don't drink. I don't even drink beer. I mean, I've tried it."

"Yeah," he said, "it takes practice. Just like your cigarettes. How many you smoke a day? A pack?" I nodded. "That stuff'll kill ya."

"Like wine," I said.

"True, bro. That's true. Especially if you don't know what the fuck you're doing. Don't know how far you can push, getting tired or scared. Don't know how to see over the rim once you've reached the edge, like great experimenters and discoverers, because you're too fucked up. With drugs, or with booze, or with sex, or with gambling, or with crime. With eating. With pumping iron. And because you're fucked up, doing it out of habit, operating like a machine, without freedom, to a predictable end, there's no joy in it—just a junkie without memory—so when you come back, you've got no news, not for yourself, much less for anyone else. Whereas, the connoisseur, you dig, goes at it with love, knows how to go the length of the table," he said, with a sweeping gesture over the food-laden table before us, "to the extreme, you dig, trying to know a thing by trying to exhaust its endless sensory and psychological possibilities, the endless subtleties, nuances—hot damn! But, you see," he said, leaning forward, wagging his forefinger at me, "you don't do it all the time. That shit just dulls the palate in your brain. And the thing is, you can do it with anything you choose. In any field. Maybe only in one. But in that one, you better love it; and if you don't have one, you better find it. 'Cause, dig, Mr. Death stands behind every corner you turn, and you never know when His Eminence is gonna collar your ass. For it's through that one thing that you'll learn who you are in connection to this world, making your young-ass self a man, an endless goddamn process of making yourself ripe, you dig? 'Ripeness is all.' You dig?" Then with two fingers he plucked up a piece of dark red, raw tuna from the bowl in front of me and said, with a certain glee, "Making yourself into a plum." Popping it with relish into his mouth.

After taking a long drink from his wine, his pectorals moving again, he placed the glass by its stem on the white oilcloth and asked, "So how come you don't like school? By the way, I dropped out, too. About your age, a matter of fact."

"I was kicked out," I said.

"That's just another name for it, boy," he said, seeming annoyed. "You didn't want to be there in the first place, right? A bunch of organized bullshit, right? Algebra, French. All that repetitive crap. Couldn't even read that skinny book, what was it?—*Silas Marner.* And when you forgot your gym shorts they made you sit in the stands like a jackass in your BVD's. Hey, I know, the whole thing was a drag. So what'd you do? Hang out in a poolroom?"

"Mr. Broder tell you that?"

"Look, man, I got nothing against poolrooms or you hanging in one."

"So what'd you do, rob a bank?" Here he paused. Then drank down the remainder of another glass, his eyes glossing over. Then nodded. "You're kidding," I said.

"Assault and battery, too," he said quietly. "Got ten-to-fifteen. Got out in six for good behavior. Damn, I was good . . . Look. You and me—we weren't ready for school. Even if the school weren't a factory and gave a damn about us. 'Cause we couldn't see any point in going. Nor did we have much patience putting up with dry teachers, taking from them what little good they offered and go on our happy little-ass way to the next dull class. And we wouldn't hear any counsel from adults, man or woman, talking about some distant future or threatening us with this or that nonsense. Hey, the future was now. And there was something honest about saying Fuck You to something dishonest. I mean, none of it means shit unless you yourself want to learn. Right? Then maybe you'd put up with that rinky-dink system. But wanting to learn for yourself, now that's groovy, that's fly. And you know what, it was in jail, after they locked up my self-pitying ass, that I came onto books, to thinking, to building up my body, to writing poetry, to fixing myself, the best I could, my own food while working in the kitchen.

"So here's my recommendation. Get busted for something. Stay in jail a few years."

I had to laugh, it was the craziest idea I ever heard. He poured another glass of wine and pushed it over to me.

"I'm serious, bro. You're smart. And you got some craft in you, too. I wouldn't recommend this to other kids your age. Prison would break them, change them ultimately into a criminal. And soon as they got out they'd be back inside lickety-split. You're different. Maybe a little small, but a few phone calls to the brothers (pulling twenty to life), like letters of introduction—shit, nobody be trying to put their johnson into your pale little butt. Besides, you know how to bluff, know how to sell a New York woof ticket. Am I right? I know I'm right, I ain't blind. Most important, because you have a mind, and whole lot of time on your hands, especially in that little cell, you'll find something quick. Maybe like me it'll start with your body, the intimidations, snatching your food; pushups on the floor, a little handball in the yard, honing a little sticker from a scrap of aluminum, a spoon, finally pumping iron. And then, like me, you'll hear some-one talking in the yard to a group of inmates in a language you've never heard before, sometimes with the passionate voice of a street corner philosopher or preacher, about history or race or politics and certainly about law, and secretly you'll marvel over the music of his words, half of which you won't understand, but that won't matter, the sound and the rhythm and the headlong pace and the rapt faces round the ragged circle will get to you, slowly drawing you from the edge toward the center; then one day you'll pass the cell where he's reading something; then another day you'll pass it, more slowly each time, when he's writing something; then one day he'll raise his head and say, 'You want something?' and you'll say, 'What're you reading?' and he'll say, 'Why?' and you'll mumble something as you slouch away, feeling a little shame, knowing you don't know why, until you go to the prison library and check out some of the same books that were on his desk, whose titles you've memorized, and try to read them, barely getting past the first few pages of most of them, until one starts to speak to you. As one did to me. The author had the same name as mine. Hughes. Langston Hughes. And the next time you enter the circle, you move close to his elbow, and just as time expires you mention the book and its author, maybe mention how some of the poems struck you. And the tall black man with close-cropped red hair will look down on you with slightly raised eyes—of recognition—eyes which seem in a flash to weigh and approve your sincerity, eyes which encourage your pursuit in improving the quality of your mind. That tall Black man, by the way, was Malcolm X, the finest, fiercest, most dignified Black activist to have ever laid footprints on this white American earth, Praise Allah, Amen. Whooo! I need a drink!"

"What about Dr. King?" I asked, my face feeling flushed.

"The Reverend King? I don't know, I just sympathize with Malcolm. He has no illusions of assimilating into the white status quo, into the white man's culture. Which in white man's eyes, and Black folks, too, is," he said, pointing to his forearm, "impossible. Though I like Reverend King's idea of mutually, all of us, creating a new culture. But then again, that ain't gonna happen unless bold men like Malcolm make society see, in Technicolor, in 3-D, the innate integrity and courage of a minority race. I dig his jump-in-your-face, confrontational style. And, in a different way, like the Reverend King, Malcolm is eloquent."

"Eloquent," I repeated. I was dizzy. My forehead was sweating, like I had a fever. I wanted to go home, but somehow I didn't know how to take my leave. I was strangely scared.

"Another thing that Malcolm taught me was that words were power. That whoever can command words is powerful. You follow my drift?" I didn't but nodded anyway. "Who was it? 'Words: the bridge that carries us across the void, from the Mountain of Birth to the Mountain of Death.' The thing is, as we move toward the far mountain, each of us continually creates a bridge from the words, the flesh and bones of our own character. Ideally, with each plank that is added, all of what we made is revised for the better, made stronger, made more eloquent, moving in a beautiful arc," he said, his big arm tracing the air like a dancer. "And there comes a time when a great one appears, creating a bridge of such stunning power that it is big enough to carry hosts of people, whole races and civilizations, across the void . . ." After a long pause, as I finished off my glass, Virgil sighed heavily. "Look, Kenj, I don't mean to throw you out, but I'm a little fucked up."

A few months later, just before signing up with the Air Force, I visited Virg one last time. For the occasion, he cooked up a Spanish casserole of shellfish, yellow rice, pimentos, peas, and sausages. Washing it all down with iced pitchers of red wine thick with floating fruit. The stuff was so sweet, I drank it like soda. Going straight to my head. Mr. Broder, despite nursing, again, his gouty foot, was in good spirits, too, sitting at the head of the table like a king, while Melanie, who stayed with us a good two hours beyond her limit, ignoring her prickling skin, kept filling our sloshing goblets, shaking her hips to the loud Latin music on the record player (on the low bookshelf beneath the rope-jumping infant), to the vibraphones of Cal Tjader, Tito Fuentes's brass band, the bongos and conga of Mongo Santamaria; Mr. Broder, eyes closed, head swaying, drumming the edge of the table with his fork and spoon; Virg howling like Dizzy Gillespie, sweating, though a light flurry was falling beyond the window, talking dizzily about books, music, food, about politics, about Malcolm X getting gunned down in the Audubon Ballroom in upper Manhattan, "a sad fucking day for America," about his deep deep voice, about the poetry of Langston Hughes "pure music, bro," the headlong lines of Walt Whitman, the rhythm, the rush of "that righteous mother-fucker, John Big Dick Milton," seeing it all in Ginsberg's screaming *Howl*," saying that, whether I knew it or not, that I hailed from a very literary neighborhood, that, in fact, in the 50s, the novelist Jack Kerouac and Ginsberg had lived in my building above the Aki Dining Room, that another writer, a walking cadaver, William Burroughs, with a pocketful of miracle drugs, would visit them, that I had probably brushed by them as I played tag in the streets with my friends; which didn't impress me as much as the two postcards he would send me later. One, that the Frame boys' father, who taught French at Columbia, had just published the definitive translation of Montaigne's essays, "Check it out." The second, more than two decades later (the last I would hear from him), that Bosco's brother Oscar, with whom I'd taken English classes (taught by Heller, Barthelme, and Vonnegut) at City College, had just won the Pulitzer Prize for fiction. Beneath his musical signature, he wrote, as if to say goodbye, the title of Oscar's book: *The Mambo Kings Play Songs of Love.*

BOOTS

It was during my flight to Dallas, Texas, thence to Lackland Air Force Base, that I wrote the first of many letters home—to Joe, to Sully, to my mother and my sister Mimi. But mostly to Jocelyn, a tall, slender, dark-skinned girl, who, with her father and her two older sisters, had recently immigrated to the island of Manhattan from the island of Haiti. A leap of cultural light years. We had dated off and on for about a year. But I don't know why. When I first met her in the neighborhood, it took me about a month to get used to her plainness. Besides, she could barely speak English and was at least two or three inches taller than I. I suppose what drew me to her was her innocence and sincerity and the loneliness palpable in her eyes, so far from home, stuck, without choice, in a foreign world.

I would feel a similar loneliness for the first six months of boot camp and technical school. Nor would its shadow, a kind of longing, ever leave me. Probably having been a part of me from the first, though it might have taken me longer than others to understand this. Or maybe because of the draft I came to understand this sooner than most. In either case, in this I wasn't alone.

We lived for letters, dreamed about the next one from our girl, hoping it would be a thick one, fondling the ones we received, smelling them, reading them over and over, our shaven heads bowed under the wide expanse of Texas sky or lying in our bunks before lights out, thinking of home, thinking of the distance—when the memory of walking about with house keys in your pocket or flipping through the TV guide became the monuments of a former life. And I thought of the strength of Jocelyn's firm, slender arms around my neck, her lips against mine, her tongue exploring my mouth, remembering the times we wrestled hungrily in the balcony of the Symphony movie house on 95th Street and Broadway. I was in love. I was in love, it seemed, as we pounded the left heel of our brogans into the road—"Listen to it," Sgt. Bickford would say, tired of calling out "Yor lef . . . yor lef"—as, in columns of four, eyes staring at the back of the head of the airman in front of us, we'd march to the rifle range, the dispensary, the parade ground, the classrooms in the Quonset hut, the mess hall, the admin building, the PX, then back to the barracks; it seemed I was in love with someone or other since fourth grade, in love with someone or other most of the nineteen years of my life. That being in love, that divine distraction, helped you endure the tedium, the drivel, the misery, the sadness, the grief of loss, like the time I was in love with haughty Suzanne when my father died.

The military, I said to Jocelyn in another letter, tried to strip you of your identity through intimidation and fear, a drill instructor (usually some staff sergeant from the South), yelling in your face, in your ear, at the back of your skull, in your other ear, calling you a dipshit as you stood at attention—naming you "Buddha," "Willie Mays," "Pimples," "Gimp," in the initial shakedown ("You don't like that, boy? Who you looking at? You don't look at nothing! Put your heels together!"), civilian suitcases, handbags, sacks opened, lying atop thin, bare mattresses, poking with a swagger stick, flipping through your personal effects, so much rubbish ("What's this?" It was a large postcard of the Confederate flag I'd picked up at the airport. "You making fun of something, boy?" "No." "I can't hear you!" "No!" "No, *sir!*' "No, *sir!*"), constantly bellowing at you, demeaning you, reducing you to your dog tag number (which you better not forget), your weight, your size place, the mistakes you make (insuring that you made them): all of us bald, tired, pitiful, showering and shaving together, defecating en masse on bare toilets six inches apart, knocking knees; constantly lining us up to wait here or go there from five in the morning till ten at night, your every move regulated, inspected, criticized, your bed, your footlocker, your shoes ("Who in the godforsaken world taught you how to shave, boy?"); constantly testing your stamina, your obedience, constantly breaking you down (and one did break, banging his head against a locker, anything, "Get me the fuck outta here!"); another (our greatest fear) repeating the whole six-week cycle, which would have been longer had there been no war going on; and I would think of you, Jocelyn, your baby blue sweater, fondling your breasts, the flesh round your pelvic bone, your tight thighs, virgin that you are, that I am, imagining us naked and sweating laid on a beach towel on the roof of 401, feeling like Jupiter, making it rain everywhere over the hot dry streets of Manhattan, over the whole Earth, words which I showed my bunkmate Sky who smiled with approval, impressed, thinking it poetry; an *ode* I said, having somewhere heard the word.

I told Sky, who was from Tennessee, that Jocelyn and her father had left Haiti in 1964, fleeing Papa Doc Duvalier and his Tonton Macout ("His what?"): the trained murderers and thugs of the secret police. Which, like most secret police, was invented for the sole purpose of voodooing its own people. Through Jocelyn, her sisters (Brigette and Florelle), and her father, through their graciousness and hospitality—"Southern, no doubt," said Sky—through their innocence of New York and their nasal French accent (through the scents of Air du Temps and Ambush), through the openness of their lifestyle, recalling verandahs and spacious countryside, they more or less civilized the boys in the neighborhood, eventually marrying three of them. They invited us into their home to sit and eat with them, rice and beans, pork chops and peppers, an occasional glass of red wine, to play bridge with them, disarming us of our coarse language, our streetwise posture, recruiting us as tutors of the American way of life, forcing us to exercise the better parts of our nature.

After mail call, Sky found me staring at the springs of the bunk above me and asked me to write an *ode* for him. Sky was recently married and was probably from a fine Knoxville family; there was nothing sloppy about him, the way he groomed himself and dressed, the way his fatigues and formal blues clung to his slim body as if they were tailored for him (my sleeves were always too long, my shirt rising above my belt, bunching out at the waist), the way he marched (though I marched as well), because of his height and build, he simply cut a finer figure, the way he stood sharply at attention, saluting, or standing during long periods at parade rest under the Texas sun without growing fatigued, without his muscles tightening or his joints locking (while I bitched out of the side of my mouth); the way he made his bed, kept his footlocker, the way he ate, his back naturally upright like the way he sat in chapel, alert, and rarely (unlike us) did he swear and complain, affable and polite, saying "sir" as naturally as he would say "How are you feeling, Kenj?" Had he been given the chance, he would have made a fine officer, a quick attaché to some high ranking general or a navigator on a B-52. Mutt and Jeff, we made an odd pair.

"Do you think you could write a poem for me?" He took out his wallet and, ducking beneath the bedrail, sat beside me on the bunk, smelling of after-shave. "Here," he said, passing me a snapshot of his wife, "just so you get a feel for what she's like." And as soon as I saw her sitting on the steps of a porch, I knew that the poem that Sky wanted me to write for her was not the kind I had written for Jocelyn. With her long, straight blonde hair, draped like a veil behind her shoulders, Sky's young wife reminded me of Kristin, my first girlfriend, someone who preferred shorts and T-shirts to dresses, walking about in bare feet, climbing trees and statues (we were nine and ten at the time), who ran as fast as the boys, as we fled the campus guards, and was daring, even crazy at times (Kris once walked the roof ledge of Laureate Hall, a nine-story apartment building, said she did it all the time); someone who was nevertheless softly feminine, innocent. Like our first dry kiss in front of everyone.

A couple of decades later I would remember her in another poem I wrote called "Before My Years" . . .

Before they ripped out the walkways,
tore down the giant maples impossible to climb,
where neighborhood mothers and professors' wives
        strolled with their babies,
crushing cinnamon leaves under the wheels of their
        carriages
or sat on granite benches by the Fountain of Neptune,
before the water ran dry, before Columbia turned it off,
where they read Ferlinghetti under an apricot sky,
or stared across the far shady lawns, fenced off by pillars
and thick iron arrows from the avenue of smoke;
before they tore up the grass and built tennis courts;
before they dug through their clay surfaces
and built scaffolding for the new school of business;
before the campus guards grew grizzly and ran us off the
        grounds,
Bobby and I played catch, tossing a pink ball, like an
        apple,
through the long bronze afternoons;
where in the game Truth or Consequence
I was forced into my first kiss,
Christine on the lips as soft as salamanders,
under a lavender sky;
before turning and running home under the lamplight,
        an umbrella of snow;
an old man before my years, having already died.

At the end of basic training, after sewing on our first stripe, we received our orders. I would be shipped to north Texas, to technical school. Never to see Sky again.

Hard to believe, but Sheppard Air Force Base, at Wichita Falls, was even flatter and more uniform than Lackland. And lucky me, like other new trainees, we pulled sixteen-hour-a-day KP duty for six straight days. Mopping and wiping and peeling and scraping, it seemed I could never get out of the kitchen, someone forever hounding me to move faster, until I died; when they would wrap my greasy corpse in a wet apron before burying it beneath the floor of the walk-in freezer, a lone chaplain reciting Bubba's "Elegy for a Kitchen Stiff." So mind-numbing was the work that I could hardly think of Jocelyn, much less write to her, as my black buddy Felix did every night writing to his wife before falling asleep: P. S. Better practice walking around looking at the floor, for when I come home in six months, you'll see nothing but ceiling.

Felix and I shared the same barracks room with four other guys training to be teletype maintenance men, each of the four at different stages in their schooling, each with a calendar taped to the inside of his locker, below the boobs of *Playboy* pinups, pictures of their girlfriends or wives, their dogs, their cars or pickup trucks (counting the days, known by the numbers they had remaining), poring over schematics and electrical diagrams (as Felix and I would), sometimes in the darkened hall with a flashlight before test days, damned if they failed, having to repeat a unit on this or that machine, setting themselves back another two or four weeks—for six days a week to pull work duty in the morning, to pass in review after lunch (sweating, your spit-shine melting under the hot sun), to march to school for the afternoon, to march back, to march to chow again, to iron your fatigues with enough starch to stop a bullet, to pore over the manuals, memorizing mechanical trains, the five-unit permutation code, the acceptable clearance for the magnet controlling the code ring cage, making the incredible machine come alive, spitting out a hundred words a minute: "The Kleinschmidt is like a woman," the instructor said, patting the cover. "And this is like her dress. Go ahead, take it off. There's a screw here and one on the other side. See? This ain't like that fat lady I showed y'all down the hall, jiggling with all those wheels and springs. This baby is refined. You can stick your hand right through it. Or a leg if you have a mind to." Ha, ha. ("Or your redneck pecker," Felix said under his breath.)

But the thing was, it kind of interested me, how all these things were connected and worked together simultaneously. How could one man think it all up? No doubt about it, that Kleinschmidt was a genius. And I guess I was a little surprised that I aced or nearly aced all their paper-and-pencil tests. Me. —Not that I could troubleshoot or fix the machines; that kind of training would come later on the job, when I'd panic and call for help. It also surprised me that I knew more than I thought I did, when, in order to escape the drudgery of morning work details, I took a battery of multiple-choice tests for several days in the personnel office and, after the last, was informed that I had just earned a General Education Diploma (which would prove invaluable to my getting into college). Felix was jealous that I got out of work duty while he had to mop, wax, and buff the floors of the Officers' Day Room, "You Japanese faggot," while I sat in an air-conditioned room penciling in little boxes and drinking coffee.

And gradually my feelings for Jocelyn would fade. Nor would she continue to write me. Everything, it seemed, was limited and temporary, which seemed especially true in the military. Friendships, at least for me, were formed for the moment with whomever chance had thrown my way, as with Sky, who liked marching, or with Felix, who liked The Temptations and The Miracles and fell asleep every night to the crooning of Nancy Wilson. Thinking always of the time growing shorter, we kept our private lives at a distance from each other, and it was okay, there were no regrets, so that (with new orders in our pockets) we knew, after shaking hands and saying we'd keep in touch, it wouldn't be true. Hoisting our duffle bags over our shoulders, walking, one after another at the same tilted angle though the barracks door, we were already on leave. Already with friends and family. Already home.

But things were limited and temporary everywhere. Benny, I heard right away, had been killed in Vietnam by "friendly fire," and Andrew Young was cut down a little over a month earlier on patrol just outside of Quang Tri. My friends were still going to graduate school, moving steadily toward marriage. My older sister Reiko, still single, still proud of the fact that she was on file with the CIA for picking sugar cane one summer in Cuba during the late Fifties.

I "broke dawn" that first night back, drinking beer with Sully, Joe, and Johnny on Johnny's stoop, across the street from Jocelyn's apartment building. "Did you hear that Jocelyn and Justin Bones are seeing each other?" Johnny asked. Joe and Sully were looking at me out of the corner of their eyes.

"Yeah," I said, brushing cigarette ash from the wrinkled lap of my summer uniform, "I stopped by early last night. Everyone looks the same. Look, it's no big thing, man. We're going to the movies Friday night. She was happy I asked."

"Ah, you should forget about her," said Joe. Sully was silent.

"Yeah," Johnny said, taking a gulp from his beer. The morning light between the buildings was a quiet blue. "Besides, you'll be gone in a couple of weeks anyhow."

"Look, man," I said, "I stopped crying over that girl months ago. I mean, I don't have to go out with her." Which was the truth.

"Here's what I'll do with you," said Joe, the businessman, "I'll give you fifteen bucks if you change your mind about Friday,"

"You serious?"

"Is it a bet?"

"I'll take five of that," said Sully.

"I'll take five, too," said Johnny.

"You guys got a bet," I said. The bet was a lock. The affair was formally over.

One night, a few days before heading out to Omaha, I was standing by the iron bars, calling to Joe at his second-story window at the end of the alleyway, when I heard over my shoulder "Kenji?" I turned and recognized her right away. Even after eleven years.

"Bonnie?" She looked the same. Perhaps more beautiful. I had a crush on her in third grade. Boy, was she sassy, didn't like that I liked her. Had her fifth-grade sister threaten me. "What're you doing in my neighborhood?"

"I live in 401, right on the Drive," she said, smiling. She was dressed in a light summer coat. She always dressed nicely. Her family was well off, even had a big car, a kind of crazy thing to have in New York City; I saw it one evening at school parked by the playground. Her folks (her mother was white, her father black) were having a little spat.

"Columbia?" I asked.

"Uh-huh, a junior." We talked about ten minutes recalling old classmates, teachers, where they were now, what I was doing, before finally parting company. As she walked down the street, out of my life for a second time (she had tested into Bronx High School of Science the first time), I wondered how hard life had been on her, how she must have struggled with her identity. Through elementary and junior high school, though her physical appearance proclaimed her white, she behaved and talked, walked and danced like a black. No, not *like*, she *was* black. And proud of it, thank you very much. Which, I suppose, was an anomaly that Harlem tolerated as *cute* in a little "white" girl walking between her two tall parents—but as audaciousness or stupidity or ignorance in a young white woman chicly dressed. And it might have been dangerous for her, too, walking the streets in neighborhoods beyond her own to catch the bus or to walk to the train station. As for white folks and her own whiteness, how did she reconcile that with herself? Did she accept, finally embrace, that part of her, too? I wondered if any of her white acquaintances had ever cast racial slurs in her presence, ignorant of her background. The young Bonnie would have struck like a cat, hands on saucy hips, ready to go to blows. Feeling yourself an anomaly with white folks, too. And the same old questions, the explanations, how tiring it was. The irksome, stupid assumptions. I know. Though the questions put to me were different: *What country you from? What language you speak? Hey, you speak pretty good.* —"I'm American, you dipshit!"

Funny. When Bonnie and I met that night, we met again like children. Our eyes filled with Mrs. Thompson's classroom, the noisy cafeteria, the school playground crowded with jubilant ghosts. The world, it seemed, was wiser then. Or, at least, *we* were. As she turned the corner on Amsterdam Avenue, I wanted to run after her, turn her around, cradle her heart-shaped face in my hands, and kiss her.

Offutt Air Force Base, Omaha, Nebraska, Headquarters of the Strategic Air Command, is located at the very heart of America, the Command Post itself buried ten stories below ground. Here, as above ground, along General's Row, a shady street of large country houses opposite the parade ground, generals with stars on their epaulets abounded. In fact, in the event that Offutt ever came under attack, one general was always in the air in a military 747, in the Looking Glass, to assume command and pursue the war to its conclusion. When it descended after twelve hours, its twin was already in the air, assuming the proper altitude.

I worked in the maintenance shop down the hall from NORAD Control, whose monitors could pick up a flea's behind, much less a Russian missile hauling ass over the pole. For three day shifts, three swing shifts, three midnight shifts, and two days off, according to Zulu time, I worked in this lightless well for eighteen months. Across two winters when the wind (the Hawk or Giant Razor Blade, the black guys called it), slashed at our faces and wrists as we walked across the flight line. Across the spring and the humid, rank summer when the hot breeze would shift, bringing us the thick brown stench of the stockyards across the steaming road. Many of the old-timers, teletype operators mostly, mainly Southern blacks, kept to their barracks room drinking Old Grandad and listened to jazz, as Plaud, an Irish kid from Boston, usually did. If he weren't in the basement with Captain Oakley (a clarinet man) practicing his alto sax.

It was through Plaud that I learned to like Diz and Trane, Miles and Bird, I had little choice. Plaud played their records day and night, playing them with the volume turned up, his door open, were he playing pool or double-deck pinochle in the lounge. It was also through Plaud, one of the few single guys on base who had a car, who introduced me one night to Mrs. Oakley, Lorraine, who was drinking beer with her husband in the corner booth of the Brown Derby downtown.

She did not say hi. Her eyes were bloodshot. Probably in her middle thirties.

"Thailand, eighteen months," said Captain Oakley. (I'd be shipping out to Guam in eight. A short timer!) "Got the orders today. It won't be that long, honey. —Look, Lorraine, why don't we have a barbecue this Saturday? You guys off?" We both nodded. "I'll cook up some ribs, make a salad, corn on the cob, the kids'll love it. A small going away party. Just us, Plaud and Kenji here. What do you say?"

"Oh, I guess so," she said. She had short, dirty-blonde hair, slight breasts, a slight frame and was slightly taller than I was. (Jocelyn, I remembered, had me by three inches and ten pounds.) And like Jocelyn, Lorraine was older than I was, too. I was merely making observations at the time. They lived in a rented house on the outskirts of Omaha with two pretty little girls, six and eight; the older one liked teasing me, started sticking her tongue at me in an odd sort of way once I began sleeping in her mother's bedroom. A virgin no longer, the surface mystery over. Captain Oakley teased, too—not that he actually gave me permission. When I helped him fill up the cooler with drinks from the fridge, he said, "Now, I want you and Plaud to keep Lorraine happy while I'm gone." He then smiled, pointing at the brown bottle of Geritol on the fridge door. "I gotta take it to keep the old blood going. Not like you young bucks." Then he winked at me. I didn't quite know how to take him.

And we loved each other, I suppose, in the way two people so different were able to, both knowing that what we shared was temporary, that eventually I would be going and that her husband would return, and that for a time it was enough that we filled each other's loneliness, each other's need for affection, closeness, and sex. And as for that, she seemed as clumsy and as innocent and apologetic as I, though she had two kids and had been married for years. But I took little notice and checked any questions and responsibilities: whether or not, for example, she experienced an orgasm herself; or how her kids felt about our sleeping together, how that might affect them in the future; or if I were the first or sixth to be with Lorraine. Or what her husband might feel, Captain Oakley who befriended me, had the single guys over for holiday dinners. Or that, after making love, after smoking a cigarette, a dullness would pervade my skull, a feeling that I could shut off with sleep or the next time we made love, a growing anger in me, a vague, subconscious self-loathing, I suppose, that gradually made me impatient and short with Lorraine, and eventually cruel. For what or why, I did not know. The fawning eyes that made me cruel. This Alabama woman with two kids who took the moment-to-moment chores of life so lightly, easily, one day after another, whom Plaud called "Grandma" to bust my chops, who mostly wanted someone to hug, to hug her back. She would do the laundry, she would do the cooking, she would raise the kids. She would drive the lover back and forth to base. She who knew better than I that, though time was short, it could be filled with loving. That I could have been kinder to her.

My comeuppance would come on Guam (The Rock), on Andersen Air Force Base, quickly accustomed (deaf) to the noise of

B-52s taking off in the morning for Vietnam, their returning in the late afternoon, blind to the mess they'd left behind. I was also blinded by the scorching heat, dreading the morning, the unrelenting light, the god-awful humidity. Bored to tears by the monotony of greasy, repetitive work, and by the long limp hours when I didn't, I found temporary distraction in a part-time job at the base bowling alley, spying on officers' wives, female dependents of almost any age, or I visited with Filipino Ray, one of many civilian contract workers far from home, who ran the ceramics shop (next to the lapidary shop), who talked frequently of his wife and two daughters back home. Of his herculean sexual prowess.

Or I took the shuttle bus to the beach, or walked across the field to the pool opposite on-base housing to check out the teenage girls, or walked in circles round the display cases of the PX, down the aisles of the commissary, wherever the women were, or I'd catch a ride with Chester from Hawaii, a Chinese teletype operator, who was having an affair with a married Guamanian (in collusion with the daughter who pretended to be his girlfriend) to check out the local girls, or I'd go to the library and read D.H. Lawrence and Nabokov between the air-conditioned shelves, a couple of Japanese writers, Mishima and Kawabata (whose short story, "House of Sleeping Beauties," would later influence one of mine), or I took a night class in college English, where two rows to my right, and three seats to my rear sat Alicia, a long-legged, short-haired blonde with tiny hoops in her ears, who had a left eye askew of center (it was hard to tell, at first, what she was looking at), wearing very tight short-shorts, who would compete in a contest for Miss Guam eight months later, running out of money, since, as the director-choreographer said, she needed more meat.

She was eighteen years old and recently graduated from high school, the daughter of a senior master sergeant; part Mexican, part German, part Jewish, a military brat who had been round the world, had made friends and boyfriends with many different people, saying to me once that she had seen the children of mixed marriages and thought, "They were cute." So for the first few weeks I worked very hard in English, trying to impress her, my hand raised to answer the teacher's questions or to offer witty observations on the readings we had for homework; writing what I thought was an excellent composition comparing the B-52s to sharks, when, on the night I was to read before the class, she didn't show up. She didn't show up for the next few classes either.

I next saw her sunning herself on the pool deck with her friends, when she reached behind her to tie the strings of her halter top. After she left, I asked her friends what her name was, then ran to the rail to watch her walk in her bare feet across the lawn in the direction of the housing area for military families. "Alicia!" I called. Then when she turned I raised my arm and waved to her. She waved back. Then turned, the beach towel slung over her left shoulder, the end swaying gently with her proud, runway walk.

The next I saw her was at the bowling alley where I had just relieved Zack. When she suddenly appeared before me at the counter, leaning toward me with both elbows on the surface, smiling at me full in the face. "Hi," she said, the top of her blouse falling forward.

"Hi . . . Alicia," I said, stunned. She was wearing her bathing suit top underneath her blouse. "I've been wondering where you were."

"Why? You've only seen me once."

"Twice." She had a long neck. I knew what Dracula felt.

"Where?"

"It was your fault that I got a C- in English. I was getting an A before you decided to drop the class."

"'You were in that class?"

"Yup . . . By the way, my name is Kenji," I said, staring into her eyes, both the right one and the left, then at her lips.

"I know," she said, beaming. And my heart jumped.

The next night, after watching a movie at the outdoor theatre, we strolled over the lawn to her house and sat on a couch in the darkened living room, kissing and pawing each other, me biting and sucking her long neck. After work the next day (I was now working shifts, manning the phones in Communications Control), I walked over to the commissary where Alicia just got a job sitting at a dais by the commissary entrance checking military IDs. She smiled as soon as she saw me. "How ya doing?" I said.

"A little sore," she said smiling, pulling down the collar of her white smock. She had a string of dark purple bruises all about her neck. "But I kind of like it."

"Did I do that?"

"My father said I had to control myself more," she said, her eyes twinkling. "Want to come over tonight?"

"Sure," I said. What was I, crazy? But her parents greeted me cordially, even with Alicia's neck in full view before us all. It was okay, they seemed to be telling me, knowing their daughter better than I, I supposed. We were more or less bound by those bruises. And the library. I sent her little notes scribbled with Renaissance love poems. Which she thought was very thoughtful and cute, if a little schmaltzy. But, God, I was in love. And for a time, so was she, calling me at work when I pulled night duty. And on those nights that I was off we made love everywhere, on the lanai, in the backyard, in her old man's car, fogging the windows, trying everything from cunnilingus to tortellini, fondling each other in sweet torture at the movies, in the pool, in the sea, in her old man's car as she drove us to Agana. I mean, she was young and sexy, and smarter than I was (having read and experienced a lot), while she was proud of the fact that she was going with a man. A *man!*

So, about three months later, we were suddenly engaged, trying on rings over the glass counter of the PX. And there were plans to be made, a date to be set, money to be set aside, signing on with the Air Force for another tour, to be stationed where? It didn't matter. Anywhere with Alicia would be fine. Chester would teach me how to drive, lessons beginning Saturday, which would end three Saturdays hence—quitting. Alicia having quitted me.

But, what had I done? What was wrong? Was she angry about something? Was she playing with me? I mean, I was desperately in love with her, my heart cracking, I couldn't take no for an answer without some explanation, so I hounded her at every turn—incessantly called her up to plead my case, her brother or sister telling me she wasn't home—when something inside me snapped and the shame hit home. Then anger. Then some cold reasoning. She was eighteen and knew, subconsciously, that she was not yet ready to marry. And perhaps she knew that when I grew hesitant and more conservative in my thinking as we tried to plan out the complex future, which, admittedly, was no fun. What she did was not mean. Her saying, "Kenji, I've changed my mind," was merely very practical. She simply did not want to measure it all out with onerous words. What was the point? Her feelings had changed, and that was that. I would have to live with pain. I'd get over it, as several times she had. Besides, her family was leaving for Omaha in three weeks, her father reassigned to Offutt. A whole new life awaited her. She who was expert in short-term affairs.

EMIKO

I awoke early in the morning. Emiko was sleeping beside me with her left leg warming my thighs. Outside the bedding I knew it was cold; I watched my breath vanish in the air. Gently, I untangled myself from her arms and legs and hair and tiptoed across the frozen tatami and drew open the shade. A draft of cold air rushed at my groin so I quickly retreated to Emiko's warmth. I wondered how long the sleeping pill would last.

The inn was an inexpensive one that afforded a view of only the crown of Mt. Fuji. Even so, Fuji reared up like a white giant. Below the inn was a sleeping forest where nothing stirred. And the scent of pine mingled with Emiko was everywhere.

With my back to the window and my head propped in the palm of my left hand, I stared at Emiko's face. I brought the back of my other hand close to her face and felt her breath. Each time she breathed my hand would grow warm, then moist and cold, then warm again. Somehow it reminded me of the time remaining to me in the mountains of Japan. The thought of returning to Guam and the insufferable heat and the officers I loathed made me despair. Fortunately, the thought flittered away as Emiko sighed and turned on her back.

My cousin's face was round with barely a nose. Her lips were full and serious. I touched the feathery lashes of her crescent eyes and swept back her hair to look at her ears. They were small and pierced and below the left, on the side of her upper jaw, was a mole. And though I knew her teeth were white and regular, I parted her lips and felt her teeth with my thumb. I was pleased and surprised that she did not wake. The sleeping pill, I thought, must have been strong. I traced my hand down along her throat, through the shallow of her small breasts, to the slight swell of her belly, then tiptoed with my fingertips along the ridge of her pelvic bone.

How different Japan was from the world I was accustomed to. The smells, the tastes, the language. Especially the language, which, outside the market place and the cabarets, flowed smoothly like whispers: the sounds touching the inner ear like Emiko's warm resonant breath.

Most of my stay was spent sightseeing with Emiko in the vastness and denseness of Tokyo where she lived. Alone, without Emiko, I would have been lost. I knew I would have been lost.

I pulled the quilt back from her child-like breasts, never tiring of the secrets of her body. Unlike most women I knew, she didn't shave the hair beneath her arms. The hair there seemed repugnant at first, but after a while, because of its sensuousness and naturalness, I found it more and more pleasing with each glimpse. The curve of her breasts was lyrical, like the inverted arc at the nape of the neck which the Japanese felt the most beautiful and graceful line of a woman's body. Her nipples were small and pink and tan, still unsuckled and taut. Emiko was ashamed of her breasts because she felt they were inferior to those she compared them to—"*chiisai*," she would say—like the fullness of those of the West. I quickly covered her up when her nipples hardened to the cold.

Did I love her? I didn't know; I wasn't quite sure; we rarely talked. Neither of us was very articulate in the other's language. To tell the truth, I lied to everyone she introduced me to. It was just too difficult explaining why I did not speak my father's tongue. I told them I was born and raised in Hawaii. I guess this was explanation enough—none of her friends asked twice. Between Emiko and me, most of our talk was made up of hand signals and facial expressions and touch. How powerful this last was. The first time I held her hand was on the grounds of the Imperial Palace where young lovers met in the evenings. When I touched her, her palms became moist; she slowed her pace and averted her eyes. Unlike cousins ever again, we walked the ancient grounds for hours in silence. I felt somehow like a boy again, walking hand in hand with my girlfriend, unable to think of anything to say. But the feeling of contentment and excitement sparring in my chest was a man's.

But did I love her?

I knew I had to go back to Guam and serve the remainder of my eighteen months. Yet hadn't I given Emiko a vow when I squeezed her hand and touched her breast before the Golden Pavilion? And then three nights ago, wasn't there something exchanged, offered and taken, when we slowly made love in the secret inn, in the room that was filled with autumn chrysanthemums? And again last night, when we were both entwined in so many arms and so many legs, vainly in search of the other far beneath the skin, didn't I say, "I love you"?

It was close to ten o'clock. Soon, I thought, we would have to go. The trip down the mountain would take some time and I wanted to see Yokohama before I left. But the moment was too soon. Emiko's breath on my face told me so. And it was still too cold. Too cold to get up.

How soundly my cousin slept. I could have easily made love to her without her knowing. I wondered what my mother would say. She wrote me in Guam and told me my cousin would show me Japan. Dear Mom, I mentally wrote, have decided to stay.

According to the instructions, I was told to meet my cousin at the USO the day I arrived. But I had bumped into a friend I had been stationed with in Omaha two years ago. I left a message for my cousin to meet me the following day. Lying beside Emiko I cursed myself and regretted the lost day.

The first place Marlowe took me was a cocktail lounge skirting the Ginza. He warned me not to order anything more expensive than beer because of the prices these places charged. We visited a number of these lounges. Some were sordid and stale. Others, warm and quaint. Each provided us with a hostess. Marlowe, familiar with the language and a confident guy besides, knew of my hunger to touch a woman. In a roundabout way he revealed the fact to my hostess. But, as I discovered, touching was easy. Most of the women took the initiative and toyed with me playfully as they were encouraged to do. But to bed they were not obliged. In any case, I didn't know how to begin. I was too ignorant of what was expected. I was too brash, too blunt, too much to the point, where patience and indirectness were the Oriental way. I felt a little frustrated and ashamed.

Marlowe then took me to a cabaret. As we walked in, thirty or forty young hostesses were lined up casually and hopefully against a long wall. Marlowe picked a girl with pointed breasts while I asked for a girl who could speak English. As it turned out, the girl chosen for me could barely talk about the weather. While we drank beer, the girls scotch, one of the waitresses brought us a tray of things to eat. On the tray was an assortment of dried fish, soy bean crackers, and other peculiar things I was hesitant to taste. But by this time I was woozy from the beer and my taste buds were dulled, and I found it quite charming to be fed by my hostess's fingers. Once, with a coy, well-tested smile on her face, she took my hand and placed it on her breast beneath her kimono. But for all I knew, I could have been squeezing a satin balloon filled with warm water. Taking my hand away I tactfully brought it to my nose. It smelled of perspiration and sweet perfume. I didn't like the smell. Emiko, on the other hand, used nothing. She knew the power of a woman's smell: a smell that encourages a man to taste. Emiko's smell was provoking.

When we left the cabaret I shouted to Marlowe, "C'mon! I need a hunk of flesh!" He told me I also needed a wash. He took me to a bath parlor at the edge of the city where the lighting was poor and the houses seamy. Inside, we removed our shoes and waited in a room within warm paper walls and sliding doors. Then a girl in her twenties, clad only in underwear, led me away to a cozy room on the second floor. Half the room was made of ceramic tiles. The other half was lined with tatami with bedding on the side made for one.

Slowly she undressed me, which was pleasantly perplexing, and pointed me to a stool in the area of tile. Naked, I squatted, my knees level with my chin. With soap and hands she washed me completely. Never have I experienced a more luxuriating bath. How wonderful it was to be washed by someone with warm, slippery hands. She rinsed me off with pails of warm water and helped me to enter a large wooden tub. I sat up to my neck in water and nearly swooned, while the girl, whose name was Omi, scrubbed my dirty underwear. She was plump, and the halter she wore barely covered her bulbous breasts, which glistened with lather and water and sweat and bobbed about in all directions. She dried me off with fluffy towels and bade me lie on my chest on the bedding for one. Then the fingers and the heels of her hands kneaded me in earnest. And I must have dozed off. I didn't know she had turned me on my back till she pressed and pulled the flesh of my hips. It was then that I asked for my clothes and wallet.

I gave her a note of five thousand yen. I didn't care how much it was worth, nor was I about to calculate. Mechanically she made love to me. Then she washed me again with efficiency. I slept that night in an iron bunk at Tachikawa Air Force Base. Empty, I knew I needed something more.

Emiko turned on her back and gently snored, then turned on her side again away from me. The top of her back was freckled and the line of her spine disappeared at the cleft of her rear. Having nothing to do, I wrote with my thumb nail "Emiko" above the vaccination on her upper arm, "Emiko" down both shoulder blades; then I traced concentric circles at the small of her back. How soft her skin was. How smooth. The only part of her I couldn't appreciate was her somewhat muscular calves. I attributed the shape of her legs to the customary way she sat on the floor. She sat with her legs underneath her, with her back severely erect, and could sit like this for hours while I lay sprawled upon the floor.

I met her the following day at the USO. I dropped my bags at her place, and we rode a train to Kyoto, where we joined a shrine tour by bus. After the fourth or fifth shrine, the serenity and beauty of the shrines and the artful landscaping wearied me. I was tired of shrines! We left and returned to her place. And as she bathed, I recalled the affectionate way she took care of me. Nothing, nothing she did was without me in mind. Every time we left the tour bus she'd straighten my jacket in the rear—something only a wife or mother would do. And every time we took off our shoes to view the interior of a shrine, she'd straighten my shoes and turn them around so I wouldn't have to do it myself when it was time to leave. At one shrine, she bought us paper fortunes from a Shinto monk who sat in a booth in front of the entrance. Taking my fortune she read it and gave me hers. Then she turned around with mine and tied it to the branch of a small leafless tree that had many other fortunes fastened to it. She told me this was done so that the bad fortune wouldn't follow me. The sun felt warm. I could feel the pebbles of the courtyard underneath my leather soles. She had sacrificed her own good fortune for mine, and all I could do was stare at the tree and watch the many white tassels dangling from its branches.

Was that why I thought I loved her?

Reaching along her pelvic bone I found her hand. Slowly she turned on her back again. How small her hand was. I flicked out my tongue and tasted her palm. Then I put her thumb in my mouth and quietly sucked. Dropping her hand, I leaned over her right breast and nipped the curve of her mound. As a tiny droplet of blood appeared, I wondered how much I could really know her. And if I did love her—that is, I thought, if *love* were the right word to use—what was it that I loved? Not her body, no. Nor her logic. But what was it then that I thought I loved? The dread of leaving her suddenly grew real again. My stomach tightened like a fist. But then, Emiko blinked and opened her eyes.

Stifling a yawn with a doll's hand and pushing herself to a sitting position, she half smiled "Good morning." She brushed the tips of the hair on my chest like a teasing child or a knowing woman, folded back the quilt, then tiptoed bashfully to the bathroom nude. I got up and dressed and stood by the window and watched the clouds obscure Fujiyama's crown. I knew I had to decide whether to stay or leave. It was then that it occurred to me—Emiko might not love me.

To get to the seaside city of Yokohama from the inn in which we stayed, Emiko had to drive further up the mountain before we could begin our descent. With each bend of the mounting road a new vista burst in our face. And the noontime sun somewhere above the curve of the car seemed to dissolve the morning haze. We stopped at a roadside citrus stand and peeled and ate oranges for lunch. After rinsing our hands in a fountain, Emiko turned and bowed a last goodbye to the sleeping god Fujiyama. Swiftly we started down the mountain road. I had six hours left to decide. Emiko must love me.

The day was clear and unusually bright, but the biting mountain wind forced us to keep the windows closed. And soon the windows to our rear left and right began to fog. Only the windshield escaped our breath. I felt that all that was real was here in the front seat with Emiko and me, while the scenes that flashed across the windshield were merely scenes of a mythical travelogue. The whole world was here, isolated in the glass compartment filled with Emiko's presence. Even the sound of the engine was muffled, hushed as if beneath a blanket of snow. And the only sense of movement I felt was the swaying of our bodies left and right, back and forth. Neither of us spoke. There was little to say.

As I studied Emiko's profile, I wondered what she was thinking. Only her eye and her extended arm and leg seemed concerned with the winding road. Every once in a while she would turn and smile at me. And I could see the sadness I felt reflected in her eyes. I didn't want to leave Japan and yet, and yet, I wasn't quite sure I could give up my home, my family, my friends, the world I was so much accustomed to. And though I still wasn't sure that I loved Emiko, I told her I did. I told her I wanted to stay. Without turning to me, while the tentative fingers of her free hand dropped from her lips to her right breast, she said, "Kenji-san, you must go. Family will be shame." It was best, I knew, if I left. It was best, I knew, if I stayed.

Nearing Yokohama, the patches of blue that peeked through the pine became ponds, then lakes, then a single sea as large as the sky. And the temperature grew warm. We stopped at an inn and made love for the last time, then went into the city to eat and say goodbye.

In Yokohama's Chinatown, beneath the calligraphy of colorful neon signs, in the midst of a festival-like atmosphere, among the sailors, merchants, tourists, and others that thronged the avenue of smiles, Emiko quickly kissed me on the cheek, undid her hair, then vanished like a dream in the Street of Novelties.

HOME

All the way up I pictured the cartoons that Mike had collected and tacked to his bedroom wall. He was about twelve at the time. One was of a man sitting outside at a small round table in front of a big window, which had painted on the glass: Cafe Disillusionment. The waiter, his posture upright, was standing opposite him. The caption read: "Your order is not ready. Nor will it ever be."

In another cartoon, in front of the Cafe Déjà Vu, a man is walking by the window and is looking at a man seated inside next to the glass, who is, simultaneously, looking at the passerby. They have identical, deadpan faces. Big eyes like white discs.

In another, a man in a long overcoat, holding a battered briefcase, stands with his back to us in front of a lobby map. An arrow points to a spot which reads: "Why are you here?"

Why are you there?

"Here we are," said Sully.

Soon as we stepped out of the cage of the elevator we could smell it. The hallway reeked of marijuana. It was coming from the half-open door of Iris's ninth floor loft.

"The dummy doesn't even close the door," Sully said.

"It's ten in the morning, for chrissake." I pushed past Sully, rang the bell, banged the door open, and yelled, "MIKE MASCETTI! IT'S THE POLICE!"

Aquinas, Mike's pug dog, started yapping.

"Kenji!" Mike said, surprised to see me. He was on the far side of the loft, sitting in an old-fashioned, four-clawed tub, smoking a fat joint—when a frothing Aquinas leaped from the tub and scooted across the room, a bubbly hamster, and jumped into Sully's arms, licking Sully's big nose.

"Hiya doin', boy. You miss me, Aquinas? —Okay, okay."

The radio atop the makeshift shelves of boards and bricks, next to the tub, was playing Coltrane's version of "My Favorite Things." The old saw was true, Aquinas looked just like its owner.

"Aquinas, enough!" said Mike. "When did you get back? Did you bring me something from Guam?"

"Yeah, a water buffalo," I said, as we meandered toward him, avoiding the easel, stepping gingerly over the warped and wrinkled, paint-splattered, plastic oilcloths and half-done canvases spread about the wood floor like tropical islands, sidestepping an overflowing ashtray, the cardboard coffee cups, crumpled wrappers and newspapers and magazines and books. A blue corduroy throw pillow. What a mess. Just like Mike's old bedroom, only the place wasn't his.

"Awww. That's disappointing," he said.

"Nah, I got you this woodblock print when I was in Tokyo on R & R. I'll give it to you later. Maybe. C'mon, are we going to the track or what?" Arts and Letters was running at Aqueduct in the Wood Memorial. *What a horse.*

"Close the door, will ya, Sully? This isn't a barn," Mike said, climbing out of the tub, a St. Mike medal dangling from his neck.

"Woulda fooled me," said Sully. "God, you are *ugly*. Look, Kenj, an albino billy goat."

I mean, the place *could* have been a barn; that's how huge and regular it seemed to me, with tall wooden posts that broke up the large, rectangular floor space. If it weren't for the pungent smells of oil paint and thinner and turpentine and dope seeping into my brain. Besides, I was still suffering from jet lag.

"Want a hit?" said Mike, pulling up his bell-bottom jeans. *Have to get me a pair.* But nothing off the shelf ever fit me, what with my irregular proportions: jackets, shirts, pants, shoes—especially shoes. Size 7 triple E.

"Still a virgin," said Sully, taking the joint from Mike's lips, then sucking on it like it was a clogged straw.

"This crypto guy back from Nam turned me on once."

"Krypton, you mean," said Sully, sitting at the butcher-block table below a long row of pen and ink portraits tacked to the gray wall. Iris, I thought. Sully was lit by the skylight high above his head. Actually, the whole loft was flooded with a lambent light that streamed through the tall west windows. Neither gray nor white, just overcast, uniform, and flat; *the same,* I thought.

Welcome home.

As I walked to one of the windows, I said to Mike, "Heard you're teaching some place upstate. At some hoity-toity prep school. Speech or something."

"Not quite. Vermont. Mostly drama," he said, pulling on a flowery tie-dyed shirt. Ruffling the top of his curly blonde afro (he looked a little like Harpo Marx), he walked barefoot to the small refrigerator and asked if anyone wanted a beer. Sully said he might as well have one, as Mike clunked some ice in a glass and mixed himself a B & B and water. "So," Mike said, sitting opposite Sully, lighting up the joint gone dead, "what do you plan to do?"

I had never seen Washington Square from this perspective. It was crowded with people, even in the November cold—which went straight through my fatigue jacket, the turtle neck, the flannel and undershirts, straight to the marrow through the bones. "I don't know. Lay back a couple of weeks maybe. Maybe bartend for the Boss. Take Sully's job. Heard you're working nights for him. —Hey," I said, "how come you're not teaching now?"

"Give me some of that," Sully said, stretching out his hand for Mike's joint. Aquinas had settled under the butcher-block table.

"I'm on break. We're on a trimester system," he said, cleaning his granny glasses with the bottom of his shirt. Somewhere, Billie Holiday was singing "Autumn in New York," and I started to hum along with her waning, cracked, broken-hearted voice:

> *Autumn in New York*
> Why does it seem sooo in-viting?

Turning back to the window, I thought nothing had changed much: scraggly guys still playing chess on the granite tables; a lady in a white fur vest walking a pair of Russian wolfhounds; a tall black man in a gray wool hat, standing atop a crate, haranguing a ragged circle of pedestrians about the end of the world or against the war in Vietnam or reciting Ginsburg's *Howl* to long-haired college kids with books under their arms, an old lady with a shopping cart, a man supported by a lamp post drinking from a brown paper bag; others seated on park benches were drinking coffee, reading with their collars up, books, newspapers, the racing form, one with a magnifying glass, next to an old man feeding gray pigeons, teenagers smoking cigarettes and pot and goofing at the passing throng, two long-bearded Hassidic Jews, one gesturing in the air, then emphatically at the sky; ogling a young lady in a green mini skirt passing the Jews, mimicking the blind man pausing in his walk to sneeze; kids tossing a Frisbee over the heads of some second graders out on a class excursion, yellow name tags on their jackets; a woman in a striped scarf leaning, in the middle of a walkway, over her baby carriage; a kid plucking a guitar next to another fingering a flute

> Glit-tering crowds
> And shim-mering clouds
> In canyons of steel
> They're making me feel
> I'm home.

a juggler by the fountain; a woman, dressed like a gypsy, selling from a card table her homemade jewelry; several dozing, sitting upright in the minimal sun at the edge of the gray fountain, or slouching, day dreaming, or spaced out. Feeling light-headed myself.

> *It's autumn in New York*
> *It's good to live it again.*

. . . good to live it again.

I imagined a frail old man propped in his hospital bed so he can see out the window, not knowing what day it is. Tuesday or Sunday. Easter, Passover, or Ramadan. Just floating. Free. Free of time. The mean between two infinities: never having been; never will be. He notices his right hand resting on the telephone receiver which lies in its cradle, unsure if it rang. Or if he just hung up.

Suddenly the door opens, and he watches a man in his fifties walk towards him. He does not recognize the man, though he returns his warm smile with another warm smile. The man says gently, "Hi, I am Russell. I am your son," to which, with genuine curiosity, the old man replies, "And who am I?"

> *It's autumn in New York*
> *It's good to live it again.*

"So, where's Iris?" I asked, turning away from the window.

"She's teaching a drawing class."

"Where?" I asked.

"On Saturday?" said Sully.

"Columbia."

"You know, I've been meaning to ask you," said Sully, popping another beer.

"Get me one," I said.

"How come Iris's mouth, you know, on the left side, is kinda messed up?" He handed me a beer and popped another for himself. "She have an accident or something?"

"Yeah. When she was growing up in South Africa, she was mugged. That part of her face is partially paralyzed."

"That's nice," I said. *God ...*

"I met her last summer when the school hired me to model for one of her classes."

"They must've been desperate," Sully said. "Take a look at these," he said, pointing with his beer can at the portraits on the wall above his shoulder. There were six of them, ink drawings, portraits of the same man, that was clear. A light-skinned black man. It was even clearer that each successive portrait showed the man growing older, grayer, the eyes dimmer, receding farther and farther into the sockets of his skull, which became more and more pronounced as the flesh of his face was sucked into the hollows of his cheeks and jaw and throat, the skin spotted and taut. It was like I was watching the slow evolution of Dorian Gray—except for the last portrait: the old man was holding up, by the wiry threads of its scalp, a head with a face identical to the old man's. My eyes must've widened.

"Medusa," said Sully, his eyes glazed.

The hair at my nape tingled, as though it had grown six inches already.

"My idea," said Mike, "... Iris drew it ... portraits of her father. The first four are from photographs taken every decade since his twenties. This one, he's in his fifties. What he is today. Pretty cool, huh?"

"*Papa was a rolling stone,*" sang Sully.

"She's good," I said, riveted to the drawing. The feeling of being alive seemed suddenly strange. Stranger than dying.

"What am I, chopped liver?—"

"What's that?" said Sully. I heard it too.

"A rally," Mike said, nonplused, still staring at the Medusa portrait, while mumbling, "The hero returning from the dark land with the truth."

I followed Sully across the room to the window. There was a huge crowd now around the black man atop the crate, and there were people holding up antiwar signs and placards, and people seemed to be shouting all at once in response to the black man's exhortations. Where'd they all come from?

"Just like up at Columbia," said Sully. "And City College."

City?

"The Four Horsemen of the Apocalypse."

"What?"

"Under the arch," Sully pointed. "Say, Mike, why don't you hand me your Mannlicher-Carcano?"

"I told you, Oswald was a patsy," Mike said.

No doubt about it.

Four policemen in helmets were mounted on huge, maple-black horses. *War horses*, I thought. But the rally seemed peaceful enough.

"Well," said Mike, "are we going to the track or what?"

"Let me have some of that," I said to Sully, taking the joint from his fingertips. "Might as well catch up." I sucked on it as he and Mike had and choked, croaking and coughing, my head about to explode. "God!"

"Which one?" said Sully.

"There isn't one," said Mike. "Though I'm still Catholic."

". . . Here," I said, handing Sully back the joint, then screwed my blurry eyes with my knuckles. Then grew dizzy. "Whew." Then giddy. "Wow." It was like my head was swelling with syrup, softening my vision, the back of my neck, my shoulders, my joints. My knees felt weak. I needed to sit down and staggered to the old couch beneath the adjacent windows.

"Here, try some more," said Sully, standing over me.

"Why not," I said, smiling like a fool, like Mike grinning at me from across the room over some secret pleasure—like reading us passages from books we never heard of, like *Tom Jones* or Joyce's *Ulysses*, late at night at the West End bar, and then, at the end, smiling with joy and sipping daintily from his glass of B & B like a fop; like the way he grinned just after sucking on a water pipe of hash, his eyes like aluminum; or while listening to Jimi Hendrix on guitar, fuselage after fuselage of cat gut nerves (who was once a Screaming Eagle in the 101st), playing with his fists, his elbows, his teeth; or after watching Brando extemporize in a hayloft—quoting some poet named Ashbery: "This is the tune but there are no words, the words are only speculation." *Just the tune. Just the tune.* "Can you dig it?" he'd say, grinning, making us grin. Or, best of all, grinning deliciously like that neurotic genius Mercutio, in *Romeo and Juliet*, as he recited Shakespeare's Queen Mab speech, rhapsodizing, crying, lost, tossed by the night wind behind the bar of the Campus Dining Room. And we'd applaud, not understanding half of what he was saying. Just his voice, *the tune,* mattered.

"Say, Kenj," Mike said, putting on some sweat socks, "that's what you can do."

"What?" I said.

"Work in a Chinese laundry."

"And you can work in a pizzeria, you wop."

A grin that would never leave him. Not even when he learned, at 35, ten years later, that he was sick. Nor when he got sicker. Nor, upon each visit, as we witnessed the week-to-week carnage, watched as the disease ravaged his body: the atrophy of sinew and muscle and meat and flesh; the skeleton, the bones, the remains of some prehistoric animal arising in his gray skin; his body a battlefield of some primordial war. And the grin would remain through all the probing and poking and sampling, through all the various treatments and therapies, some agonizing, from hospital to hospital, clinic to clinic, from doctors to gurus to cranks, all across the Eastern seaboard.

And he would shame us with his grin. I would have packed it in. What the hell.

I was rubbing my face with both hands, but the face didn't feel like my own. Nor did the hands. It seemed I also had lost my voice.

"How 'bout driving a taxi?" quipped Sully.

"Nah, too small," said Mike. "His foot can't reach the pedal." *Ha ha.*

"Heard about the midget who committed suicide?" said Sully. "He jumped off the curb." *Ha ha.*

And then we would witness the havoc a second time as the disease had its way with Iris.

Mike had gone to Corpus Christi, then Arch Bishop Molloy, then City College; then, awarded a scholarship to graduate school, he studied at Yale, earning degrees in art history and drama. And he would teach his passion to rich kids in various New England boarding schools, smoking dope and drinking booze with other long-haired, itinerant school teachers, following their trade from school to school as attendance and salaries and whim suited them. For three years—until it occurred to him that he and Iris were in love, and so they were married.

Joe was married and had a daughter. Sully was married and had a daughter, and another kid was on the way. I wanted to get married, too, I supposed, have a kid of my own.

The light in the loft seemed to have dimmed.

"Great," Sully said, still standing by the window. "It's starting to snow. You guys still wanna go to the track?"

"How about something to eat?" Mike said, rising from the table.

"Say, Mike," I said, "you still angry at that guy?"

"What guy?" he said, pausing with his left hand on the refrigerator handle.

"You know."

"What guy?"

"The guy who hit you in the face with a truck." Sully cracked up, slapping his denim thigh.

"That's it," he said. "No chow for you, Sullivan. No, I'm serious. The fridge is empty—"

When the door opened and in walked Iris—like a rose had been tossed into the room. All color and scent. Sully had beaten Mike in their race to help her and had taken the grocery bags from Iris's arms. "Thank you, kind sir," she said. Sully had passed on the bags to Mike. Then, turning to me, she said with a warm, homecoming smile, "You must be Kenji. Mike told me a lot about you." My god, she glowed, and it wasn't merely because of the November snow. I was dumbstruck.

"Well," said Sully, "at least say hello, you dummy."

Like an idiot I stuck out my hand and said, "Hello," then, like a kid, said to Mike, "I want one, too," which made her laugh. I kept thinking, *bell-botttoms, long hair, the new music to play over bigger speakers, a new stereo—none of it was enough.* It felt like a church were growing inside my chest. All this tingling—when suddenly, as though someone had pulled a plug from my ankle—I could see the change in Iris's eyes—something began to drain from the top of my skull, down through my forehead, the bridge of my nose, my cheeks, like liquid draining from a vessel, altering its color, when—I wanted to leave. But I couldn't—I blacked out and, as Sully put it, collapsed like old clothes.

I didn't know when or how I got home.

At first, I awoke in the barracks at Andersen Air force Base and heard again the B-52s taking off for Nam. Then I realized that someone, probably my sister Mimi, was vacuuming the hallway. My mother walked past my bedroom doorway, loudly closing the apartment door. I wondered if I ever left home. I wondered if I was just now going off to war. Then I wondered if the war had happened a long time ago and that I was really an old man, when Mimi, turning off the machine, stuck her head in the doorway and said, "You up? Want something to eat?" She sounded curious and unusually cheery. It then finally dawned on me that it was late morning or lunchtime, that it was sunny outside, the snow had stopped. It dawned on me that I could start over again.

CHRISTINE

I'd been back now for six months and quickly got used to all the long hair, the bell-bottoms, the new music, the antiwar protests, and drugs everywhere, not only in Southeast Asia, and I was getting restless. So sometimes I helped the Boss at lunchtime at the Campus Dining Room, a basement bar and grill across the street from Columbia University. I worked the register ringing up bills and bagging take-out orders or helped Sully at the bar, three deep in grizzled construction guys who worked the site for the new law school. When Sully said something under his breath, which I couldn't hear, what with all the noise. He always spoke like he was giving me a tip on a horse or the lowdown on a customer.

"What?"

"Check out the booth under the window. No, the right window, you dummy." She was a dark-haired Asian girl with big eyes.

"Wow."

"Not bad, huh?" She was sitting with three other girls. Grad students from Teachers College, you could tell. I elbowed Sully away from the register when they came up to pay their bills. She was first. Her eyes were huge.

I beamed at her and asked, "How'd you like the cheeseburger?"

"Good," she said, nodding. She was smartly dressed, chic even, if a bit conservative. I mean, she was no hippie.

I gave her change, and while handling the other bills, I said, "I was just wondering . . . Where're you from?"

"C'mon, Christine, we'll be late," one of her companions urged.

"Hawaii," she said. Waves crashed on the beach, drawing up our legs as we embraced, kissing passionately. "Bye." I watched as she and her friends passed through the glass door.

"Come back soon," I called, just as the door shut. She turned and smiled. *Wow.*

I found out later she was studying for a master's degree in elementary education and was at Columbia on a partial scholarship. A long way from home and palm trees and beaches and slack-key guitars.

After she left I felt despondent again. Besides, I had an interview downtown that afternoon. I needed work. Something to calm my hands.

So I trained for two days as a dictionary salesman, trained by a slick greasy guy in a double-breasted suit who demonstrated his spiel through showy gestures like a magician. The next day I followed one of the salesmen who was assigned the financial district, who importuned people busy at work from one office to the next, from one floor to another, without selling a single copy, and I knew this wasn't me. I guess I projected on others the feeling I've had of being interrupted myself by strangers wanting to sell me something while just sitting down to a meal. Impatient. Exasperated. Sometimes angry. I couldn't hustle that way. Perhaps I hadn't the guts or the chutzpah. I knew I couldn't hide the feeling of mortification.

I then worked (because of my military experience with teletype machines) for Global Communications on Broad Street, perpendicular to Wall: first as a wire man, then as a teletype man, then as a computer maintenance man—this last work nearly driving me crazy, it was so boring. And except for the shop, there were no windows, while the shop window looked upon a sooty brick wall six feet away. *Why even have a window?*

Every morning or evening, depending upon the shift I had, I'd stare at the ceiling of my bedroom and rue the moment when I'd have to rise and put on my green work shirt, despairing over my petty life, the meaningless work, dreading the hours, the long subway ride nearly the length of Manhattan, to pace the tile floor in front of the empty worktable, to stare out the window, count the bricks in the wall.

For six months.

Which would have been longer had it not been for Christine.

Often at midnight, after working a swing shift, the Boss's son, Butch, blinking me with the headlights of his Volvo, would pick me up on Broad Street, and we'd race uptown on the West Side Highway, the Hudson to our left, flying past 34th Street (a sprinkling of lights on the Jersey bank), 72nd Street (catching a glimpse of the Washington Bridge lit like a Christmas tree), getting off on 125th Street, swerving right beneath the viaduct, skirting potholes, knifing past silver puddles beneath lamplights, argon particles, turning right on Amsterdam, then flashing up the Avenue, catching the green then yellow then red lights, pulling to a jerking halt in front of Christine's dorm, fifteen minutes tops each time, "Thanks, Butch," ringing the buzzer, watching Christine through the glass door, in a white dress, walking toward me through the lobby, growing larger, "Hi, babe," beneath the floodlight, crystals gently falling on her hair and shoulders like confetti.

"Hi," she'd say, and we'd go for a bite somewhere, to the Campus Dining Room for a hamburger, to the West End for a pastrami on rye, to the V & T for a pizza, sitting together in the corner in a high-backed booth, her face aglow in the pink candlelight. It was like the red anthurium (sent from Hawaii) sprouting from the Bloomingdale's bag by her thigh that lit the subway car like a campfire, drawing every starving eye, like Monroe in a room full of typewriters: proof that the anthurium was alive, that it was real, that Christine was beautiful, a pink shower tree bursting from dark volcanic soil.

It was like that wherever we went. (I was forced to groom and dress myself better.) And she wanted to see everything. So, holding hands, we ran about the city.

Touristy things at first: climbing the stairs inside the Statue of Liberty with a bunch of screaming grade school kids; rounding Manhattan on the Circle Line Cruise (it seemed with the same damn kids) with Puerto Rican families and jabbering foreigners from Poland and Germany, my stomach queasy from a cold hot dog, the trip endless, the East River rank, as if like immigrants (Christine in a shawl) we were sailing toward Ellis Island; zooming up the express elevator to the top of the Empire State Building, scared again as my father sat me on his shoulders to look over the edge, feeling Christine's cold, thrilling cheek against my own; schlepping her packages down Delancey Street, "You want I should wrap it?! Lady, this is not Macy's"; walking down Mott Street in Chinatown, the air thick with refuse, oyster sauce, and college kids fresh from a foreign flick (Kurosawa's *The Seven Samurai*, *The Fantasticks* in Washington Square, or Coltrane at the Village Vanguard), to eat lobster and black beans in a basement restaurant in Chinatown, and afterward, spumoni in Little Italy. "*Capisce?*"

"*Capisce.*"

* * *

Though the day was bright as Easter Sunday and the room was lofty and light, it felt—as we looked at the painting—as if the wall were engulfed by night.

"It's scary," Christine said, her troubled eyes scanning the painting's black features; you could almost hear the screams and the suffering and the creatures bellowing. It wasn't something you'd hang in your living room. Even if you had the space. I mean, the rectangular canvas was huge, taking up nearly the whole museum wall.

"Yeah. It's supposed to be disturbing," this angular ensemble of hideous, inhumane crimes all in a row. Picasso's *Guernica*. Like Goya before him, he descended into the darkness of his own time.

"What is it? Hell?"

"Yeah." *Like Breugel's,* I thought. "It's a nightmare document on the Spanish Civil War. All wars." The contrast between the painting and Christine's cheek was *nine times the space of heaven.* She squeezed my hand and softly tugged. We walked along the length of the canvas beyond the frame into another room.

This one was filled with Impressionist paintings glimmering with light made of swaths and dabs and molecular colors—each painting a little world. Of church facades, lily pads, wet streets, tigers, and painted people.

"They're beautiful," Christine said. "They remind me of poems." I was standing close behind her, her hair smelling faintly of flowers.

"Love poems?" I asked.

"Some," she said, tilting her head, as though judging the long hair of Renoir's nude.

"Any of 'em passionate?"

She turned and smiled. "No. Not with these." We walked to the next painting.

"I guess you need bigger canvases. You know, like a novel?" not sure of what the hell I was talking about.

In the next room, I drew her finally to a painting hung modestly among others which immediately faded from sight. "Here's my favorite," I said. "Van Gogh's *Starry Night*." Like the first time I saw it, she too stood stunned. Stars like whirlpools of light. I mean, here was the whole universe."

"He saw auras," Christine said.

"What?"

"The energy that surrounds all living things. Maybe all things. Some say it's spiritual energy."

"Yeah." *I can dig it.* "Like the halos you see around Christ's head in those Renaissance paintings. Mary's. And all those cherubs and angels. . . . Aura." She sounded like my sister Mimi.

In the taxi I remarked, "Wonder if you have to cut your ear off to see 'em."

"What do you mean?"

So I told her what I remembered from reading his biography and the little book that my sister Mimi gave me one year for Christmas— "Which I lost"—which was made up of excerpts from Van Gogh's letters to his brother Theo. "Van Gogh was frequently ill, suffered from depression, and often he was very poor. Worse, I suppose, was that his work was not understood. He was a compassionate man who loved all living things and work."

Before the glass door of her dorm, her hair framed by the foyer light, I said "Good night."

When I mentioned that Mimi had given me a couple of books to read while I rode the subway to work, Christine told me she used to curl up on the couch with a book in her lap bigger than she was and read, read, read. Her mother would say, "Go to sleep, Christine. Your eyes are red."

"I knew when I was young that I wanted to be a teacher when I grew up," she said. "I would gather my younger brothers and the neighborhood children and conduct classes, pretending I was a teacher. Lots of times I would lead them in songs." We were walking, hand in hand, across the granite promenade of Grant's Tomb toward Riverside Church, where I wanted to show her the church bells.

"One time, a couple of years after my younger brother Jay had drowned, I was feeling sad inside, and I guess it showed because my teacher took me to see the counselor, Mrs. Hirai. She asked me what was wrong, and I remember touching my heart. Then she told me a story about how she learned how to heal people by placing her hand on someone and touching the ground with her other hand. She learned this technique, she said, when she was on a plane and her daughter had a terrible earache. The lady sitting next to her told Mrs. Hirai to place her hand lightly over her daughter's ear and her other hand on the armrest, and her daughter's earache went away. Just as my own ache had gone away. This counselor, as I talked to her, said she didn't know anything about these things. But she did remember that a long time ago, when she was going to college and was waitressing, a lady looked at her and said, 'Oh, how beautiful!' She asked the lady what she meant, and the lady said, 'I see beautiful colors around you—'

"An aura—"

"'—and I see Kwan Yin, the Chinese goddess of mercy, above your head.' And, just like that counselor, I wished that I could have those healing powers, too. There were a lot of kids I wanted to help when I did substitute teaching in the public schools."

We rode the church elevator to the top floor, then got out and walked up the spiral staircase to the bell tower. The bells were huge, surrounded by wood scaffolding and narrow catwalks. I felt like the Hunchback of Notre Dame and wanted to yell, like the actor Charles Laughton, "Sanctuary! Sanctuary!" Christine, the wind ruffling her dark hair, was fearful of the height. Leading her by the hand, we stopped in the middle of a catwalk and kissed for the first time.

I was her Prince Charming, to protect her, to show her a new, exciting life. True: a little short, a little stocky, a little disheveled: but promised the first dance in the ballroom of her heart.

Back on the ground, we visited the high-ceilinged church. We would get married here in December, the whole semicircle of the apse lined with towering Christmas trees. I had proposed to her in the spring outside the Brooklyn Museum (after viewing a Van Gogh exhibition), when the museum's magnificent cherry blossoms were in bloom. Few things made her happier than flowers. Well, here, along the walkway, were enough to last her a lifetime. We sat beneath a pair of pink trees where the flowers fell into her lap and upon our picnic blanket.

And she said, "Remember that teacher I told you about? the one who made me feel better when I was sad? Sometime later, to thank her, I bought her a white ginger lei, and I felt the lei had to have white ribbons, too." We were lying on the blanket, her head in the crook of my arm, as we looked up at the branches thick with blossoms. "On the bus to school, I became aware of so many white flowers. In front of a luxury apartment, I noticed, for the first time, bushes of double white hibiscus. I had never seen hibiscus blossoms like that before. Usually hibiscus come in brilliant colors, like red, yellow, and orange. When I got off the bus and walked down the street to school, I saw white roses on a bush with hardly any leaves, so from a distance, it looked like only white roses covered the bush. One garden had a patch of white bachelor's buttons which were at the side of the yard and which I had never seen before. Another yard had white Christmas flowers covering a tree outside the fence, and there was a bush filled with my very favorite, white *pikake* blossoms. When I reached school and gave the lei to the teacher, who I hardly knew personally, she said, 'Do you know? This is my favorite lei.' Then when I got home that afternoon and walked through the door, I heard a gasp from my mother and my aunties. My cousin Iris had just given my mother a bouquet of white roses. Iris said, 'Aunty, if Jay were here, he would want you to have these flowers.' They were very beautiful. . . .

"Don't you wonder sometimes that, no matter how hard things are, life speaks to you? Reassures you that it cares?"

"I don't know," I said. "I have friends."

"You're lucky."

"You're lucky, too. You seem to have a nice family."

"The reason I ask is not only because of the flowers. There were butterflies, too."

"Butterflies?"

"On one Christmas day, I was feeling sad again, so I went and sat outside of Jay's old bedroom. It was a sunny day. The skies were blue and the garden was alive with greenery and yellow daises. And then, through my tears, I saw the butterflies, the tiny white butterflies. So many of them flitting here and there among the flowers. For a moment I forgot where I was until I heard my mother calling. She just wanted to see if I was all right. Without thinking of the butterflies, I went to her. But later, I often thought of that time in the garden. *Where did all those butterflies come from? Were they there to comfort me?*"

"That's a beautiful story," I said. But sometimes, I felt, she read too much into things or picked out things her unconscious mind wanted her to see. This was especially true the first time she got ill, and then after that the meanings would vary in urgency, depending on the intensity of her illness.

From Riverside Church, we walked to Sully's house for dinner. Sully's apartment was on the fifth floor of a six-story walk-up on 123rd Street with a view of Morningside Park, P.S. 125, and the endless, trapezoidal rooftops of Harlem. Daisy was cooking up a Dominican pork dish, black beans and rice, plátanos, and an avocado salsa salad arranged on a big platter that, slipping between her wet fingers, Christine would drop at the threshold between the kitchen and living room. Chirping in horror. Arching backward on the couch, Sully laughed with generous glee, slapping his denim thigh.

I rose and went to Christine. "No big deal, babe," I said, smiling, as she momentarily buried her face in my neck.

"Don't worry," Daisy said. "This one does it all the time."

Christine and Daisy became good friends, two island girls. They would go off together to the market in Spanish Harlem for tropical fruit, vegetables, and spices. Places that Christine would never go alone, while Daisy never felt any fear. "We should have been scared though." Just a month ago a professor was stabbed right outside of Teachers College at four in the afternoon—for his wrist watch. And Daisy would take her into tenement buildings that she had only seen on television or in the movies: trash overflowing garbage cans, creaky wooden stairs winding steeply upward, dark hallways covered with graffiti. These apartments were so different from what she was used to, with their long dark hallways with bedrooms and the kitchen projecting off to the side and the living room, at the very end, the only room where most of the sunlight and fresh air entered the apartment; the only room that faced the street, usually above a bar or a store or a restaurant. (Lucky for Christine that the rent-controlled apartment the Boss would get us, on the third floor, was laid out sideways, every room affording a view of the street, though we were positioned directly over the entrance of the Campus Dining Room, its noise of laughter and jukebox music.)

Once Daisy took her into an apartment of a terribly poor family. As the mother turned on the naked bulb hanging on a cord from the ceiling, Christine saw the baby sleeping in its crib, looking sick and weak. She remembered looking at the baby's skinny legs. "He was almost two and still couldn't walk." She and Daisy shared a lot, and we ate at each other's homes, as well as at Boss's. And Christine would babysit for Daisy when the two kids came. Until Daisy—"YOU'RE SUPPOSED TO BE MY FRIEND!"—screamed at Christine for not letting her know that Sully was playing around with Anya. But what could she do? Sully was *my* friend.

And my friends adored Christine (though some of my friends were limited in their thinking).

Ski the cop (who, with flashing lights and sirens, escorted our wedding party from Riverside to the Aki Dining Room) didn't believe that Christine was Japanese because of her large features—her eyes, her lips, her breasts, her hips. McGlynn even asked her if they spoke English in Hawaii. Her university professor suggested that, if she were going to the mainland, she may as well go as far as she could, meaning the East Coast. Good suggestion. And the Campus Dining Room, in my mind, was as far east, and as far out, as she would ever want to go.

For if there were any sunlight, any glow of innocence, any flowers, she brought it herself as she descended the seventeen steep steps into the basement bar. She was literally not of this world, though she'd be welcomed in any, as she was here. Christine, in many respects like a child herself, was simply good. Radiating goodness. Making you want to be good yourself—even Highland (the construction worker forced into retirement because of his bad back), the most bitter man in the neighborhood—even he—would thaw: "Hi, Eddie," Christine would say. And his wife Rosemary would join him at the bar after work and find him cheerful, almost as he used to be, and stroked the softening iron roads of his cheek, and she'd tell Christine, "No kiddin', just like Paul Newman," and drew from her hefty purse a smaller one containing her farthings and a picture of Highland in his twenties and said, "See what I mean. Just like Paul Newman," and, peeking over Christine's shoulder, shifting back and forth between the photo and Highland, I said, "Yeah. You're right." Really, the resemblance was uncanny. There was something about Christine that encouraged enthusiasm in the simplest things.

After several more late night dates (thank god for Butch), Christine would wake me round ten in the morning, after her early class on children's literature. She would open the door to my bedroom, lean over and kiss me, her lapels, her cheek, her lips still cold with March. *God, what time is it?* After a while, to save Christine the wait and my mother the long walk down the linoleum hall, Mimi gave her a set of her own house keys.

On those mornings absent of Christine, I would dread the vagrant dust motes floating aimlessly on the shafts of light that lanced through the cracks of the venetian blinds, the creaking of the narrow bed, the dangling of a leg off the edge; dreading the meaningless work I had to face downtown that afternoon, like all afternoons, servicing the tape machines that stored the million and one telegrams to be sent overseas; dreading the empty workbench; dreading the shop's single window above it; dreading the brick wall.

I knew what Hamlet felt, though I didn't know his name then, nor the name of the ailment he suffered. Hamlet's anger, his depression, his sense of meaninglessness was not exclusively caused by the loss of his father, though the loss, I knew, created a monstrous, irreparable hole in Hamlet's breast, so deep was his love for his father.

But it is also true that many of Hamlet's speeches recall a more general condition, a wider malady, that arises—*whatever its cause*—from the face-to-face confrontation with your own hollow life and its attendant burdens—with having to comb your hair, with having to put on your socks, with having to walk to the bus stop—with being alive—much less avenge a father's murder. And the dark recognition slowly coalesces into words, arriving in foot-high letters as big as those on the Columbia library frieze, but like the looped electronic tape that circles again and again the Times Square building: NO TEMPERATURE THE TERRAIN IS BARREN THERE IS NO WIND NO TEMPERATURE THE TERRAIN IS BARREN...

And so believing leads easily to sleep or Seconal. You are the pain you must flee.

And only you can fix it.

But you do nothing. Repeat like a slave your implacable routine. See no out. Convinced there is none.

I believed as much.

Until Christine began waking me.

Four years later, after putting me through college, Christine herself, in the worst of all ironies, would fall again and again into the darkest wells of depression.

As if on my behalf.

The missionary contracting leprosy herself.

Her roots ran deep in Hawaii. She was Japanese-Filipino on her mother's side, from a plantation family on the Big Island. From her father, she was Chinese-Hawaiian-English/missionary, who passed on to her the dormant seeds of instability, manic-depression, suicide, the record clear in her great aunt's journal about her mother's "unaccountable episodes of madness, as if the sign of Cain were upon her," as she would suddenly lose herself in the grain of the dining room table, her left forefinger on the precise vein of the koa wood, her right hand still clutching a cloth: as she bent over the table for hours as if to enter the wood through the vein, or become the crack in the counter, or the single stitch of her apron hem. Several times her husband, returning from a sick bed or a funeral, would discover her with "nary a cloth to cover her shame," hiding in the ti leaf bushes of their Hawaiian garden.

The family record is speckled with kinfolk afflicted with periodic bouts of depression, several members submitting to lengthy stays at drug-inducing sanitariums. The symptoms reared up (most recently, in her two aunties, her cousin, her brother) through breakdowns, first, in their mid-twenties after experiencing some trauma connected to change, sudden or gradual, in their day-to-day routine: a change in the predictable world around you, in its attitude, at least as *you* see it, toward *you* . Then given to some ill timing, the defective gene, your temperament, and circumstance conspire the overthrow of your emotional brain—dropping you like a parachuting seed the vertical length of your being. As you settle upon the flat, gray, measureless lake of despondency. And terror.

Obtaining in the father.

Descending to Christine.

I must be out of my mind—let the psychiatrist talk me into signing Christine into a place like this!—Ward Eight. St. Luke's Hospital.

But here we were, Sully and I, two hours after her phone call to take her home, sitting, like our nerves, at the edge of our chairs in a wide, empty corridor waiting to see the doctor who seemed to fit the place better than his patients—had there been any. That's what got us. I mean, besides Christine, there was no one here. It was vacant. Blank. Like some sub-Sahara of the mind.

And cold.

And forlorn . . .

Her bed and nightstand, like the others in the large, dark, empty room, were set in the far corner, her lamp the only one lit. On the stand, beneath the small circle of light, were arranged her cosmetic bag, her brush, a comb, a tube of moisturizer, and, on the bed, her robe from home—the only things of human warmth in the entire ward. Small things that broke your heart.

"Let's get out of here," I said, retrieving her overnight bag from the empty closet, my brain swirling afire with fright and fight, both— fearful of what the doctor might say, getting in the way, my face wary; reflected in the face behind the wire mesh window of the padded steel corridor door, which looked back into mine. It belonged to the stocky Hispanic who entered, pocketing his keys, and walked past our chairs with a gait, a stride that said, "Be cool. Don't fuck with me." The Ward's hired muscle. And my sense of panic and danger rose, as it did in the angles of Sully's straight face. To whom I said softly, "We're getting her out of here no matter what." And the doctor, despite the stonework of his face and his blank eyes, knew my resolution, hearing the desperate strain of the carrier wave that hefted the burden of my words. They were clear and simple. He knew, and I knew he knew, I'd brook no compromise.

But how could I have left her in the first place—alone, unat- tended—after her two sleepless nights of pacing, turning her wed- ding ring round and round and round on her red finger, her knuckle growing raw, her confidence gone, unable to return to the Cathedral to work with kids at the summer day camp, to the one boy who failed to find fun in her games; unable, as we planned after the summer, to begin her new teaching job in a Baltimore public school, to keep up a new apartment near Johns Hopkins where I had planned to continue my schooling for at least the next two years. Was I in my right mind when I refused Princeton's scholarship? Or the one from Columbia, just right across the street?

Was I in my right mind when I allowed her parents to come and fly her back to their home in Honolulu? Did I expect them to take her to some shop for repairs and then, all new again, send her back to me, air mail?

"What're you doing, Kenj?" said Sully across the bar. He seemed irritated and disappointed in me, angry even, his face telling me I was stupid. "What're you doing *here*? You should be with Christine. Look at you. You're drinking yourself half to death. For what?" And of course he was right. What the hell was I thinking? I belonged with Christine. What else mattered?

So I dropped everything, packed a bag, and left. We would not return to the City for fifteen years.

All the interim, it seems sometimes, was a single, long convalescence, given the number of relapses Christine experienced over the course of those years. Making those periods of wellness periods of appreciation and quiet joy: just to wake up in the morning and go to work, to read a novel in the evening or visit with family, or jog around Magic Island as Christine dozed beneath a palm tree, as if to catch up on the sleep she had lost in those numberless days of illness.

Once, recuperating on the Big Island at her aunty's house on the outskirts of rainy Hilo, I watched Christine across the continent of the living room as she worked on a watercolor. I was trying to write a letter to one of my old professors at City College. I just wanted to tell him what had happened to me over the years—so full was I of feeling and, at the moment, no place to go, for when it rains in Hilo it comes down in torrents. I mean, nothing was small on the Big Island: its erupting volcanoes, its tsunamis, so too with its rains—and the image of Niagara Falls and the honeymoon we took (before we married that December) reemerged in my mind with its thunderous noise, and I was transfixed to the dining room chair as we stood transfixed along the bank of the river rushing to the precipice and over its side, and we were everywhere at once, on the opposite bank on the Canadian side, behind and beneath the Falls, huddled in rain gear, or on the opposite balcony, feeling its awesome roar and power resonating in our breasts, awed by its size, by its girth, by its endless abundance of water pouring over the edge, fearful that, before our very eyes, it must run out, it must run dry, so great was the volume, its outpouring, boundless.

Just before lunch I completed a half page of the letter addressed to my old professor (a Greek poet we simply called Gus), unable to capture the swirling events that centered upon Christine and swept us away. There were too many, and too many, it seemed, required some kind of explanation, which I wasn't up to or didn't have, so I just signed the thing—then looked back over to Christine (still painting), then turned to the kitchen doorway where I heard her aunt stirring something in a pot, and recalling stories, I was off on another page which, later that wet afternoon, turned out to be a poem called "Paintings." Three days later, I sent it off with the half-page letter. It was in three parts.

I.

"It's eleven-thirty, Mr. K. I thought you'd like a bowl of soup."
Celery.
I feel like biting into a head of Manoa lettuce or
     crisp fern shoots you could pick in your backyard.
Of course it rained a lot
a land of volcanoes, black sand beaches
lush with earthquakes:
the stone porch split down the steps
and the corrugated roof of the toolshed pattered with
     rain
sharpening the shears
sleep

the hibiscus and orchid.
We moved a pile of rocks that day and found a family of
        khaki toads—
big, boy
Christine got stung
and we watched a spider real fast spin a web
lots of work after the rain
so fast everything grows.
My beard.
The tidal wave that dashed our house away.
The neighbors, Kaloi, Beverly died.
They took our things, Christine's nice leather purses.
The mosquitoes didn't bite her after the first year.
The bugs, or something's, eating the cabbage—
a spotless bungalow
four rooms with sunlight and trade breeze
and the smell of ginger.

                    II.

"Mr. K?"
        Something else gnawed at her nerves
        pulled at her hair   stared
        traced in her watercolors
        too delicate for this world
        bruised fruit
        a rose in a cut glass
        a thin lambskin book
        leaves
        ferns
        broken quills
        rings missing stones—

you see transparencies
overlapping wraiths
her ghost everywhere
in the porcelain walls
upon her cheek, her pink knees
her hands, fruits, in the flower pattern of the
        crystal floor
in vellum
illuminations
palimpsests
her palms
her mind
a glass shoe.

III.

"Felt a drop, Kenji."
        The clouds turn charcoal; a black dog chases
        something through the mist of the soccer field, trees
        mountain pastures somewhere behind.
        Christine stows her paints; we pack the cooler
        roll the mats. I try to protect her
        as we flee the rain
        in flimsy dress
        through a large, dark
        no name canvas
        in a golden frame.

More than a decade later we returned to New York, Christine
having regained her health. As we touched down at Kennedy Airport,
as the Arab cabby drove us to my brother's house in Brooklyn, I kept
thinking about the changing light glinting off my mother's glasses, so

many years ago, as she sat on the picnic bench watching the endless passing of a freight train hailing from some vague distance; and I kept thinking, *O what a strange trip it has been.*

TURNS

Since I had time to kill, I jaywalked across the busy avenue and followed the walkway between the dead lawns and the tall red project buildings, hearing again the five-part harmony of teenage voices as they echoed off the walls in the summer night, Willie and his brother Booga, dark-skinned Puerto Ricans who lifted weights and played handball, Andrew, Mulligan, and me, singing The Skyliners's "This I Swear Is True." There, in that window on the eleventh floor, lived Luz, my junior high school flame, who now had a kid. Maybe more now. Who taught me to slow dance at the ninth grade prom when the lights spun like fruit on the gymnasium floor—circling her pelvis against my thighs, my keys, like grinding glass, my brains in my pockets.

Farther down the walkway, where the projects abutted the concrete playground of P.S. 125, my alma mater, I sat on a park bench, lit a cigarette, and stared at the empty, concrete softball diamond. I looked at my watch. It was 11:30, I was right on time. There was Mr. Bellay, two softball bats on his shoulder, leading his motley troop of sixth graders from the school building. There was Harold Ford and Dilday, Steve and Danny, Lawrence (the son of a Baptist minister), Vickie, saucy Gladys, and Bonnie Bloom. And the big bully Roland Tombs, who couldn't play ball worth a damn, who was a dropout, too, in and out of jail for petty theft, assault and battery, just like his brothers. Emily and Gracie, the smartest girl in the class, who broke her arm falling off the jungle gym. I could see them. Living ghosts. As he led his charges along the painted foul line toward home plate, I dropped my cigarette and moved to the chain link fence and grabbed it with both hands. "Mr. Bellay," I called. He stopped, turned toward me, and a moment later his shoulders relaxed.

"Well, well, well. Kenji?" he said, moving toward the fence, the kids crowding around him, their faces aglow under the autumn sun. "How are you? What're you doing now?" he asked, shading his eyes, straining to reconcile, through the fence, across the span of twelve years, his memory with my present appearance in the shade of a tree. My fatigue jacket. My long hair and stubble.

"I was in the service for a while."

"So I see."

"Worked downtown as a computer tech. But now I'm going back to school. City College, if I can." Mr. Bellay hadn't changed at all. The same white shirt and tie and wingtip shoes.

"Hey, that's great."

"Mr. Bellay?" inquired a voice from the rear.

"Look, Kenji—"

"Go ahead," I said, smiling.

"How about lunch?" he said, sidling away through the whirlpool of kids. "The teachers' caf. at 12:10."

"Can't. Got an appointment," I said, thinking how odd it would feel to eat lunch with Mr. Bellay. Still my teacher.

"Come back and visit then," he said, as he ushered the kids toward the diamond. He loved playing ball as much as the kids did, especially hitting the ball over the fence. Funny. Softball was the one subject he didn't teach. He just let us play. Funny. Every Friday he checked our teeth, ears, and fingernails. Because of him, to this day, I carry a handkerchief ("Hey, mister, you put that thing back in your pocket?!"). Across the years, even through the fence, I could still feel Mr. Bellay's hand on my shoulder that snowy December day when my father died ("See that squad car idling by the school entrance?").

I watched the kids for a while, assessing their skills, trying to find the scrawny one with the bazooka arm. Until a project cop approached from a distance.

Back on the avenue, I lit another cigarette and watched a gypsy cab careen madly down toward the trough of 125th Street, timing the lights exactly, then up the opposite slope past Junior High School 43, and I thought of paying a visit to Mr. Block, my old algebra teacher, and Mr. Mann, who could've easily flunked me in French, had he not directed me in a Harlem version of *My Fair Lady*—"People stop and stare; they don't bother me/For there's nowhere else on earth where I would rather be/Let the time go by; I don't care if I/Can be here on the street where you live." That was me, the first Japanese-American Freddy Eynsford-Hill.

But I was no longer a tenor, the high C beyond me now, the throwing arm shot, and Luz no longer lived on the eleventh floor. No, I hadn't the energy to descend the slope again. Besides, Tombs might be there himself, hanging around the basketball courts, still seeking me out in the cafeteria or the playground, or lying in wait after school, to take his revenge on me for judo chopping him in the ribs with my size seven Converse sneaker on the last day of school. With a broken mop stick in his hand, Tombs and his brothers chased Blumenthal and me all the way up the hill to Columbia, up 119th Street, into my lobby, to knock on my door. The gall! The rage! The humiliation! I was half his size and brought tears to his eyes in front of his friends and kin. He had a name to uphold. A rep! that commanded respect and aroused fear among the ninth graders. No doubt, had he a knife, he would have plunged it into my chest.

As I backtracked along the avenue, the projects vanished, replaced by the tenements and shops that preceded them. The bodega, the stationery store, the butcher shop, the barbershop. Looking through the window I could see myself draped in a pin-striped sheet, seated on a board laid across the thick, padded arms of the barber's chair, my head being shorn, wailing as if electrocuted; my father standing stoically behind me containing his chagrin; his image multiplied infinitely by the facing mirrors.

It seemed that, if I wanted to go forward, I had to do it walking backwards. I couldn't shake this strange feeling. All I knew was that, after my appointment, I would never visit this Harlem neighborhood again. Of that and my grade school past, of my old teachers and classmates, I was reconciled.

Stepping into the carpeted hall from the elevator, I checked my watch. I was five minutes behind myself.

"Kenji?" Miss Klingler inquired through the crack in the door. For a moment, she looked like the old vice principal who yelled at my mom and kicked me out of school.

"Yeah," I said, suddenly tense.

She unhooked the chain and said, "Come in." I followed her down a short hall (she wore thick stockings and heavy brown shoes, walked with a slight limp) into a brightly lit room with papers and files and books piled helter-skelter everywhere, on the dining table, on three of the chairs, on the parquet floor, beneath and atop the coffee table, on half the couch, on top of the TV next to a cactus plant, and along the radiator cover below the sunlit windows that looked over Amsterdam Avenue and the low income projects across the street. God, what a mess. "Have a seat," she said, pointing to the one empty chair, the seat tired with her hefty impression. She made space for me at the table cluttered with papers and manila folders, an ashtray (her lipstick smudged on the cigarette butts), a tea cup, the tea bag like a dead mouse resting on the saucer. The chair seat was warm. "Have you had lunch?" she asked.

"Yeah," I said.

"Would you like some tea? Coffee?" I shook my head. "Juice? I got some soda in the fridge."

"No thanks, " I said, wondering how in the world this woman could get me into college, wondering how she got anyone in, wondering how she could even manage her own life. She walked into the kitchen and spoke from there.

"I didn't tell you over the phone, but Fred Broder and I worked together for many years. It was shocking to hear how he died. He was a good man . . . kids, I suppose." She stood at the kitchen doorway, no bigger than my mother, holding a tea kettle by the handle, speaking to no one in particular, "Why would anyone want to hurt Fred?" Then speaking from the kitchen again, "He probably refused to give them what they wanted, angering them. Fred could do that, you know. He could be stubborn . . . but that can't be it," she said, pausing momentarily at the threshold again. "Fred had a lot of experience; he was sensitive to kids. Especially troubled kids. Knowing boys who thought they had nothing to lose could commit the most heinous crimes in the blink of an eye. For the flimsiest reasons. You know what I mean," she said, pouring hot water into her cup. She picked up the dead mouse by the tail and dipped it up and down in the hot water. Then she examined my face: "Don't you?" It was a teacher question, her answer already embedded in her premise.

"Kind of." I was trying to picture an elderly Mr. Broder, his red hair, his slim build, standing alist in front of his Greenwich Village brownstone, favoring his good foot, the one unafflicted with gout; trying to picture him as he paused, turning to face the surly voices at his back, the drawn knife; trying to picture him as a stranger, a faceless white man in a tailored brown suit and paisley tie; trying to picture him reaching into his inside breast pocket and offering his assailants his long maroon wallet. Unperturbed. His voice calm, reasonable. Feeling no fear. Showing none. Which was perhaps the cause. Perhaps not. I could not conjure further, bloody as my imagination could be; I had already seen enough blood-spite. Blood-rancor. Evil for the sake of evil. Though I've witnessed heroism too. Goodness as irrational as evil. "Kind of," I said. But I did not volunteer other reasons why Mr. Broder might have been stabbed to death. Yeah, I knew some boys . . . some men, too.

"He was kind to you, wasn't he?"

What? I'm here, aren't I? I just shook my head. I wanted to say, simply, *He's dead. So is my father. And one day you'll be dead. I'll be dead. "'Scuse me, just passing through." And all for what?*

I looked at the window, then at the innumerable windows of the low income projects across the avenue. And I imagined hosts of people, common as myself, waking up and eating their morning Cheerios and Quaker Oats, then catching the subway downtown to their job at the post office, the garment factory, the fish market, the maintenance shop, the warehouse, to heave, heft, and haul, to sell, deliver, and fill out forms—writing receipts, answering the phone, opening and closing the same file cabinet, broom closet, the elevator door all day long; then returning home to their shop-worn wives and belligerent kids to eat their dinners, read the paper, watch TV, sleep. *Sleep, the momentary pause between the monotonous heartbeats of life.* Year after year. Until retiring on meager savings, a company pension, Social Security. Living out their lives betwixt memories and the remnants of dignity that they could still imagine, perhaps even proud that, for the most part, they had acted rightly through the course of their passing lives. *Was that It?* Passing anonymously from a non-descript planet rounding a minor star at the fringe of a spiraling galaxy, among a host of galaxies, in a universe that, itself, must inevitably consume itself. Passing from this world into the larger oblivion from which they were spawned. The length of their visit, their presence gleaned, no more than the lightning bug's path tangent to the orbit of Jupiter. —*For what?* Was there something here that I was missing?

"I don't mean to pry." She cleared a chair for herself of papers and pamphlets, placed them on the Persian rug by the leg of the table.

"I brought over what you told me," I said, suddenly remembering. I took out the folded papers from my fatigue jacket: copies of my birth certificate, high school transcripts, my General Education Diploma and test scores, my military record and discharge papers.

"Good," she said, taking them from me, putting on these half-glasses that hung from her neck on a thin chain, reminding me of the glasses that Mr. Draper wore. "Your scores aren't bad at all, Kenji," she said, placing my papers on the stack to her left; I suppose my eyes widened. She looked at the pile. "Don't worry. I won't lose them. I haven't lost a student's papers in my life. Though it may seem hard to believe. Now, there's one last thing you'll have to do," she said, sliding toward me a thin blue brochure (which she had plucked from another stack). "I want you to fill out the registration form in the back and take the Scholastic Aptitude Test—see?—at the Coliseum on 59th Street next Tuesday morning at nine sharp. Now you have to do this, Kenji. If you want to be accepted for the spring semester . . .

"You do want to go back to school, right?" she asked, looking at my eyes.

"Yes."

"Why?" *Why?* First they want to know why I quit; now they want to know why I want to get back in.

"I don't know. My friends, this guy Joe, and Michael who teaches, and my girlfriend who's going for her masters at Teachers College; my mother, my two sisters, especially the older one kept bringing it up."

"They've all gone to college?"

"All except my mother, I think."

"Why do you think they wanted you to go back to school?"

"I don't know. Maybe they're afraid I'd become a bum. Maybe even a criminal. A hitman. *Who knows?*" I said, feeling tired.

"Are you afraid of becoming these things?"

"What're you, a psychologist?" (*Why are you angry?*)

"I just want to know why you decided to try again."

"There is no trying again. This'll be my first."

"Now you sound like you're bragging. You dropped out once. What makes you believe that you'll see it through this time?"

"Look, four years is a long time; I'm not thinking that far ahead. Could be five, six years even. So long as it's not boring. Like the job I just quit downtown. Besides, I heard if you don't like a class you can drop it for another, right?" She nodded.

"So you're going back to school to find a better job? A more interesting job?" That seemed the motivation. "Have any idea what kind that may be? Not that you have to know right away. I mean, I didn't at eighteen."

"And I don't at twenty-three. But there's time."

"Yes," she said, smiling. "There's always time . . . —Oh, one last thing. You need to fill out some forms before you go. Here they are." They were underneath her saucer.

While filling in the blanks, I sensed Miss Klingler drift silently away into the kitchen again. Heard the refrigerator open, when the telephone rang. Probably another Broder referral wanting to return to school. Then minutes later the phone rang again. And would probably ring several more times into the night. And without thought to the hour or visiting neighbors or even her guests, she will stand in the kitchen in her heavy brown shoes and thick stockings, advising, directing, asking and answering questions. This was her mission. Her chosen obsession. To get kids back into school, kids who would forget her existence in a blink of an eye. Faceless, even if remembered. Then barely a name. Then that, too, would fade. Simply some lady who helped me get into college. Maybe for her, that was enough. Maybe their forgetting her altogether didn't really matter. Maybe one's desire to be remembered was not universal. Maybe, if looked at closely (as my Methodist mother would advise)—maybe such desire was simply vanity.

After signing the last paper, I thanked her and was about to rise, when she placed her hand on my arm and said, "If you have any questions later, call me. Even if it's just to talk about Mr. Broder."

Then—as though I were eavesdropping on myself—I overheard myself asking her, "You like doing this kind of work?"

As I descended the elevator and walked toward Amsterdam Avenue, under a lofty, blue November sky, I was afflicted with feelings of things half said or incomplete, of lost opportunities, on the one hand, and of new beginnings, on the other, of good things that I might shape of the future. It was like leaving forever my Air Force buddies, finally going home. The single thought that arose was, You could have been kinder—when I suddenly realized that I was at home. For, exactly where I stood on the sloping sidewalk, there used to be a side street, 124th Street, where I was born and lived as a child. It would have cut through the middle-income projects, slicing Mrs. Klinger's building in half; I would have landed, unbroken, in her lobby after being hit by a car one summer. And here would be the corner bodega where Father witnessed a stabbing. I jaywalked across the busy avenue, daring the traffic, as I would with Christine while visiting Rome, to the barber shop that once stood where the walkway now split the low-income projects.

As I passed Michael's building on 121st Street, I wondered where in New England he might be teaching; whether (unlike Corpus Christi, in the middle of Michael's block) the private school kids were all white; how much the tuition might be; how much he got paid. To my mind, whatever he was getting wasn't enough. I knew that if I were a teacher and had me as a student, I would have kicked me out of class. I remembered that Joe had once taught summer school in lower Manhattan near Houston Street, pinning a sixth grader against a school fence, scaring the crap out of him, who whined, "Go ahead, I'll sue you, I swear." Maybe I should go into law.

Turning the corner, I walked along 120th Street and the towering walls of Columbia Campus toward Broadway. Across the street was Teachers College: Christine was probably at lunch or in the library. Five months from then, in April, she'd sign a contract to teach first graders at Nightingale Bamford. And there was Barnard College to my right, another school for girls. Funny. I couldn't think of one female teacher I had that I wanted to visit. In fact, though the singular images of others came to mind, like my seventh grade English teacher sitting on my hand, I could only remember the name of one, my fourth grade teacher, old Mrs. Sampson. It was she who said, in answer to some query, "You should clean your *bowels* every day," at which point, mysteriously, Gladys and Bonnie Broom chortled. They were the only ones in class who knew what "bowels" meant. This was probably the first time I used the dictionary for a serious purpose, leading me to look up all the names, terms, synonyms, function words, slang, colloquial, and scientific for our private parts, male and female, and cross-referencing anything else pertaining to them and sex. It's interesting what we remember about school.

More interesting, I supposed, is all that we forget. Believe me, I wanted to remember, but it seemed to me, then, that I had no say in the matter, that my memory had a mind of its own, sometimes making me remember the pettiest things. Like my breathing or the flow of blood running through my veins—I mean, who was controlling this show anyway? Who was driving the car? Who was in control when Tiger stabbed a sixteen-year-old boy in the chest? Who was in command when they stabbed Mr. Broder?

I decided to visit Mr. Draper at the Business Library and entered the campus through the west gate. I hadn't seen him since my discharge over a year ago. As I passed through the grounds, down red brick paths, brushing the shedding hedges with my Levis, the cherry trees already bare, it suddenly grew overcast as though winter had already arrived.

I didn't recognize the woman at the circulation desk nor the kid pushing the book truck to the lift.

"Well, come on in, Mr. Kenj," said Draper, lifting his eyes above his half-glasses. He had just unwrapped the sandwich on his desk.

"How ya doin', Mr. Draper?"

"Oh, just as well as can be," he said smiling. "I heard you're going back to school."

"Who told you? Joe?"

"He and Florelle came for dinner the other night." Steak and salad and wine, I thought. Martinis.

"Yeah, well, it isn't for certain. Still have to take the SATs. I'm not even sure what scores I have to make. I'll probably get killed in math. Maybe I oughta get one of those review books."

"Oh, I think you'll do all right." *You do?* I thought. *How do you know?* Nothing was ever a big deal to Mr. Draper.

"Well, I hope so," I said. "Go ahead, eat your sandwich."

"So, what's your young lady friend like?" (*Joe again.*)

"She's from Honolulu. From an old missionary family who dropped God for the sugar industry."

"A lucrative business. Her family must be well established."

"Innocent as a flower. —But, *naive!* You won't believe this, Mr. Draper. On our first date, I pick her up late after working downtown on a swing shift, and we're walking down Broadway for a bite of pizza at the V & T, when, just after passing this big Black dude wearing a leather trench coat and shades, she whispers: 'Is that a mugger?'" Draper laughed, wiping his mouth. "I mean . . . I didn't know what to say . . . Which, I suppose, is as bad as McGlynn sitting at the bar at the CDR asking Christine if any of her relatives in Hawaii lived in grass shacks! For crying out loud. Right now, she's writing her thesis paper on children's literature. Comes from a long line of teachers on her mother's side. Say, Joe told me you went to Greece again for the summer."

But Draper didn't say very much about his trip. Talking in vague generalities he never shared much of his personal life. He had only taken a single bite of his sandwich. I felt I had overstayed my visit. No, I didn't ask him for a part-time job. Both of us knew, that was not possible.

As I slowly descended the broad steps in front of Low Library, facing the promenade and the vast quad, I felt a lightness in my chest as I breathed in the space and air of the wide sky. I stood at the level of the Alma Mater, who sat on a throne, dressed in a stone gown, a scepter in her hand, and stretched, yawned, stared at the pigeons swooping above mighty Butler Library that stood across the wide expanse at the opposite end of the quad, fluttering over the yard-high letters of the frieze—HOMER * SOCRATES * PLATO * ARISTOTLE * DEDMOSTHENES * VIRGIL * CICERO—thinking of a chicken salad sandwich like Mr. Draper's, suddenly hungry myself. *Know thyself*, I mouthed.

It was a small event that I'd recall years later while browsing the shelves of Salter's Book Store (the same book store where, that afternoon, I failed to pick up an SAT review book, distracted instead by a book called *Confessions of a Mask* by a Japanese writer named Yukio Mishima). The cover of this other book was blood red; maybe that attracted me. Or perhaps it was the title, *The Heart of Philosophy*, which echoed, in some odd way, Joseph Conrad's *Heart of Darkness*. Anyway, as I was flipping through the pages (written by one Jacob Needleman), I read the following; he was talking about Socrates: "Would I live," Needleman said, "and never understand, or die and understand?" . . .

> I think of the story of Al-Hallaj, the great Sufi saint of tenth century Persia. He was sentenced to die for heresy; his skin was slowly stripped away from his body and, scourged and mutilated, he was hung upon a cross to await his death. That much is historical fact. Al-Hallaj had sung of his identity with God—a heretical notion to Muslim orthodoxy. Some say that he openly sought martyrdom in speaking this way. Make of that what one will, a story of his last days was once told to me when I myself was in a condition of great distress. It was told to me in the most pedestrian of places—a crowded businessman's cafeteria in New York—on

a freezing winter day when it seemed the sun would never again appear from behind iron-gray clouds.

When Al-Hallaj was on the cross, his pupils came to hear his last words of instruction.

I asked myself what would be the last words of a martyred saint: an exclamation to faith? a vision of God? a command of forgiveness?

"As he lay dying, he said one thing to them."

One thing? What? A blessing of some sort? Peace? Love? Nothing of the kind. Amid the clattering of plates and the confusing buzz of laughing and loud voices, the words struck me as though in the chest: "Study yourself."

That night I beat the pants off Sully in straight pool, running 65 balls in a row, the most I've ever run, beating him out of a fin. But it wasn't the winning. It wasn't the money.

VOICES

Because I felt that I wasn't very bright, because I had been more or less told as much by adults, and by companions several years older than I, and because they were probably correct in their impression of me at that particular time in my life, I returned to school with a secret vengeance to prove everyone, including myself, wrong. So for that first semester, the spring of '71, I studied like a maniac. No less out of fear and trepidation. A matter of survival. That is, I studied everything since I didn't know how to study—reading every sentence, every word, of every assigned text. Many of them more than once. Underscoring nearly everything with a ballpoint pen, which then required me to reduce the gridwork with a yellow marker; thence, to transcribe and paraphrase the yellow reduction into manageable notes. Hours of this. In addition to rewriting the day's lecture notes or redrafting a paper for English that was due the following week.

I mean, for a whole semester!

(Despite Christine knocking on my bedroom door, finding me bent over my books and papers, saying, "You're still studying?" meaning, "You really don't have to study so hard" and "When will you be done?" for, of course, she wanted to go out, *do* something. I could feel the February cold on her cheek as she leaned over me, and, with my Papermate still firmly lodged in the calloused groove of my fingers, or with my right thumb fixed to the line I had just read, we'd kiss for several sweet seconds—then suddenly back to work. I mean, this was serious business. After all, it wasn't *her* pride that hung in the balance. She had already proven herself a certified pro. While I had yet to show a thing.)

And, to be sure, as was its historical function (according to Professor Bunting), I did not want my testicles hung at the point of an obelisk by some victorious pharaoh-teacher, much less some snooty classmate, signaling even my most minor mistake. I suppose it was a machismo thing for me, that streetwise instinct, via the Pleistocene, to do battle, to be top dog, like the need to be loved, always just below the surface. So I remained tactful, deferential, circumspect, properly inquisitive and ambitious, and clandestine, though I held a genuine regard for most of my teachers.

(Didn't Mother teach kids Japanese out of an abandoned boxcar in New Mexico? Didn't Joe teach sixth graders one summer down on Houston Street? And Frame's old man, the Montaigne scholar, he was still at Columbia. And how many profs hung out at the CDR, like Arty and his wife? And Michael, the itinerant drama teacher, didn't he say that teaching was a noble profession? Wouldn't Christine become a teacher? —"Almost ready?" she'd ask, anticipating my reply, removing her green wool beanie, fluffing her dark hair. "Give me twenty minutes. A half hour," I'd say.)

And from my seat, first-row-left-center, for four years in every classroom, lecture hall, and auditorium, like a season-ticketholder at halfcourt to watch the Knicks at the Garden, I always had my hand up interrupting the professor's speech. For the most part, I'd spit back the professor's words in the form of a question, just to make sure I got it right, or I'd ask him (there were mostly hims at the time) if he could elaborate a little on what he meant; then sometimes I'd circle back to an idea when another didn't seem to mesh with it, curious to know why, where from. Then later, I wanted to know where he, the professor himself, stood on the matter, trying to figure him out—his values, his biases, his likes—what kicked his switch—especially probing after his soft spots where, in time of need, I might prey on his sympathies. An advantage, I confess, that I acted on just twice, both occurring in the same semester, a matter of fact, in two introductory courses.

The first was in Psych 100. The instructor, a short blonde fellow, was just a few years older than I, familiar, no doubt, with the uncertainties that new, young students experienced in their first year. Then, too, young people were dying in Vietnam—and down South fighting for civil rights—and sympathetic or not, we wore the costume of protest, of the counter-culture, long-haired soldiers of peace at the barricades of the status quo—of big business, big government, big institutions, big military, the German shepherd police—undermining, co-opting, burning the symbols that betrayed their history and their grand ideals and came to represent the Big Lie. And the kids took Christ's words and made love everywhere while listening to Dylan, the Beatles, and The Band, the sweet smell of dope thick in the air. Agents and provocateurs of an alternative reality.

And I looked the part. Since my discharge, I let my hair grow out over my ears and down my nape; it now hung over my shoulders. I wore bell-bottom jeans, a fatigue shirt with stripes and all, and an olive-green field jacket. Anyway, the weekend before my Tuesday finals, I dropped some LSD (blotter acid, to be precise) for the first time in my life in Jankowski's basement apartment. "This little thing?" I said to Jean.

"Just lick it off the paper," he said, lying on his waterbed. "You sure? Twelve hours?" It was hard to believe. "Trust me," he said.

So fifteen, twenty minutes later, I feel it coming on, this low-grade trembling inside, gradual at first, like the molecules inside the blood cells are jostling each other banging each other into the gelatinous cell walls so that the cells pulsate and wobble and cartwheel as they circumnavigate through the vessels the skeins of vibrating capillaries which permeate every organ especially the big intestines then the diaphragm the lungs the upper reaches of the chest titillating making you feel giddy the esophagus the Adam's apple the lower cheeks the nape of the neck the roof of the skull so you must laugh chortle really your whole insides a network of firing neurons your brain the Milky Way the water welling in your eyes with each quickening surge each heave of your chest you wipe away with your knuckles and the backs of your hands your sleeves and down again rocking your head in the darkened room on Jankowski's waterbed turning to laugh with him whose eyes have receded into his sockets almost as if cowering which makes you suddenly anxious and you ask, "How ya feeling?" and you try to explain but it's useless no language to match it or quick enough to run it down so elusive so evanescent the thought the image of the round earth the color of an X-ray the people black dots moving together but remaining distinct thickening then growing a dark tail then spreading over the left hemisphere and you try to tell Jankowski who now seems frightened and your own anxiety has heightened and you want to go home home home where Christine is and you walk into the apartment three floors above the CDR into the bright light where Christine emerges from the living room and you see the objects around you as though from the back of a cave and she sees your face and hugs you and asks if you're okay yeah you say then sit in your canvas director's chair by the bookcase in the next room squeezing its arms pinching your eyes shut squeezing harder and harder when suddenly a distant swirling nebula of light appears in the crosshairs of your temple and as you squeeze harder it grows nearer larger more intense and as the light seems to scream its presence nearly full-face you jump awake pulling your face back a cosmic inch eyes wide your hands open and you want to tell Christine but Sully is here to give you some Valium and you are sitting opposite each other on the floor while he tries to talk you down but he looks strange with his right leg bent in the air he is a shaggy Russian wolfhound and slender man at once who is talking to me and I am talking to him and then he is gone Christine is in bed and everything physical material bearing outline or boundary is without meaning while the real meanings are universal beyond and through this world of appearances and impossible therefore to grasp in the weak light now touching the living room window.

I slept through most of Saturday, waking only to eat, so that by Sunday, though a little shaken, I was myself again. After class on Monday, the day before my psych final, I pulled the professor aside and told him I had taken some LSD, "It was my first time," and I had a bad trip and didn't feel I was capable of taking tomorrow's final. I suppose I had succeeded in giving him the impression that I felt still disoriented, and I sensed he had been there himself. "Look," he said, his face kind with concern, "don't worry about the final. Forget it."

I would regret my conduct here even more than my failed attempt in my introductory philosophy class with Professor Mavriks, who I guessed was in his early fifties, liked to suck on his pipe as he lectured on his feet pacing the front of the room or when he leaned against the wall near the doorway, talking of morality and ethics as applied to Plato's magical ring of invisibility and how we ourselves might employ it. Sad to say, as was the case in psychology class, I was acing philosophy too, though I had a much weaker grasp of its foundations. In fact, after Mavriks returned our midterm exams, he asked if I minded reading my essay to the class. But I declined, fearful of being found out a fraud, afraid that my writing would reveal my true ignorance.

Anyway, after class, after telling him in an obscure manner that I needed to speak with him, he led me to his office, where, from a crimson leather chair, and he leaning against the front of his desk sucking his pipe, I unfolded my pathetic tale and its tragic result. Obvious in my face and my questionable condition. And, alas, he too showed sincere worry over my well-being.

But he didn't give me the free pass that I wanted. Not yet anyway. He simply said, "Why don't you wait till tomorrow? See how you feel then," which meant that it was up to me whether I felt well enough to come in and take the exam. Which I did. Fearing that, if I didn't, I would fail the course. Had I not come in, or had I left the exam room five minutes after sitting down, penning an apology because of my psychological condition, I suspect he would have given me the A I had wanted, though I had not fulfilled every requirement of the course. As it was, I sat for the exam and even wrote, as I responded to the first of five questions, "Hey, I know this," which, together with my other unprepared responses, promptly earned me the C I deserved for the semester.

I'd like to say I needed only one lesson to learn how dangerous LSD could be—as I learned with PCP (commonly known as angel dust), as I learned with thorazine (an elephant tranquilizer), as I learned with dilaudin (the doctor's heroin in pill form)—and that, frightened near to death, I would never experiment with LSD again. I'd like to say this. But I can't. A weak psychological profile, stupidity, perhaps, I don't know why, I would take it again two, three, four more times. While, not infrequently, I went to class mellow on marijuana or rarefied on coke. Though (I suspect a deeper fear finally asserted itself, taking control of my steerage, setting a course more beneficial to the organism's survival) I would taper off, first on this, then on that, and would stop messing around with drugs altogether by the time I graduated.

I'd also like to say that, because of my experience with Professor Mavriks, I had changed myself, finding more admirable principles to guide my actions. But, again, I can't say this. For the influence of the street would prevail in me for a while longer—to bluff, to feint, to con, to prevaricate and pretend, to win or acquire anything by deception as you preyed upon another's sympathies and *good* intentions—and to operate in this manner when you had done more than enough work to succeed in your pursuit honestly, now that was insane. Had I been less a slave to my fears; had I the psychological muscle that makes for moral action; or, afterward, had my power of reflection been more mature, the development of my character would not have been retarded.

But I was who I was and no person else. If there were within me a force—like guilt, anger, grief—undermining my good efforts, wanting me to lose, wanting me to fail, it would appeal to my tragic sensibilities: the hero promising the villain the first dance in the ball-room of the mind. Where, among the mirrors, the chandeliers, images applaud your superiority and sacrifice, acknowledging you the Prince of Could Have Beens.

Sentimental and perverse—here, nevertheless, was something safe, preserving the secret of my fears. Elevating them to virtues.

Now, I could have realized all this were I conscious. But I wasn't. And even if I had been, I'm not sure I could have stopped the performance. For what other roles, of worthy note, were there to play?

Just as my study and reading habits (now more refined) put me in good stead, so too did my studied observation of my teachers. Funny. Of all my grade school teachers, only a handful come to mind, and then only as caricatures without names. Like my ninth grade English teacher who taught us Shakespeare's *Julius Caesar*, an experience I don't recall at all. What I do remember is his calling us up to the front of the room to retrieve our papers or tests, and, one time, as he handed back a paper to me he wouldn't let go of it, and, of course, I would be stuck short holding my end, which forced me to raise my head and look into this face with this U-shaped grin that literally, like Bert Lahr's, reached nearly to his ears. Befuddling us. He'd bring us up short in other ways too, like a girl would raise her hand and ask, "May I go to the restroom?" and he'd respond, "No. You may go to the restroom." Or he'd nod his head vigorously and say, "No."

Another I remember was this science teacher in junior high school; he had the hairiest arms we'd ever seen, and a square head, like a block, a Cro-Magnon type who never seemed to bathe, emanating a trail of yeast as he walked the aisles, sawing the air with his hairy arms. But we liked him because he told off-color jokes and could animate his body—his fingers, his limbs, his torso, his hips—becoming the scientific process he lectured about—becoming an enzyme, a bacterium, a sperm cell, a photon—and his eyeballs especially; he could move them independent of each other; they were rotating electrons that would collide across the bridge of his nose. O, could we have such eyeballs!

The math teachers I've had, on the other hand, were on the whole a humorless lot, high on discipline, all business, like the numbers they cuddle up to. One comes to mind (and in all probability helped set the standard when the Earth first cooled) was my calculus teacher, no bigger than a broomstick. No iron strand out of place, meticulously dressed in dark business suits, she brooked no arguments, no excuses, gave no quarter, she had no time. (He was wise, the author of *Little Red Riding Hood*, to have separated out of the grandmother, the wolf. What grandchild, much less some fledging undergrad, could stand up to that fierceness of face, that withering look when the grandmother was crossed?) It was easy to act the robot she wanted me to be—when one day, receiving input from some invisible source, crossing her wires, the most remarkable thing happened. In the middle of some review session, her face softened, as did her eyes which took on this distant look as she spoke, almost to herself, of a young mathematician, Poincaré, perhaps, speaking in tones we had never heard before, speaking in tones of admiration, praising his genius, emphasizing his youth, speaking in tones almost like love.

We were stunned, fixed in our seats, until, breaking from her reverie, she, with no small regret, pushed aside her vision with her hand and turned back to the blackboard. But I tarried. For, through an accident, through the unaccountable breach of her professional character, I was permitted a glimpse of what she felt was sacred and possibly the pivotal motive behind her endeavor as a pure mathematician: who would chart the heartbeat of the cosmos.

What intrigued me was the moment, the single moment that revealed her as a human being, revealing her humanity, her desires, her regrets, her vulnerability, which made her a figure both tragic and noble. These were the moments, out of the corner of my eye, I waited for. Though never again would they hit me with such force.

I knew, for example, what our introductory art teacher felt—a lass, I imagined, straight out of grad school in Wisconsin (enamored of color, line, texture, balance, and those other pictorial features we were to master in order to appreciate art)—when she found Faulkner's *As I Lay Dying* left on the podium, where, in quiet surprise, she smiled to herself, drawing her hand, sensually, down the length of its cover; then remembering the rest of us in the auditorium, she held the book aloft and asked if this might belong to one of us. (Slim chance. Faulkner, "the Southern Express," as the writer Flannery O'Connor dubbed him, would break breathlessly from the big woods like a bear, two semesters later.)

Now Professor Yao Shen had affections, too. She was nearing her seventies at the time, her head bobbing atop a long, narrow, Chinese dress, teaching a grad course on the History of English, teaching us as if we were children, babies even, particularly with the grandmotherly machinations of her mobile face; there never was a moment we didn't know what she felt, especially if our answers were right or, even better, if we said something original; just as her face would tell us if we were wrong, or if she felt doubtful about our conclusion, or felt disappointed, or was comically shocked when a bizarre speculation appeared just left of Mars. There, too, we'd find her face. And she'd drive my deskmate Burnbagle nuts. For, somehow, once every session she'd refer to the poet Keats as "My Johnny," as if Keats were her next-door neighbor or a nephew or her boyfriend, and Burnbagle would roll his eyes, as if losing consciousness, and drop his bushy head into the frying pan of his hands. "I can't stand it!" he'd say after class. "John Keats!" whom Burnbagle held in the highest esteem, seating him between Sophocles, on his left, and Shakespeare, on his right, on the frieze of his personal Pantheon. "My God, Kenji," he'd say, his face twisted in genuine agony. "*My Johnny!*"

But Shen's passion was just too positive for me; she was always up, always jolly. Which can wear on your nerves. I was looking for a different kind of passion, something akin to the hard-edged cynicism, resignation, and compassion of someone like Professor Kriegel, my first writing teacher, whose fine pen was also his cudgel. I recall running across a personal essay of his in *Harper's* a few years back that presented a strong, narrative argument against handguns, which, toward the end of his tale, had there been a gun readily at hand, he would have used it, having been pushed to the wall. And I know. For he would shoot from the hip, too, when responding to my short story characters, who, for the most part, tended toward loud, ignorant pronouncements on famous writers. ("One would wonder why that ass Fitzgerald bothered to write at all.")

That he was intolerant of mediocrity was evidenced not so much in his words as it was in his voice, in his streetfighter's grimace (which was his smile), and in his thick upper body that challenged you and hoped that you would do your best—that to do otherwise was dishonesty. (I would eventually publish two works that had taken seed in his class: one about my affair with my cousin in Japan and the other on the ritual suicide by the Japanese writer Yukio Mishima. Another, which was not published, was about *him*, only my hero was a heroine, a tyrannical virtuoso singer confined to a wheelchair. Her correspondence to Kriegel would seem obvious, so obvious that I wouldn't recognize it until twelve years later.)

On this particular day, after setting his battered briefcase on the desk at the head of the class and propping his crutches against the chalk rail, after bending to shift his steel-braced legs beneath the desk, he withdrew from his briefcase a book—*his* book, which had been recently published. He remarked, without raising his eyes, that there were a few sentences that he didn't recall writing. In any case, his talk was short, and we returned to our own work, though I'm sure others, like myself, watched him, fascinated. Oblivious to us, he seemed to fondle the book with his large, powerful hands, feeling the spine, tracing its edges, testing the thickness and the quality of the paper. Cradling the book in one hand, he flipped through the pages with the other, his eyes glazed with a fiercely possessive, fiercely proud light.

One day, after leaving him at the doorway of his office (I was halfway down the path), he asked me, "What do you want to do with your writing?" (Me? I was just a sophomore.)

But I guess I knew in my bones. I turned without breaking stride and yelled, "I wanna make them feel."

And then there was good old Gus. He was my favorite. Professor Konstantinos Lardas. Even his name was like a song.

At the bell, he leaned into the classroom, shoulders and head only, and smiled at us oddly. Leaning back, he tilted his head, and raising his dark eyebrows, he looked up at the room number stenciled above the doorway. Then stepping over the threshold, in dark blue slacks, he looked at us again with that odd smile lighting up his amber face.

Who was this man? At first he seemed a little senile, though he wasn't really that old. Maybe he drank; there was a rubberiness about his jowls. He stepped toward us, like a doddering old man, and greeted us as though we were familiar to him. I don't recall much else of this first class, except that he seemed to stammer like a child as he groped for words (this poet!), appealing (with one hand on his forehead) to the students seated near the front of the room (while motioning them toward him with the other) to give him the words that had slipped his mind. "Oh, you know what I mean" (his hand shaking). "Yes, yes, that's the one."

Then suddenly it didn't matter any more whether his gestures, his fumbling after words, his soft voice, his being "old" were all a ploy to get us to talk or to lean forward in our seats to catch his meaning. For he was ingratiating, as warm as the maroon and brown fabrics he wore or the old, thin, leather-bound books he held, from which he would read to us, moisture collecting at the corner of his mouth, his horn-rimmed glasses flashing at the end of his nose. For how he could read! You could hear each word, each syllable, sharp, edged with the roughness of his voice, charged with large and lofty feelings, as if he were alone reading aloud to himself in a large, lofty cavern, his shoulders and head imperceptibly nodding, emphasizing the phrasing, the pause, the rhythm, the trembling sounds, unable to contain them in his body, making the whole room shake, the ceiling, the walls, the windows, the floor, our desks, making us shake, thrilling us with the passionate fragments of Sappho, or the music of Hopkins, or breaking our hearts with Sacco's last words before his execution; or he is Milton, ensconced upon a peak, as his Satan falls "Nine times the space of heaven"; or, upon a heath, he is Lear and Shakespeare and his language all at once, rending the thundering garment of the sky, "Blow winds, and crack your cheeks. Rage, blow!"; or he is Mark Anthony swearing vengeance over Caesar's mutilated corpse—"Woe to the hand that shed this costly blood!"—; or he sits at the window sill, in the fading light, reading lyric after lyric of every dusk and passing bee that belonged to Emily Dickinson, the Belle of Amherst, who wrote, "This is my letter to the world,/That never wrote to me"; or he is Melville's contemplative Ishmael, leaning over the railing of the Pequod:

> Chompollion deciphered the wrinkled granite of hieroglyphics. But there is no Chompollion to decipher the Egypt of every man's and every being's face. Physiognomy, like every other human science, is but a passing fable. If then, Sir William Jones, who read in thirty languages, could not read the simplest peasant's face in its profounder and more subtle meanings, how may unlettered Ishmael hope to read the awful Chaldee of the Sperm Whale's brow? I but put that brow before you. Read it if you can.

Or he is Faulkner's rumbling, rushing, head-long lines with the blood of the slave and the Chickasaw and the white man coursing through his veins in pursuit of "the deer and the bear juxtaposed and reliefed against" the monument of the big woods, the wilderness, which must fall, as did Joe Christmas; or he is the Federico Garcia Lorca who sings:

> Whoever inhabits that bull's hide stretched between the Jucar, the Guadalete, the Sil, or the Pisuerga—no need to mention those lion-colored waves churned up by the Plata—has heard it said with a certain frequency: "Now that has real *duende!*"
> Black sounds: so said the celebrated Spaniard, thereby concurring with Goethe, who, in effect, defined the *duende* when he said, speaking of Paganini: "A mysterious power that all may feel and no philosophy explain."

Then Lardas, himself again, would look up from the book and eye us over his glasses to see if we had understood, to see if we had appreciated the music. Yes, it was there in our bright faces and glossy eyes.

He was himself again because, when he read to us, when he read like that, he was not Lardas anymore; he would transcend himself, his personality, and become the language and the ideal voice of the text, whatever the text—bodying it forth—becoming the text itself. Becoming the subject to be learned. So that we were transported to a world that was finer, purer, and nobler than any we had known. So that many of us aspired to the creating of such worlds. So that, for all these reasons (after graduating summa cum laude, Phi Beta Kappa, and a partridge in a pear tree), I too would become an English teacher.

MAUI

I am sitting at the crossroads of Makawao, population 2500, where
Baldwin Avenue meets Olinda Road, which sweeps steeply uphill,
for the town leans like splintered siding on the slope of Haleakala,
"House of the Sun," an extinct volcano, on the stillness of Sunday,
fled to a vacant beach, despite the shade of musty eaves and monkey
pod trees.

The rock 'n' rollers I teach call Makawao "Hippie Town," of
surfers, craftsmen, farmers, entrepreneurs, from Newport, Boston,
Canada, Missouri, from elsewhere from long ago, like some of their
grandparents, in rusty pickups and four wheel drives, in shacks and
pole houses, breeding orchids on their back porch or pot in forest
pockets, where maile grow on the shoulders of ghosts.

It's really a town of Portuguese cowboys, of mainland steaks and
Hawaiian fish, *ono, uku,* mahimahi, of barnyard nights at Longhi's
Saloon, where the men are grizzly, dusty, leathery as jerky or a chaw
of tobacco, where the women are horses, saltier than the men, who
don't need Colts or bullwhips to kill each other. Alex, known as Geek,
was already bustin' broncs at seventeen, while Derek back from U. of
Davis makes Maui wine, and Suzanne turns English into Spanish for
the Sandinistas. —Ahkoi? She simply chucked the whole thing, went
back to the peninsula, wraps laulau with her own taro leaves, dances
ancient hulas under purple shower trees and jacaranda.

I teach up Olinda Road, through a tunnel of eucalyptus, across Oskie Rice's Rodeo. Take a right between two rows of cypress trees, across a rattling cattle guard, through the gate, which opens upon a lettuce-green campus, the chapel, the West Maui Mountains, the ocean, a pasture of drifting cows. It is dusk and in the vesper light you can almost hear . . .

The resignation.

The violet sky.

What had it been? Eighteen years? Eighteen years together. Almost inconsequential now. What did the eighth grader write?

> A bird is singing,
> how can it be so cheerful
> when I feel this way?
>
> How can the sun shine
> and the gentle winds blow
> as if everything in the world
> were perfect
> when I feel so mad inside?
>
> At least the weeds and thorns
> are on my side.

Angry? Only for a short time. Other words attach to the feeling also, denial, resentment, self-pity, rancor, betrayal, pain that radiates along the limbs to the ankle from the sciatic nerve, pinched in the lower back, persistent as a ten-point migraine, pulsating and scintillating, but originating, archeologically, from the heart. How huge the echoing cavern. Hello! Hello! Is anyone home?

So two months after nursing me back to health, while sitting next to each other at the picnic table on our redwood lanai at the rear of the school's duplex, facing a forest of towering Norfolk pine, Christine dropped her watery eyes and said she didn't love me anymore.

I was too stunned to breathe, to utter a sound, so utter the collapse of the church in my lungs. What's going on here?

"I'm sorry, Kenji."

A woodpecker stutters in the piney distance.

"I guess I felt the change when you were able to teach again. When you went back to work. When you were strong again."

Then a flash of red in the dark wood. A scarlet cardinal. An arrow.

"When you didn't need me anymore."

A fluorescent green dragonfly hovers by the railing.

A barrette for your hair.

She is dressed in white, like a bride.

"Do you understand what I'm saying?"

Nod.

"Kenji?"

Nod again.

"Kenji, there was nothing I could do about it. There wasn't anything that you did. And I didn't do anything either. Nor was there anybody else. Ever. It's just . . . the feeling just stopped."

"Just like that . . ." I said softly, mechanically, a branch cracking in the forest.

She nodded, looking at her hands in her lap, her chapped fingers and cracked, bitten nails. I wonder about Toby, our three-year-old.

"It's not your fault," I said. What will happen to Toby?

"I'm tired, Kenji," she said, as she dabbed at her eyes with a paper napkin. The diamond ring flashes. The diamond. Imperishable. "I'm just so tired. Sometimes I wish God would just take me up in his arms and rock me back and forth. Just rock me in his warmth. Back and forth."

"Yeah, I'm tired, too . . ." Tired and sad, and now we're both alone. So we'll be strangers. What does that amount to? I'm strong enough now. "So what will you do?" How many times had I thought of that, too, thought about leaving you? After all those years of your breaking down, year after year, all those years of depression and medication and hospitalization, dropping everything just for you. Just for you. But how could it be otherwise? How many times had the thought passed through my own mind of leaving you? But I always loved you. Always. One might think that you owed me, too. "So what do we do now?"

"Let's walk," she said, rising, taking my hand. I stood, steadied myself with the picnic table until the nausea passed. We walked through the house. Toby would be napping on the couch, a green blanket covering his legs, but he's playing at Aunty Rose's house. The young lime tree in our front yard had given its first fruit. Today the fruit was gone. We didn't mind the students taking plumeria or the white ginger blossoms. They mowed the lawn. Ate chocolate chip cookies. Helped Christine after the operation on my aorta. Her hand is warm. We'll light the fireplace tonight.

The dusk was heavy with stillness; no birds sang, no horse, no cow in the adjoining pasture seemed to move, as we walked through the motionless air in the waning light, past the chapel, past the reflection pool, past the long row of French windows of the breakfast room attached to Cooper House, the long glass table, the long mirror on the back wall, our image doubling, tripling, Christine in white, reminding me of Pele, the volcano goddess, waylaying the faint of heart, ever testing the strength of human spirit, reminding me of the Snow Woman of Japanese folk tale, a snow goddess who marries a mortal and by him has a child, but warns him that if he ever reveals her identity she must kill him. But, instead, when he does, she vanishes forever into the snow. We pass through the kudzu-covered portico of Cooper House, across the soccer field and sit on an incline overlooking Kahului and the West Maui Mountains. It is heartbreakingly beautiful. Holy. And before this mighty expanse, this temple, we remain humble and silent, knowing that we shall never see this evening, this particular sight, ever again.

"I'm going to stay with Aunty Rose," she said, staring far out down the mountain to the sea. "She can watch Toby."

"I just don't understand. I mean, what's happened between us?"

"I don't know. I love you still, but it's not the same."

"Not the same," I repeated. And I think of home, see the Manhattan skyline, the Chrysler Building, the Empire State building, the Twin Towers, back back back. "When will you go?" The Brooklyn Bridge. Maui, just a dream. Christine a snow princess. Christine having an episode—isn't that it? She's sick again?

"June. When school is pau." Pau. Finished. Finis. Pow. Right in the chops . . .

"Two months. Two months. You might as well stay the summer. Who knows. Maybe you don't even have to leave. I could sleep in the other bedroom." She shook her head.

"Look at me, Kenji," she said.

> Was this the face that launched a thousand ships,
> And burnt the topless towers of Illium?

Those eyes that merely reflected my own adoration. My own idolatry. Eyes which now held no facet or gleam of love for me. Eyes, lips, mouth, cheeks, the tilt of the head that held me at the edge, at the circumference, of her former intimacy, that said, unflinchingly, that it was late, that visiting hours were nigh, that there was no turning back, no exceptions, like the maid who understands that all special privileges have been revoked, whose eyes assume the formality of distance, not cold, but objectified, like the night watchman who glances at the wall clock, tolerant of your presence, your momentary befuddlement, disorientation, in which way to turn in finding the exit; eyes that discover to you the truth of your dilemma and its solution both, without recourse to fairy tales, fantasy, or fabulation of any sort, without reprieve, without words, just this look, just this that makes you the former, the used-to-be, the X, the before. The Other. None of which would matter were you not in love.

"Now you know," she said.

Then she stood and hugged herself when a breeze arose.

"Let's go back," I said, without rising.

"No. You go," she said.

It was nearly dark now. I did not move.

"You are okay?" I asked, with fleeting hope.

"Yes," she said, as she turned to go.

"Can you pick up Toby?" I said. "I just need to sit a while."

"Okay. You'll be all right, Kenji?"

"Yeah, sure."

She turned toward Cooper House in the gloom, the woman in white, like a ghost.

PIETÀ

In Albert Camus's *The Stranger*, the protagonist, Monsieur Meursault, begins the novel by saying, "Mother died today. Or maybe yesterday; I can't be sure. The telegram from the Home says: YOUR MOTHER PASSED AWAY, FUNERAL TOMORROW, DEEP SYMPATHY. Which leaves the matter doubtful; it could have been yesterday." We soon find out that when she died is of little concern. He says to his boss, who seems, to Meursault, annoyed by the inconvenience of his two days' leave, "Sorry, sir, it's not my fault, you know."

And upon meeting the Home's Warden, from whom he feels blame for his mother's death, he tries to explain himself, but the Warden cuts him off: "There's no need to excuse yourself, my boy, I've looked up the record and obviously you weren't in a position to see that she was properly cared for." Which may have been true. Though it wouldn't have mattered, insofar as his fidelity to his mother was concerned. Truth is, like other offspring, he does not love his mother. So that, when he is tried for the murder of an anonymous Algerian man, in a singular, petty confrontation, he is found guilty primarily because of—absurd as it may sound—his lack of filial affection for his mother. The Mother. Icon of icons. Whence his feeling of guilt.

There are many of us who probably feel guilt. But, like Meursault, not shame. Not really.

On the other hand, I have witnessed mothers who have, simply, point-blank, declared their lack of love for their children. More. In one parent conference with her daughter's teachers, who were concerned with the child's academic progress and dormitory behavior, the mother, without apology, unflinchingly stated, "I do not like her." Then dismissing with a wave of her ivory hand our naive protestations to the contrary, she added, "I can't stand her." She felt no shame, no guilt even (unlike her second husband sitting uncomfortably beside her, a helpless expression on his face, as if to say, "It's not my fault"), as the mother expressed her abhorrence for her daughter. She simply did not want to be near the child, sharing the same house with her, breathing the same air, hearing her, smelling her, catering to her whining, pawing, egocentric needs. It was simply a fact of life. Though she would provide for her, assume responsibility for her physical well-being. Another fact of life. She could, at least, pride herself on her honesty. Unlike other parents who commonly foist their children on a host of other professionals—maids, nannies, chauffeurs, tutors, instructors, coaches, counselors, psychologists, and other shamans—parents who, really, couldn't be bothered as they pursue their own professional interests.

No. There is no crime here. At least not on the statutes. No Andrea Yates, who, directed by the mad voices in her skull, drowned her five children in a bathtub. No Medea who kills her two children out of spite for her husband Jason, hating him more than she loved her children—her utterance, in the ancient Greek, sounding as one long hiss.

Two years before my mother's death, we had spoken long distance over the phone about my flying from Hawaii to visit her again in my former home in New York City. I had visited her five years ago. And I was stunned to emptiness when she said, "No, Kenji. You live your own life." I was shaken, the cavern in my brain echoing her words. You live your own life. I understood this as her saying Good bye, bringing to an end my ever returning home, my ever seeing her again. I knew her first concern was the cost of such a visit, with a wife and child, no less. But I still felt rejected. Unneeded. Unnecessary. Fading from her imagination, a shadow in her fading memory. A stranger.

And I felt guilty.

Time has a way of wearing away the doorstep, the tile in front of the kitchen sink, doorknobs, mirrors. While physical distance, relentless as water, wears away the heart's affections, like abrading and reshaping stones along the bank of the stream. I was not moved by her passing and wondered when it was that my feelings for my mother had changed, whether or not I had ever felt that deep abiding love which the world assumes we all feel as a matter of course, as unquestioned as the love a mother feels for her child.

Live your own life. How final. How profound a gift. How deep the sacrifice.

Icon of icons.

The first and only time we had seen Michelangelo's *Pietà*, housed in St. Peter's Basilica, it was protected behind a crystal wall. For it had recently been attacked by a madman, who walked into the chapel and attacked the Virgin with a hammer while shouting "I am Jesus Christ!" The restored *Pietà*—the statue of the Virgin Mother and the crucified Christ in her lap—takes the breath in a sudden gasp, and, at the same instant, the eyes liquefy, the lungs rise into your throat, and you feel the full weight of your swollen heart, so deeply moving, the pathos in the pose of her hands, the tilt of her head, her loss and resignation monumentalized in pure white marble.

Her suffering ennobled. Her love. Her life. Everything devoted to her child's prosperity. I remember our returning from church one morning, finding my mother seated in the center of the living room couch, quietly knitting, serene, the apartment, for once, orderly and clean. In her old age, in her tranquility, she would turn to beadwork jewelry and doll making. At rare moments, she would pluck out hymns on the old upright. Her work momentarily done. A rare moment of domestic peace. The late morning sun streaming upon her lap.

Then two years later we went to visit her anyway, having learned that, after repairing two broken hips, she contracted stomach cancer. Nor did her dementia diminish her suffering.

Then two days after returning to Hawaii the inevitable call came. It was Sunday, All Saints' Day, when my first understanding of humility and sacrifice and grace passed from the world.

Even as she lay upon her bed, accepting miso soup, tea, apple juice, or Jell-O, Mother could still show her chagrin, as my sister nosed after some alien smell over her bedclothes or my standing bare-chested at the foot of the bed. Otherwise she would wave hi to my sister standing at the threshold of the living room or wave to me and Christine as we left for dinner; a hand that would close in mine as I sat next to her bed and read; or place upon her abdomen when the pain arose; that would rub my sore stomach in the middle of the night when Daddy was alive.

I remember her kneeling by his bedside holding an empty water glass upside down over Daddy's nose. The glass would not fog. There were four of us, then, to worry over and rear. For she had the strength that Daddy always reflected. Just as she reflected the gentleness that Daddy held inside.

I'll remember, too, my sister's late return from work, her leaning over Ma's bed, whispering kindnesses, laying her hair, her head, her cheek next to Ma's, her arm securing the embrace. Her mother. Her lifetime buddy. No marble statue to monumentalize the passing moment.

Parents pass away, that's a fact of life.

> Abide with me; fast falls the eventide;
> The darkness deepens; Lord, with me abide!
> When other helpers fail and comforts flee,
> Help of the helpless, O abide with me.

Swift to its close ebbs out life's little day;
Earth's joys grow dim; its glories pass away;
Change and decay in all around I see;
Help of the helpless, O abide with me.

So they sang at my mother's funeral. Had I been present I would have probably grieved some, too, as I dwelled quietly on her picture and her urn. Years later, as an aging man, I would think of her when I wrote "Pietà":

Old moon . . . Old vagrant
hands deep in your pockets
you wander by the glass
loiter at the corner over names
Monroe   de Milo   Mona Lisa
humming like Mathis
into a sweet bottle of wine
Ave Maria

O, Marie!   Mary!

Mother of God!

I am your hatless
snowman
a crumbling pylon in a white desert
a pea coat clinging to a light pole
a bent yield sign kneeling at the curb

head filled
with the thousand burning candles
of your name

so much beauty
so much love
so much sadness
I cannot leave you

though my heart craves
stillness stasis surcease
all the names for rest
for your grief
that is
mine.

DREAM

He sees Christine exiting Macy's with packages. She is wearing a dress the color and movement of water. Her hair is long, as when she was young, and he can follow her easily just by her scent and the white scarf trailing behind her. He walks parallel to her on the opposite side of the street. The street seems busy but everything seems transparent, except Christine, who stops in front of a lady's shoe store where she talks to someone on her cell phone. He can hear her say, "Bernie? Just come over to the house for dinner. I can fix something simple and we can watch a movie." As the traffic light turns green she walks leisurely across the street, as if on a runway, and enters a Chinese restaurant. She waves to her friends and sits down with them in a window booth. Everyone is smiling and chatting at once, showing each other their purchases, gesturing to the waitress with the dim sum cart. Kenji sits in the next booth. He hears her voice but doesn't understand what she's saying. After, he follows her to her car, a silver Corvette, which was once his. On the freeway, he can see her white scarf fluttering in the jet stream behind her. He watches from across the street as she enters her front door, low heels, watery skirt, packages, scarf and all. It is dark now. He sees Bernie's hulking black SUV pull into the driveway. He is a big man. He is carrying a bottle of white wine, white roses. Christine greets him at the threshold, takes the flowers and kisses him on the lips, a deep lingering kiss. Then she draws him inside. Kenji rounds the side of the house to Christine's bedroom window and watches as they kiss passionately on

her bed and they grope and fondle and undress each other. When she
rises, turns off the light and draws the curtains.

MEDITATION

The other day, Terra calls me at home, where I am recuperating from my operation, to interview me for the junior school newspaper. She asks me four, maybe five questions and *no* follow-up questions (I mean, she's an eighth grade reporter). And I recall only two: "How did you feel when you got the class's get-well card?" "Warm and fuzzy," I say, lying. When my wife Christine had brought the card to my hospital room and asked me if I wanted to hear what the kids had written, I told her "No." I already knew: warm and fuzzy things. What could a kid say, really, that is not trite about wishing one's return to good health? Exactly. What most adults would say.

The other question was: "Were you afraid?"

"No," I say. "First of all, I was in too much pain, thinking I had a kidney stone, wanting only the pain to stop. Then when I was told that I had something far worse, I was impassive, having been numbed by morphine." I was not even sensitive to Christine's fear and worry.

Soon after, when I heard a doctor say to Christine that my chances of surviving the operation were fifty-fifty, I was ready. That is, whatever the odds, live or die, it was out of my hands, though, when I heard the odds, I thought strangely that they were fair. Otherwise, success or failure, I would not be conscious of the turning point, which, in my case, would span forty-eight more, unconscious and half-conscious hours after the operation.

My fear of dying, when I do fear it, occurs in the restless moments before sleep, as I lie in bed in the darkness of night; when I feel most the loneliness of isolation and the inevitable separation from those I love most, from Christine lying next to me and my son down the hall watching TV; when they, too, break my heart, in their own darkness, must suffer this profound sadness, this loss, through aforethought; when I think of the fears felt by my father and mother, separately, as they passed from the Earth.

The frightful reaction that follows these thoughts is a form of paralysis, like a missing heartbeat, facing the momentary eternity of blankness; like the hiatus, the breathtaking silence that seizes the lungs and rib cage when the CD stops and breathing is labored. When, just after, the natural sounds of my surroundings creep back into consciousness.

During the daylight, on the other hand, it is easier to be brave; easier for me to accept my mortality and the loss of my family; easier to rationalize alongside the great sages of Earth's history, with Socrates and Buddha, Rumi and Gandhi, for example, and other wise and holy men; easier to believe in providence and purpose and reprieve.

The darkness is another story.

Most mornings, before the sun rises over the left shoulder of the valley, and the weather is accommodating, Christine and I, from our modest house, pressed against the forest preserve at the end of our windy valley, walk down the gradual slope to the street's first curve to the right. Then we turn and trudge back, she to strengthen herself against the cancer in the lining of her bladder and I to regain the strength and shape of the muscles in my dwindling calves.

I had recently survived an abdominal aortic aneurysm (or Triple A, in hospital parlance). An aneurysm is a permanent abnormal blood-filled distillation of a blood vessel resulting from disease of the vessel wall. My doctor likened the distillation to a bulging air pocket or rodent trapped in a water hose. He said that I was fortunate that the distillation or bubble had leaked and did not burst, which would have caused my immediate demise. The pain I experienced for ten hours, before finally admitting myself to ER, was caused by the leakage, first felt in my lower back, then my left groin, then down my left leg to the bottom of my left calf. I would learn later that most people die before reaching the hospital.

Out of precaution, the ER doctor ordered a CAT scan for me, which, I suppose, was not the usual practice in confirming the presence or absence of a kidney stone. When the aneurysm was found, a team of specialists was speedily called in, who, in concert, sliced me open from sternum to groin; cut out the diseased portion of the artery that connects to the aorta; replaced it with a plastic tube (hoping the tube would integrate with its organic home); then sealed the longitudinal incision with sixty, stainless steel staples. I learned that most people do not survive the operation, and fewer still the long, critical hours just after.

During our walks I ask Christine about things that remain unclear to me. I recall my doctor saying that, by the time I return home, I will have forgotten most everything about my ordeal, meaning the degree of pain and suffering I had experienced. Of that, naturally, I would only have an inkling. Like tourists, I think, who forget the hardships of travel? Like the waiting, the encumbrances, the uncertainties, the minor and temporary discomforts? But that's not so, for, from the inclined angle of a hospital bed, there are no highlights, no curious wonders, no surprising, brilliant vistas that suddenly burst upon the imagination and indelibly paint one's memory of an entire trip with a single, vivid color.

In fact, as in Conrad's *Heart of Darkness*, wherein the spiritual universe is inverted, what is remembered best is what is darkest. I cannot forget the stroke that accompanied the aneurysm that affected nerve number three of my right eye, affecting the muscles that control the eyelid and the movement of the eyeball. I cannot forget the pancreatitis, the continual vomiting of dark green bile, that sometimes accompanies a protracted IV diet. I cannot forget the nurse's faulty insertion of the catheter, effecting sufficient pain to require its removal, which caused a tearing of the ureter wall, much blood, and another operation.

I cannot forget my second night in ICU, watching the blonde-haired nurse across the way, standing, talking with her patient, whom I couldn't see, for the curtain was half drawn. I only heard his voice, which was deep and calm. Several times she would leave his bedside to return to her work station to fill out some forms or whisper to the nurse who was caring for me. And each time she appeared more and more disturbed. Then, when she last entered his room, she turned off one of the monitors, as though it were a radio, and talked to him softly until, I was sure, he had died.

Christine calls me a walking miracle. I wonder about this, most times feeling embarrassed. For it suggests that my life is more special than other lives or that I deserve to be privileged above others, which, given my history, seems nonsense. I am a teacher, sometimes a very good teacher who leads kids to realize and nurture for themselves their innate talents as readers, writers, and thinkers. But there are many such teachers, in a variety of spheres. While other individuals, through their excellent work, could better justify their value and worth for the community or even for this world. But who would make such judgments and choices, if at all? For lives are saved or dashed according to no material reckoning that we know. On the face of it, there is no reckoning. All seems haphazard.

Maybe, also, it's the word "miracle" that discomfits me, that is disconcerting, since the word suggests divine intervention, where events are sometimes directed by forces beyond nature. Yet, because of what I have read and heard and experienced myself—of those inexplicable, *miraculous* instances of life superseding death—I cannot deny certain consistencies, certain convergences, certain patterns, certain occurrences that seem implausible, even impossible, exclaiming scientific logic and mathematical percentages trivial if not irrelevant for this person at this particular moment in time.

Miracles seem to break or dismiss scientific laws and bring attention to themselves and, often, are the cause of celebration and awe. They can be seen as gifts given by a mysterious giver (or produced by an unknowable logic). And as gifts, they call for no payment in return, in act or allegiance, in obligation or fealty. There is no debt. They are expressions of kindness and love, is one interpretation.

Another is that I owe something to others, to the world, to god, meaning that there is reason for my life being spared. Perhaps there is work yet to be developed, or completed, or even begun. Perhaps my surviving has more to do with my supporting others whose work, in the larger, unknown scheme of things, is more significant than my own; that there is some lesson to be learned, an example to be exploited; that, for the time being, my presence serves a purpose; that there is cosmic reason for things occurring as they do. Whole religions, histories, and philosophies say as much.

Christine has this six-inch, white marble brick on her bureau. It is engraved with the words, as on a tombstone: "Be patient. God isn't through with you yet."

While I hear my former teacher, Joseph Heller, now dead, still speaking, at once, in multiple tongues, saying from the pages of *Picture This*: "Man is a political animal and a social animal, and he normally enjoys fantastic answers in preference to none."

If, in fact, there are no answers—not merely that we are incapable of acquiring answers or ascertaining the truth—that, ultimately, there is no meaning, no reason for being, *what* does that mean? Would such knowledge make life *more* valuable? *Less*?

On one of our walks, Christine tells me that, while in the hospital, I was overcome by emotion twice. I could recall only once. I had asked her, again, how our dear friend Charlotte was doing managing the cancer that was plaguing her over the past several years and, recently, was growing increasingly virulent, when, this time, I learned that she had died. The sound of a wounded animal, arising from some deep cavern in my heart, escaped my throat. How very sad. We had just visited her last summer. She was sitting placidly in a recliner, immersed in a novel, the quiet, and the late afternoon sun, framed by the deck beyond the window, the giant Cambria pine, and the cold ocean below. When I asked when it was that Charlotte had died, Christine said, "About a week ago. But Art emailed and said that she died rocking in his arms. . . .

"He said not to tell you until you were better."

Then I think of Art and his terrible grief, his terrible loneliness, the emptiness through the loss of his partner in life—such a graceful, beautiful soul—despite his saying early on, reassuring us, that he was okay. Then came those terse expressions of his profound sadness. This graying athlete trying to be strong, like some mythic mariner facing all manner of misfortune and storms. Like an everyday Ulysses. I send Art excerpts from Tennyson's "Ulysses":

> —you and I are old;
> Old age has yet his honor and his toil.
> Death closes all; but something ere the end,
> Some work of noble note, may yet be done . . .
>
> Though much be taken, much abides; and though
> We are not now that strength which in old days
> Moved earth and heaven, that which we are, we are,
> One equal temper of heroic hearts,
> Made weak by time and fate, but strong in will
> To strive, to seek, to find, and not to yield.

I tell my dear friend that he is my hero, that like a medieval knight he can still fight the good fight in the name of his fair lady, as when she was alive; that her absence is just as much an inspiration, now, for serving others and living an honorable life.

I then send him an excerpt from Wordsworth's "Ode":

> What though the radiance which was once so bright
> Be now for ever taken from my sight,
>   Though nothing can bring back the hour
> Of splendour in the grass, of glory in the flower;
>   We will grieve not, rather find
>   Strength in what remains behind;
>   In the primal sympathy
>   Which having been must ever be;
>   In the soothing thoughts that spring
>   Out of human suffering;
>   In the faith that looks through death,
> In years that bring the philosophic mind.

In the philosophy that allows the soul to accept, with equanimity, the absolute, irreconcilable words: *forever, always, never again, must ever be*; in the philosophy that voids all regrets and nullifies all fears; in the philosophy that assures that, even through the loss of loved ones and the dissolution of memory in old age, the heart will be suffused in beauty.

HONOLULU

She was poised at the salad bar, dressed in lavender, the dowager empress, the goddess Isis, from ancient Luxor (Ramses but a toy), plucking black olives, figs, and grape tomatoes with tongs like fingers, her arms, like a dancer's, long and sinewy, and around her wrist spiraled a silver asp. I walked up quietly behind her.

"You're right on time," Estancia said without turning around.

"How did you know?"

"Your cologne, Canoe."

"So much like Ambush," I said smartly.

"True, their scents are cousins." *Kissing?*

I tiptoed over her shoulder and spoke to her nape, "And what are *you* wearing?"

"Desert Musk," she whispered intimately. "It was sprinkled by priests over the mummies of queens before they were entombed."

I laughed. Risen from the dead, I wanted to bite her long neck. I was taken by the shiny blue stone at the end of her dangling earring. Larger blue stones, sparkling tetrahedrons, circled her throat.

She added little cubes of goat cheese and watercress to her plate, then four ribs, two each, of yellow and orange bell peppers and several strings of dark scarlet beets. She made me hungry, her plate like an artist's palate; I could have eaten the paint. She turned around, almost a pirouette, graceful as Dame Margot Fonteyn.

"I need a favor, Kenji."

My stomach growled. I imagined eating peacock.

"Are you free Thursday evening? I need an escort to the PBS fundraiser."

"Could I dance, I am your Nureyev," I said bowing deeply, my right leg extended behind me, nearly tripping Kenneth Grunewald, who taught Esperanto, and Takeshi, the science teacher, who were just passing by, as Takeshi said, "Oh, look, we're having pork butt for lunch."

"Ham, I'd say," corrected Grunewald. Then offering his arm to Takeshi, he said, "Shall we on to the haute table?"

Taking his arm, his nose high, Takeshi replied, "Why thank you, Romeo." To Susie, who was poised with tongs on the other side of the hot table, he said, pointing, "Bratwurst, that big long one. I like them big and long, don't you, Kenji?"

"*He jests at scars that never felt a wound,*" I expounded, over the din of dining room.

I loaded my plate with greens, iceberg and romaine, celery, cucumber, soybeans, parsley, asparagus spears, broccoli. A little olive oil, lemon. *We are the salad people.* Pepper, some soy sauce.

Estancia was already ensconced in a booth opposite Ursula, another gay divorcee, of royalty herself, a Hawaiian Jew descended from kings on both sides. She was as elegant as Estancia, though with bigger bosom and teeth and a throatier, freer laugh. She was the head librarian who took joy in turning iPod/cell phone/laptop/hip hop/video game kids on to books. She was eating from a plastic trough of colorful fresh fruit.

"My kingdom for a melon—Hi, Ursula," I said, like a supplicant at an altar. "No, don't move. I'm meeting with my teacher team, who, as usual, are late. So, Estancia, email me about Thursday night."

"Have some," Ursula said, offering me her fruit.

"No thank you, kind madam." I loved Ursula's soft, fleshy, pale pink lips like salamanders. I knew how Adam felt and would not succumb a second time.

"Let me see your plate," Estancia ordered. So, like a little boy, I showed her. "Don't you listen to Dr. Munch?"

"Not lately."

"You need to eat all seven colors, young man."

Young man, I like that.

"Yes, mother."

"That's Queen Mother," she joked.

"By any name, I'd call it incest," Ursula said, laughing

"There they are now," Estancia said, matter-of-factly, without lifting her head.

And there they were—*How does she do that?*—rising, like the three Fates, from the stairwell. *She couldn't have smelled them.* Following them up the stairs was Thornbush, the supervisor, tall, desiccated, bald, and bent, the Hunchback of Our Lady of Little Faith. *Truly, sir, a walking cadaver.* I motioned the three Fates to a round table near the glass doors to the lanai. "Ladies, if you'll excuse me." But Estancia fixed him with her beryllium eyes. "Yes?" he said.

"Yes," she said, holding the final ess like a hiss.

I was smitten and thought *Viagra.*

Ursula laughed. *Lips. Fruit. Salamanders.*

"We give our human sexuality presentation to the faculty second," Nalani said, relishing her marinated eggplant melt. Pamela and Sandra Song were meat-and-potato people, very picky about vegetables, *their palates still narrow. Picky picky picky.* After all, they were still in their early thirties, though Pamela was expecting her third, while Jen, well, she was a former beauty queen. *Picky picky picky and out to save the world.* I admired her energy, her ambition, her idealism and youth. In June she was off to South Africa to do some volunteer teaching, and then, without pause, she was off to Beijing, before going on to graduate school at Harvard to pursue her master's degree in math curriculum. *But she was peahen picky.*

"Did you get my email picture of Oreo?" Pamela, already looking big, asked.

"Who?" said Nalani, who was three-quarters through her sandwich already. She came from a family of big brothers.

"Oreo?" I said. "You must have just sent it."

"My baby pig," she said, adding to her five cats, her French bulldog Fizzles, fish, and, in her backyard, her aviary filled with golden finches.

"I saw Oreo. It was *sooo* cute the way Heather was hugging him," Sandra Song sang.

"Yesterday Fizzles tried to mount Oreo," Pamela reported.

"They can't do it, right?" I said, doubtfully. "Two different species, I mean, producing perverted offspring."

"Why not?" said Sandra, deadpan. "It's been done before. Dog and pig produced man."

We laughed.

"Um. Pam," said Nalani, "you'll present first. Just go over quickly your human reproduction unit in Science."

"Perfect! You can just stand sideways," I said, "and show family pictures."

"Oh, pshaw," Pamela said, rolling her eyes.

"Actually, Pam, you'll follow me and Kenji. Kenji, what are you going to say?" asked Nalani.

"I'll say something like, In English, we're reading *To Kill a Mockingbird*, and that one of the things we follow is how tomboy Scout and her older brother Jem grow more and more conscious of their sexual difference. The students are reminded of their own innocent growth, before they became sex-crazed eighth graders."

"Who are desperate for knowledge," Pamela said.

"They need to know," Sandra said.

"That's why I'll start," said Nalani, dragging the small stack of index cards towards herself, knocking over the saltshaker. *The Shakers practiced abstinence.* Then I remembered *The Hunchback of Notre Dame,* Charles Laughton in the old black and white movie, crying out from the belfry: *Abstinence! Abstinence! Abstinence!*

"I'll say that, in our sexuality unit in Ethics, we begin by standing and having the kids yell as loud as they can penis! penis! penis! vagina! vagina! vagina! Matter of fact, I'll have all the teachers stand and role-play."

"Yeah, I'll bet penis sticks in a lot of throats. I mean no pun," I said.

"Yeah, right," said Pamela, flipping her blonde hair in mock disappointment.

"Then Jen and I will read, rapid fire, some of the anonymous questions that kids want answered." Nalani gave Sandra half the stack. "Ready? Okay, me first: *Why don't people have babies every time they have sex?*"

"*What is the legal sex age?*" asked Sandra.

"*What is doggy style?*" asked Nalani.

"*Is it true that it hurts girls their first time?*"

"*How do gays/lesbians have sex?*"

"*Is it true that if you get AIDS or STDs you can't get pregnant?*"

"*Why do guys like sex more than girls?*"

"*Why do people cry after sex?*"

"*Can girls masturbate? If so, how?*"

"*What's with guys and boobs?*"

"*Which ethnicity has the biggest boobs?*"

"*What's a rim job?*"

"Here's one: *What are birth control pills used for?*"

"Strike that for the teachers."

"*Why do guys look at porn?*"

"*Is it true you will bleed when you first have sex? What do you do about that?*"

"Can you have sex without an erection?"

"Can you get impregnated while in the Jacuzzi?"

"Stop. That should give them a feel," said Nalani.

"I don't quite know what you mean by that," I said, in mock bewilderment.

"A feel for the course, you doodoo head," Pamela said.

"The feel for how we've tried to integrate our teaching," added Nalani, when a shadow passed over our table. It was Thornbush.

"Has Kenji been boring you, ladies?"

They nod; all play their part in the conspiracy.

"You know, Thornbush," I said, "I didn't want to tell you this but you seem to grow gaunter everyday."

Thornbush laughed. For some reason Thornbush reminded me of my housekeeper Elsa. Both seemed to thrive at night, like bats, though Thornbush, at least, enjoyed laughter, though sometimes it was sickly or echoed of graveyards.

We have sex and then we die.

Estancia was standing by the reception desk, dressed, as she had said, in a cerise and scarlet caftan, a belt of braided jade and gold about her waist, her hair up—showing off her long, Modigliani neck—the same blue stones at her ear and round her throat, turquoise eye shadow, and blue-purple feathers like a bird tail rising from the back of her head; she wore lavender gloves that rose to her elbows. She was like some exotic bird or rare flower found deep within a tropical forest, whose fragrance inspired hallucinatory visions of Eden.

She extended her right hand, which I took without thought and raised to my lips and I whispered, "My queen." *Nefertiti.*

"My liege," she whispered, for which I thought, *Thank you,* since I felt ill at ease in a suit I hadn't worn in years and was now a little snug around the shoulders and waist so that I kept the suit jacket unbuttoned, as I had the dress shirt at the neck, hidden artfully by the large knot of my silk tie.

I offered Estancia my arm, and together we walked the corridor as imperial guests, as a pathway through the crowded hall naturally opened before us, as both men and women stared openly at Estancia.

Put your tongues back in your eyes.

"What are you wearing that's so tantalizing?" I asked.

"Wet Orchid and Blood Passion. I combined the two scents. Depending upon my mood or the weather or the occasion, I play with different combinations, like with makeup and clothes. What are you grinning about?"

"Was I grinning?"

"You were."

"Oh. I was just thinking of this French guy, Des Esseintes, a character invented by this decadent writer, J.K. Huysmans. In one chapter of his book, called *Against the Grain*, Huysmans has Des Esseintes—who is constantly dreaming up various, outrageous ways to overcome his boredom—Huysmans has Des Esseintes construct a perfume organ. Each key he would play would release from its respective organ pipe a particular scent, so that Des Esseintes, in a way, could play a concerto of smells."

"Ingenious. But I'm sure, it shortly became suffocating," Estancia said, almost in disapproval.

"I'm sure. Another time, this time to gratify his jaded eyes, he had a giant tortoise brought to his apartments. On the tortoise's shell he affixed an assortment of semi-precious stones, all polished, and of such shimmering variety—amethysts, topaz, garnets, the watery fire of aquamarine, pink quartz, opals, agates, blue sapphires, transparent green peridots, and so forth. So that, as the tortoise moved slowly across Des Esseintes's carpet in the afternoon light, the effect was dazzling."

"Yes, but, again, temporary. He seems like a lonely bachelor. Wealthy but idle, without occupation."

"Are you lonely?" I asked, as we entered the Grand Ballroom and were given wine glasses as we passed through the double doors.

The wall panels were gold and white, each bordered by crimson drapes. From the lofty ceiling hung sparkling chandeliers. And round the spacious room groups of people were loosely grouped at the various wine tables, sipping, tasting, swishing their glasses, talking, asking questions of the vineyard merchants. The room full of jewels and tinkling glass and chatter. The round tables in the middle of the room were filled with various cheeses, pâtés, dips, sundry canapes of salmon and duck and wild mushroom, almonds and dates, pickles and olives from everywhere but here, dainty buns and breads, and on and on; the women ravishing, even those in business suits; most of the men in aloha attire, which I should have worn myself, though the suit seemed to please Estancia.

"Lonely?" Estancia replied. "Sometimes. I have a dog, a small Italian greyhound, Eliza, but she's fairly old. Are you often lonely?"

"Often. But not now," I said, looking deeply into her eyes, which remained imperturbably sedate, perhaps slightly quizzical, I couldn't tell, though there seemed a subtle change in the topography of her face, maybe around her pale pink lips—how infinitely plastic the human face. How mysterious this mobile mask of clay. *A mask for my mask! Or as Mercutio says:*

> *Give me a case to put my visage in,*
> *A visor for a visor! What care I?*

Meaning, an ugly mask for an ugly face! Good ole Mercutio, so alive, yet a poetic invention who will live and die a thousand times over. —What care I?

"Shall we taste some Italian?" Estancia suggested, leading me away, her step a dance from table to table. *A masque. "The Masque of Red Death," wherein all those beyond the ballroom walls are dying of plague, of poverty, of war, until . . .*

"Taste this," Estancia said, with aplomb, pointing to a bottle of Barolo, then tasting a Barbaresco, "from the Piedmont region," each time watching my face to gauge my reaction. "Now taste this," she said, "a Brunello di Montalcino," delighting, as I sipped, swished, and swallowed, as my eyes suddenly popped round, my face aglow, as if I had achieved Buddhahood beneath the bodhi tree. "From Tuscany," she said smiling, as if to say, *Now you know, too.*

"This is amazing!" I said. "I don't need to go any further."

"This is a tasting, my dear. You must go on."

"But I've found my truth for the night."

"The night is yet young," Estancia said, stepping toward him, taking charge of his elbow. "There's Chile to taste," she said, gesturing to the next table. Then South Africa, Australia . . ."

"Mrs. Robinson, you're trying to seduce me."

"Come, it's my job. You forget, I work in the Advancement Office," she said with a wry smile, her green eyes iridescent, like peridots.

But after tasting several international wines and more from California and Oregon, my palate grew dull and my vision grew fuzzy, like frost round the edges of a New Hampshire window. Besides, I was famished.

I thought: *Madame, why don't we visit the pupu tables and treat our palates with delicacies from the Isles of Brie and Camembert—there, near the Coast of Peking Duck, Foie Gras, and Salmon Mousse—*but said, "Estancia, I'm hungry, how 'bout you?"

"We're seated at Table 17. It's near the stage. What will you drink?"

"The Brunello."

"Of course. I'll join you in a bit," she said, squeezing my hand.

"Where are you off to?"

"France," she said, moving off like a blue cloud. I watched her stately walk, her regal carriage, as she held her glass, demurely, to the light. The sparkling glass beneath the chandelier, like ice. *Isis!*

Not the idea, not the flesh, I thought. *No, beauty killed the beast.*

I helped myself to a variety of dainty hors d'oeuvres, relishes and dips, tasting as I moved about the table—when, with mouth full, I saw Christine, dressed in a white chiffon sheath, enter the double doors, like an apparition. *My god.* I spied her through the centerpiece of purple iris and bird of paradise. *Of all the gin joints in all the towns in all the world, she walks into mine. —And who's this? Lenny? Lenny the piano man? my neighbor? —escorting Christine?*

But why not? It's all probably innocent enough. —And none of your big nose business!

Open the pod bay doors, HAL.

"Are you okay, Kenji? You look a bit wan," said Estancia.

"I feel like won ton min," I confessed.

She took my arm and said, "Lean on me."

"No, I'm fine. Just need to eat. Where's our table again?"

"Come," she said, holding me close.

I could feel her warmth, her breast against my arm, her scent, her breath as she whispered, "I saw her, too."

I nearly dropped my two saucers of finger food. I halted at the table and asked, "Who?"

"That slender woman in white. You were staring at her shamelessly, making me jealous," she said in mock chagrin. "Who is she, pray tell? She's very attractive—alluring," Estancia added, as she turned and measured Christine with an editor's eye. "I'd put her on the cover of a magazine. Wouldn't you?"

I turned and followed Estancia's gaze. Christine was at the French table, crowded about by young men, *a bunch of bean counters and dustless chalk salesmen. Gerbil hunters.* Lenny's hand was resting on her right hip. "Yeah. *Popular Mechanics.*"

"You're bitter," Estancia said. "But, of course. She was your wife, wasn't she?"

"Once. Let's eat. Oh, that's nice, I've lost my wine glass. Where'd I leave it?" I said, scanning the room, my eye inevitably drawn to Christine and the piano player's hand.

"Sit," Estancia said. "I'll get you another," though I suspected she wanted to critique Christine up close. Curious.

I sat and ate the anchovy-sweet red pepper-provolone hors d'oeuvres, the bacon-wrapped scallop glazed with vermouth, the coarse country pâté with Maui onion and lychee. But it was the brie, that particular brie with black truffles, that took me back so many years—to Paris—to that small neighborhood restaurant near our pension on the Right Bank, our first dinner in the city, sitting side-by-side, pleasantly overwhelmed by the menu, the wine list, the intimate chatter, like candlelight, shimmering around us, the Japanese couple at the corner table, still dressed in their wedding clothes, whom Christine and I had seen in Chantilly, at the Chateau, where their ceremony was held, and here they were again, which the newlyweds probably thought similarly of me and Christine, Asian tourists; and I remembered the dapper young man in the gray, three-piece suit, who sat dining contentedly alone, opposite our table, who was perhaps in his early thirties, aware that he had an audience, albeit a foreign one, who observed, nearly, his every bite, for during much of his meal he held his left hand poised on his hip like a proud, modern-day courtier, who, with much gastronomic prowess, yet with *sprezzatura*, had devoured an enormous meal, and at the end, to our disbelief, the young cosmopolitan was pointing to his preferences of cheese from a platter, big as a sombrero, held forth by the waiter. That evening in bed, we talked of what it would be like (were we ever to separate) to eat out alone, night after night, how we, too, would grow accustomed to the solitude, even come to appreciate the privacy, appreciate the nuance of one's own special company, then finally, as the dapper young man had, developing the skills and subtleties of dining alone into high art.

We'll always have Paris.

—When a bottle of Brunello seemed to descend from a lavender sky.

"Estancia, you angel! How did you manage a whole bottle?"

"As I said, I work in the Advancement Office. I'm paid to be persuasive. I also told him that I have a cousin who lives in Tuscany," she said, pouring herself and me a glass of the deep, ink-red wine.

"Estancia."

"Yes?"

"What are you?"

"A woman. If you have any doubts—"

"I mean ethnically."

"Why?" she said, tilting her head.

"You are coy."

"Okay, I'm half Polynesian-Chinese-Spanish-German. The other half I reserve for Trivial Pursuits. And so?"

"And so . . . I was wondering," I began. "I'm going to the Oregon Shakespeare Festival toward the end of June. I was wondering if you'd like to go, too."

"What exactly are you proposing?"

Bad choice of words.

"I mean, I think it's not too late to arrange a room for you across the hall from me at this cozy B & B. It's about a ten-minute walk to the theaters."

"An *arrangement*. Hm. Like a contract?"

"Nothing so serious."

"Like a contract on my head?" she said smiling.

"Yeah, I'm a *gumba* for Tony Soprano," I said, pulling out, from my breast pocket, my hand like a toy gun.

"I mean my maidenhead," she said, glancing at him coyly. "Though I'm no maiden."

"No. No. You are a queen, Queen of the Nile."

"No, I'm not a queen. I'm a woman. What you see is what you get. I mean, what you see is real."

"True. You are an Amazonian queen. And it is also true that it would be cheaper if we shared a room, right?"

She seemed to smile assent. "You have a point."

And the rockets' red glare, the bombs bursting in air.

"But let me think about it. It's a titillating proposition," she said, finishing her wine then filling both our glasses. "And not without risk."

"Want to hear what I have in mind? —I mean about Ashland. *I'll make you an offer you can't refuse.*"

"Please, call me Ms. Faustus," she said, her chin on her hand, leaning across the table.

"Of course, we'll visit a couple of wineries."

"Of course."

"I also want to visit this peach farm that's run by Kenneth Grunewald's friend. And we'll go river rafting. I am dying to go, I've never been."

"I have. It's intoxicating. Just hold my hand."

It seemed to me that the wine was getting to Estancia's queenly head.

"Then we'll watch every Shakespeare play on the program: *As You Like It, Romeo and Juliet, The Tempest, Taming of the Shrew.*"

"They're all about love," she said, feeding me a Greek olive.

"And mistaken identity," I said, chewing thoughtfully.

"Do you know me, Kenji?"

"Know you? No, not really. Who are you? Who am I?"

Then Estancia suddenly burst out laughing, slapping me on the arm; I, myself, started laughing, both rocking against each other like two tugboats knocking against each other in a slip.

Together we finished off the bottle of Brunello, talking of Ashland, of Oregon fruit, of Shakespeare, of love, of reversals and revenge; I was wondering how Estancia would drive herself home. *I mean*, I said to himself, even slurring the words in my mind, *she drank enough to sedate a triceratops.* While I began seeing double: the Lady in Blue. The Lady in White.

ESTANCIA

The Contessa, where Estancia occupied the penthouse apartments, was said to be haunted by benign ghosts of Hawaiian royalty, whose presence could be felt in stairwells, in corridors, in elevators, or momentarily seen in muumuus and *lau hala* hats, sitting on folding chairs at the periphery of family gatherings. The scent of white ginger or *pakalana* lingering in the air.

As the elevator door opened I caught the faint scent of rose blossoms. I could also hear Ravi Shankar's distant sitar music trilling down the corridor. So she must have her door ajar. To India? Arabia? The desert? Just inside the doorway, where I stepped from my sandals, I also heard the sound of water bubbling from a copper fountain to my left near a standing palm, an oasis, and my feet felt cool on the grey-blue tile.

Radiating ten feet in each direction from the doorway, the tile gave way to blonde sandalwood flooring and a long, sand-colored leather couch which faced the sliding glass doors, two of which were wide open, the diaphanous white curtains billowing with the trade breeze, like veils. And more glass doorways billowed with more curtains, more veils, in the dining room with its long glass dining table like a reflection pond, merely an extension of the living room. The walls were painted Persian blue; the blue picked up by the blue pillows and the blue flowers in the Persian carpet beneath the glass coffee table with curving brass legs, a blue pool, matching the paisley blue skirt that flared from her black top and Estancia's blue stone earrings and necklace, as she entered like a dancer from a dim room to my left. She looked ravishing.

"Salaam," I said, touching my forehead and bowing from my waist.

"Shalom," she said.

Salome:

> And when a convenient day was come, that Herod on his birthday made a supper to his lords, high captains, and chief estates of Galilee; And when the daughter of the said Herodias came in, and danced, and pleased Herod and them that sat with him, the king said unto the damsel, ask of me whatsoever thou wilt, and I will give it thee.

"Please, sit. What can I get you?" she asked.

"I should ask you that."

She looked puzzled.

"Would you like to try some Argentinean red, a Malbec?" I said. "Or a Pinot Gris from Oregon?" I said, holding out my offering of frankincense and myrrh. "I'll even open it for you."

"Come this way, kind sir," she said, following her rose-blossom scent to the dining room and the long koa wood side table along the back wall beneath a beveled mirror in a gilt frame. The gold.

"Now there are two of you that I can admire," I said.

"And there are two of you to tell me so."

"And which would you prefer?" I said, removing the two bottles from the sack.

"The Malbec," she said. "Something with meat, if you know what I mean."

"You want everything," I teased.

"I do. Don't you?"

"I guess," I said, afraid to say I do. I walked around the dining table and through the glass door to stand on the balcony overlooking the University of Hawaii campus and Manoa valley, beneath the Koolau mountain range. And the curling white clouds lit by the afternoon light. The view seemed privileged, grandiose, monarchial. "And you glimpse this every day? Well, if anyone deserves this, you do." I stretched wide my arms and opened my breast to the trade breeze and the mountains and clouds. Then I felt a certain fear as I looked down onto King Street and the vertiginous, precipitous drop, remembering my phobia of heights. So easy it would be to leap the railing. To end it all. A thrilling temptation. The audacity. And why not?

"Kenji?" I turned. "Your glass."

"Yes, of course."

"Come, sit with me," she said, settling into the cool couch.

"So tell me . . ." I said, taking a sip of the wine, swallowing deeply, then pursing my lips. "It needs to breathe a little more."

"I like it. You were right on both counts."

"Meaning?"

"Your choice of wines. I made steak au poivre and scallops Provençal."

"And here I was expecting couscous or something Greek."

"Next time."

Next time.

This time I drank deeply, wanting the wine to go to my head, feel my face flush. I wanted to luxuriate in the smooth leather couch and smell the invisible rose petals that dropped leisurely from the hollow of her throat and gathered along the elastic rim of her black, low neck top and her plunging cleavage, the mother lode of black holes. I was careful not to stare.

"I met Elsa, your housekeeper," Estancia said, bringing her wine glass to her blue scarlet lips.

"Where?"

"I meant to tell you at lunch that day, but my mind was elsewhere."

"Of course. Your biopsy. That's what I meant when I said, 'So tell me.'"

"We have the same gynecologist. I had come in early for my appointment, and there we were in the waiting room. She didn't know me. Still doesn't, though she knows my name now."

"Why didn't you tell her you knew me?"

"Let me get you another," Estancia said, touching my fingers as she took my glass. "I didn't think I needed to," she said, as she sauntered to the dining room. "Besides," she said from a distance, "people tend to reveal more intimate things to strangers than they would to friends. Strangers aren't much of a threat."

"So what intimate things did she reveal to you?" I called to her.

She returned with a wry smile on her face. "Don't look so worried. She only had complimentary things to say about you. Except that you like to recite poetry to her rosebushes."

She handed me my glass of dark purple wine.

"And?"

"And, like me, she had a hysterectomy," she said, sitting as before, one leather cushion away. "I had complications with my uterus. But Elsa, I think, had other reasons."

"What made you think so?"

"Well, when I shared my reason, she didn't reciprocate and turned her head. —She had an abortion, didn't she?"

"How did you know?" I said surprised.

"I didn't," she said, but gave no impression that she had baited me or set any snares.

"Me and my big mouth."

"Oh, it's not so big," she said, leaning toward me. "I think it's kind of cute."

I stared at her lips, which were slightly parted. And naturally I leaned my face towards her and kissed her across the continent of the leather cushion, her tongue sliding into my mouth, the feel exhilarating, as if I had never kissed before, her taste making my tongue and mouth sweet, red red wine, my brain in her moist mouth, and the fragrance of her, drunk with her, and I was 25 and aroused, as if from a long sleep.

"Wait," she said, drawing herself back, smiling. "There's still dinner."

"True, true. Let me help you."

"No, just, just sit here. You'll just be a distraction," she said, rising, straightening her skirt, which needed no straightening. "Help yourself to some more wine. And if you finish that there's some good cabernet in the cupboard below. Oh, and fix me one, too." She glided through the dining room to the kitchen, while I poured two more glasses, emptying the bottle. I found the cab below in the wine rack, opened it to let it breathe.

"Here," I said, carefully placing her glass beside her on the grey-blue granite counter, as Estancia expertly sliced a baguette on the bias. The smells of lemon, garlic, pepper and the sound of sizzling steak and scallops in two different pans filled the kitchen. The oven beeped. She opened the oven door and with two mittens removed a baking dish filled with small potatoes.

"Herbed Yukon Gold. Now, go, go. I need to concentrate."

"We could always eat after," I said.

"After what?" she said, looking at me from the sides of her eyes, her dark eyebrows slightly raised.

"Oh, you know" was my lame response.

"I do," she said, shuffling the sizzling meat and the succulent scallops simultaneously, steam rising from both pans, the air filled with spices and herbs and tempting animal aromas.

"Well, since I'm not permitted to use my hands—"

"Not here in the kitchen—"

"Well, then, I'll leave you."

My face felt feverish. While the sights and sounds and smells of food made me feel suddenly aware of my hunger, suddenly aware of my years of deprivation. I stood at the railing of the balcony and wondered if Thornbush was right about my real intentions, that all I really wanted to do was make love to Estancia. No, he was wrong. For the most part anyway. I took another long swallow of my wine. I wanted to feel the rush in my veins. The pulse and the throb. Be young again. The young athlete! The jock who played one hell of a shortstop. And then I remembered my body—the paunch, the flattened butt, the scrawny legs, the questionable stamina—had I anything left to give?

I wandered through the dining room back to the living room and stood, staring at the copper fountain and whispered Shakespeare:

> The sixth age shifts
> Into the lean slippered pantaloon,
> With spectacles on nose and pouch on side;
> His youthful hose, well saved, world too wide
> For his shrunk shank, and his big manly voice,
> Turning again toward childish treble, pipes
> And whistles in his sound. Last scene of all,
> That ends this strange eventful history,
> Is second childishness and mere oblivion,
> Sans teeth, sans eyes, sans taste, sans everything.

But then my spirits rose as Shankar gave way to Dave Brubeck's "Forty Days," his piano a rhythmic striding, both holy and hot, with snare drums and cymbals and the strumming bass, as Christ danced effortlessly over the sand dunes; then Paul Desmond on sax came in, and I could not stand still as my shoulders bobbed and my head, with eyes closed, moved every which way, then Brubeck was back on his trilling, tripping piano with its complex changes and inspired runs, improvising, creating at the cutting edge of his fingertips, and all the time the bass and symbols and drums; it was altogether too much, and when it ended I had to wipe my eyes. And, so to speak, "Take Five," which the Quartet played next.

What did the poet say that keeps us going? Desire, desire.

What was his? —Ecstasy.

As Hamlet says, though he speaks of suicide and death: "'Tis a consummation devoutly to be wished." As is oneness in the fire and flare of sexual climax and the loss of self to ecstasy, which, he believed, is a truer, though a smaller, version of actual death.

"Kenji."

"Coming."

She had already set the table and had poured us both a fresh glass.

"Amazing. I didn't even hear you," I said.

"You were dancing. Sort of. Please sit. No, over there, facing the window."

She dimmed the lights and lit, first one, then the other white spear of candle in filigreed candelabra, as more and more lights were lit in Manoa Valley.

We clinked wine glasses. "*Kampai*," she said.

"To your health." And at this Estancia lowered her eyes.

"These," she said, pointing to a small ceramic dish between them, "are kalamata olives."

"So what did the doctor find?" I asked over the salad of baby greens, crumbled feta cheese, currants, and walnuts. She passed me the olive oil decanter and pointed to another small, ceramic bowl filled with lemon quarters.

"He found cancer cells in my ureter," she said, reaching for the pepper mill, then passing it to me. I sat stunned and suddenly full of trepidation. "He wants a Dr. Simeon Gupta to take over my case."

"Why?" I had already put down my fork.

"Seems that Gupta specializes in urological cancers and is the best we have in the islands. I met him yesterday. He told me that he wanted to take his own tests, and won't look at Dr. Schultz's charts. So I go in for another biopsy Monday."

"He didn't confirm, then, Schultz's finding of bad cells?"

"No."

"So Schultz could be wrong—or the lab workup?"

"Maybe. But unlikely. If anything, they would miss something. Anyway, I found out that Gupta, like you, hails from New York City. Queens, he said."

"That's not exactly Manhattan," I said, digging into my salad, dipping the bread in a small saucer of olive oil with a dark dot of balsamic vinegar.

"Don't be a snob, Kenji," she scolded.

"Ouch!"

"He's a second-generation Indian from India."

"And how about you?" I asked.

"Depends. On my mother's side, I suppose I'm one-fourth, third-generation Chinese. If that makes any sense," she said, rising and taking their salad plates.

"No, what I meant was how are you feeling now?" I said, raising myself to fill our glasses.

"What you're really asking is whether or not I'm well enough to make love this evening. Or if it's safe."

"You must be a touch tipsy," I said, following her into the warm kitchen, where Estancia was transferring the meat and scallops and the herbed potatoes into serving dishes.

"And you're not tipsy? Take that dish in, please," she directed, looking deeply into my eyes—our breasts separated by a bowl of potatoes. "I plan to get you pleasantly drunk by the end of the evening," she teased. Then following me into the dining room she said, "After all, I have to get something in return for all this food."

"Madame, you cannot buy me. I am already your slave," I said, bowing awkwardly, then resuming my seat. I raised my glass. "Salud."

"Chin chin. —Oh, let me get the Pinot Gris from the fridge to go with the scallops."

So we ate in the glow of the candlelight to Oscar Peterson's piano. We ate slowly, quietly at times, as I thought of the film *Tom Jones*, specifically the supper scene between Tom and the fiery-headed, sensuous woman, who, increasingly, throughout the meal, transformed the acts of biting and chewing and swallowing and licking her lips into culinary acts of lovemaking, each course more heated and frenzied than the preceding, so that at meal's end, the two bolted from the table, the film on fast forward, as they raced, comically, to their room in the inn to relieve the wild horses of their pent-up sexual energy, the deliciously tortured tension and strain. I could not help smiling.

"And what's so humorous?"

I explained my thoughts as best I could, my lips slightly rubbery.

"I remember that scene. She was older than he was, but some women can carry their surplus flesh in a way that exudes and invites sexuality, don't you agree?" she said, taking a bite from the fleshy scallop on her fork.

"Yes." And as if on cue, Ravel's "Bolero" began, and I said, "Bo Derek, in the movie *10*, 1979, right? and, good lord, she was a 10."

"And she and Dudley Moore made love to the music, slowly, at first, then building in urgency as the tempo increased. Very sexy. The idea was ingenious."

"But we don't need to rush," I said.

"You mean dinner, of course," she said, smiling wryly, her head tilted.

"Of course," I said, nearly choking on a potato. Great balls of fire. Then swallowing, I said, "I just have to say—"

"Don't. Eat." Then she said, suddenly distant. "I've been thinking about Ashland and your proposal." Proposal. "Schultz's revelation does not bode well for me—for us—I mean going to the Shakespeare

Festival together," she said, avoiding my eyes. "I just want to prepare you for the possibility of my not being able to go with you. You know, if they have to treat the cancer immediately or have to operate, or some other such thing."

"Then I'll not go either," I volunteered.

"That's very gallant of you. No, I know you have your heart set on going. So you should go."

"That heart's been preempted by another," I said, not looking at her. Instead, I filled our glasses with the Pinot; then, a tad wobbly, I rose from the table: "I'll put the rest in the fridge to cool down again."

"You hardly know me," she called.

"And you hardly know me," I returned.

"I know you're obsessed with the sublime more than the sensual, but we can correct the balance."

"Yeah. And I know you're an excellent gourmet cook," I said, sitting crookedly. "And you know about clothes—your sense of color and texture and originality are impeccable—and you have a good ear and, and . . . I love your eyes."

"And I yours. Come let's get some air. No, leave the dishes. Tammy will clean them in the morning."

"Then she'll know," I said, holding with both hands the balcony railing, breathing deeply.

"Of course. Tammy knows everything," Estancia said, leaning her head on my shoulder, her right arm around my waist.

"I must speak to Tammy then."

I could feel her warmth through my clothes, along the length of my body.

"Then you'll have to wake early."

The lights in the Valley climbed up the invisible mountains. The shimmering lights seemed suspended in the night sky. Estancia smelled intoxicating; I nuzzled her hair, then turned and kissed her deeply, her mouth soft and slack and wet, drawing her body into my own, her body cleaving to mine, melting into mine without a joint, trebling the heat, the nerves beginning to smolder. This time I broke away to catch my breath.

"Whew!"

"Come," she said, taking my hand. She led me along the balcony, then through the living room to the study, turning on the ceiling light.

"So this is where you email me late at night."

"Let me go get our glasses," she said, slightly slurring.

This room was darker and closer than the others, since Estancia had tall bookcases set against the balcony windows. There were low bookcases against the back wall, upon which hung old photographs.

"That's my great-grandmother, and the child is my grandmother. My great-grandmother was a concubine for a provincial lord."

I immediately thought of the Chinese film *Raise the Red Lantern*, which was about a concubine that lived on the periphery of the lord's mansion, along a street that housed other concubines.

"And here's my grandmother at thirteen, just before she came to Hawaii by herself in search of her parents. She's my idol. Can you imagine? A thirteen-year-old girl traveling alone to Hawaii."

"What about her parents?"

"First, her father goes to Hawaii to find work and promises to return. But he never returns. Then her mother goes to Hawaii in search of the father, and she never returns. So my grandmother decides to go in search of them. But, sadly, she never finds them and ends up in a Chinese orphanage, where, luckily, six months later, she's adopted by a Chinese diplomat and is educated at an international school in Hong Kong."

"What a trip."

"Then she goes to Princeton, meets and marries a French-German aristocrat who ends up working for the French Embassy in Italy. Then, when he died, I think from cancer, she returned to Hawaii and ran a lucrative real estate firm in Chinatown. And here she is at 85, as courageous and elegant as ever, a Confucian and Taoist both."

"You're squeezing my hand," I said.

"And this is my mother."

The mother, tall and serious, was standing next to the oddest looking human he had ever seen—like the last surviving vestige of a species from the Cretaceous Period, her dress a spurious sheath over a skeleton of lizard skin. She was frightening, indeed.

"And who, in the Lord's name, is that?" I said pointing to the creature standing next to Estancia's mother.

"A Chinese fortune teller. She predicted that my mother would meet a tall, handsome man before the year was up, and it came true. My father was a visiting professor and was teaching International Business Relations at the University. My mother, a graduate student, was fearful that she would never marry."

"And you were married twice."

"We all make mistakes. Even you," she said, suddenly close to me again. I could feel her breath at my neck, the hair tingling on my chest.

I felt dizzy.

"Why don't we sit," I said, leading her from the study.

"Not there."

I stopped and turned. "Where, then?"

"Down the hall. Second room on the right."

I walked down the hall, listing a little to my left, as I whistled "God Bless America."

"You're so funny," she said behind me.

Inside the bedroom, before her bed, I turned, spread my arms, and fell like a cedar cross.

Estancia then entered and paused at the threshold and, in one practiced motion, pulled her black top up over her breasts and head.

I gasped.

Then in the next, her skirt dropped to the floor and, as I gasped a second time, she turned off the light, a silhouette in the doorway. Then she closed the door. Now a shadow, she floated toward the windows and drew the curtains, against the Contessa's ghosts. Then, as jazz guitarist Wes Montgomery played a slow mellow tune, Estancia slid like a fish into my arms, and with her soft and slack and wet lips she began to suck on mine, and I, too, became a fish, as she unbuttoned my aloha shirt and unbuckled my belt, then drew down my zipper, her hands searing, as I helped her take off my remaining garments, my member a gold ingot, and again she leaned into my side, our bodies cleaving together, melting in the rising wet heat, then slowly turning on my side, I gently caressed her neck, her back, running my fingers along her spine, across the globe of her rear, as she caressed my hip, my thighs, the ache unbearably sweet, as slowly our mouths and tongues teased in their exploration, my mouth wide now at her neck, as she arched toward me, her body shuddering, and then Charlie Parker, Bird, began playing his smoking saxophone, and my hands, my palms, my fingers were everywhere, an octopus, painting, dripping, like Jackson Pollack, making things up as my body screamed, and in the back of my mind I could hear Kerouac, the first rapper, reading headlong poetry in a smoky room, and Bird is taking off on impossible runs, blowing blowing blowing as I entered the molten sea of ecstasy and, like Ezekiel, was borne to heaven on a chariot of fire.

CRAP SHOOT

*That's what his teacher friend Nalani had said. "Life's a crap shoot."
That's what she said when Kenji was struck down with an aneurysm and,
also, when he survived and recovered from it, lightning striking at both
ends. For what end? Whereas you knew Estancia's cancer would spread,
even after Dr. Simon Gupta had removed her left kidney, left ureter, and
part of her bladder. Who knew that it would jump to her right kidney,
thence spreading, it seemed in days, like wildfire, through the rest of
her organs. Like the snap of your fingers, so relentless, so viral, so fast,
so unpredictable. So terminal. Just ease her pain, her last few days. No,
she does not want you to come and visit. Her disintegration, the stages
of her emaciation, her melting into her bones, is not how she wants you
to remember her. Her housekeeper Tammy and her brother, alone, will
witness her final days of dissolution. You must remember her as Nefertiti,
that princess of the Nile, that goddess Isis, Botticelli's Venus, Salome in
her dance of the seven veils. She who had simply said, "I am a woman."*

THROUGH THE TUNNEL AND OUT THE OTHER SIDE

The steering wheel feels odd. Besides the usual vibration, it pulls to the right, where a moving van is also struggling up the mountain. I do not want to go. It's like this all the time. Heading to Honolulu, the humidity, the traffic, the crowds. Kona winds. Especially during the weekend, especially on a Saturday. It's like going to work. My frustration deepens as the windy, winding road darkens, as the clouds darken above the Pali Tunnel, where it's always cold and rainy this time of year.

The Pali. The Pali cliffs, where Kamehameha the Great and his army of Hawaiian warriors pushed their enemy off the steep ledge to drop hundreds of feet to their deaths. A lot of bodies. A lot of bones. Surely, there must be a few left, naturally buried along the cliff side. Rain. The mud. The rising jungle, the banana, the wood rose and orchid. *It's raining it's pouring the old man is snoring.*

Funerals. As inevitable as this rain. Every Saturday, it seems. *Eight little, nine little, ten little Indians. Ashes ashes, we all fall down.* Pangy's gone. Good ole Pang. Good ole Pang and his turd-thick cigar (just like the Boss. Dead, too). I mean, just like that. And suddenly the shop is less one guy. Or the faculty lunchroom fills with strangers. Don't blink. Mel's probably next. Then Taku or Mango, it's a tossup. Then me or Jimmy. Take a ticket, move up the line, wait for your number. *Ten little Indians.* Up the mountain. *All fall down.* The rain. The tunnel just ahead. It's like entering the Lincoln Tunnel in a yellow taxi cab every time I return to New York. Home. The old neighborhood absent of old neighbors. Old friends. The Boss, Larry, gone. His son Butch. Michael. Jankowski (with his dope and monkey wrench). Hanscombe. Hagen the mailman.

Put on the lights, shift to second, dummy. It's all downhill from here.

Which is longer, the Pali or the Wilson Tunnel? —*What the hell is that?*

Larry's Campus
Bar & Grill

and as usual the Budweiser sign in the window is on the blink and the waterfall rises upward. I see Larry laid out on top of the bar—a huge pink walrus in a soiled apron. I pull on his gray mustache, and he says, "Don't bother me, will-ya." There is food everywhere. Two turkeys, two roast beefs, a ham, a pile of Italian sausages, a leg of lamb, mountains of cole slaw and German potato salad, another ham, dumplings, chocolate cake for every panhandler, bum, junkie, bag lady, cop, graduate student, neighborhood regular, the poor within a ten-block radius of the university. "Have a bite," says Joe, "it's on the Boss." Good ole Larry. The place is decorated with pink, green, and yellow balloons, each stenciled with Larry's likeness, eating, drinking, singing, laughing; and Larry's Caruso music careers from the juke box. Mike Fatanti, Joe, and Sully are celebrating around the stiff, tickling Larry. "Wait," says Tony. "We gotta make a positive ID." "Right," says Sully, lifting Larry's T-shirt, pointing to the middle of Larry's huge, pink paunch. There is no belly button. "That's him," says Joe. Then Mike sticks a panatella in Larry's mouth, lights it, and leads us through "Happy Birthday," "My Funny Valentine," "Que Sera Sera," and that chestnut song that Nat King Cole sings. Then we march out the door, sloshing our drinks, as we step into the Cow Pasture in the middle of Central Park, where the Hagens are shooting dice with Max the

Finger and Police Chief Reilly, with his two floozies, Uta and Renee, behind them is Father Forbes. He is lifting both pant legs showing off his argyle socks to John the Bookmaker, while Professors Trump, Bridges, and Horseshoe, sitting in wicker chairs, drunk out of their minds, politely applaud. We join them just as the Wing family arrives from the Chinese restaurant across the street. After the pork pastries, the plum wine, the Spanish rice, come the bread man, the beer man, and the steel gang from the building site, and Jankowski the janitor leading his Doberman Thor. All together now, on the count of three, we belch and let go our dragon kites and roar, "Yea, Larry! Yea, Larry! Yea, Larry!"

Then I remember and look at my watch; it is five o'clock. I keep to the right lane, take the right fork, parting from the Pali Highway, which sweeps quickly to the left before it rushes downtown. I descend into the valley of graveyards. The sun is out, the trade winds are back, and the steering wheel feels calm as I slow the sedan to 25. Good ole horse. When the vista of tombstones and flowers breaks upon me like music from both sides of the road, spreading out, it seems, for miles in each direction, like carnation farms on the side of a volcano: torch and fire ginger, birds of paradise, daisies, pink chrysanthemums, tulips, daffodils, vermillion anthuriums, gaudy sunflowers, and pots and pots of red poinsettias propped at nearly every gravesite, plot, and stone, like a wedding or graduation, splashing the landscape with shimmering colors, glistening after the rain.

O happy graveyard.

What did my young friend from Harvard say? *Hawaii is a great place to die.* Whereupon he fled the islands after a year of teaching. I wonder if he'll return; he's pretty old by now. Hahaha. I don't know why, but my spirit rises. The sky, now, a bright blue. As blue as the sea beyond the hotels and condos of Waikiki.

I reach for my sunglasses and see aloha shirts, muumuus, and parasols like pink hibiscus and yellow plumeria massed to the right of the crematorium. As a few arms, then heads rise to view a gauzy rainbow, the limousines pull up to the mortuary with the family. I watch as Pang's sister Myrtle is led by her elbows through the tinted double doors, followed by Pang's two daughters, slender as irises, and the rest of the frail family, young and old, gossamer as Japanese silk.

What a contrast to ole Pang and his barrel chest. A doctor with the thick hands of a mason. Long, simian arms. A heart surgeon, no less. Borne aloft, forward, left and right, really, on bow-legged, stumpy legs, like a Chinese junk on a rocky sea. He is standing over an open chest, smoking a cigar, his glasses foggy, telling his young assistant, "That's a pitching wedge, you *fut mondoo*. I said a nine iron! For what you went Punahou School?"

Then he takes his stance on the fairway and, with one mighty swing, he gouges the earth to the depth of the water table, sending a clod of earth fifty feet in the air. It doesn't matter what his score is, where the ball flies, or how many he loses; the point is to hit the holy crap out of the ball. "So Pangy, he go pick up the sod, like one twenty-pound ulua—you know, for fill in the hole he wen make," says Al in his eulogy, "and puts the buggah on his head, holding the corners round his big face. He says, 'How you like my bonnet?' and we crack up, Mel wen gag on his beer so hard it come out his nose like *hanabata*. Even though docta, Pangy was, you know, sometimes *lolo* in fun kine way. Was unpredicable. Pang would say, 'Unpredictable, you ignomamous.' Eva since McKinley High Schoo he correc my English, but neva use those big hyperbolic words, like Kenji, the kotonk school teacha," he says, pointing to me. "Anyways, at the next tee box, he look up at the Koolau Range, the mellow sky, and the flock of gaudy green parrots flying home other side da mountains. Then Pangy says, 'Some nice day, yuh?' So we look too. Everything is quiet. The sky is lavender and pink. True, was beautiful. And we stay quiet too. Sometime make your eyes watah and sometimes gotta wipe the nose, yuh? Pangy was like that, just outta the blue. Make us slow down. Make us see da birds. Make us hear too. 'What song that?' Mel wen ask. Pointing to the Norfock pine with his driver, like one spear, like him Kamehameha, Pang would say, 'Sharma thrush.'

"Pang was one bird specialish too.

"When Iris, his wife, was still alive (she was one kotonk too), she would tell Pangy, how many times, 'Daniel, please. Couldn't you get rid of at least half of them? Give them to your friends? They're really unsanitary, not to say noisy. My god. Especially that nasty Poki. He keeps biting the girls.' Pangy's house was like a bird house, an abiary, full of love birds, papaya birds, finches, mejiros, cardinals, parakeets, a couple of parrots, cages everywhere. And one cockatiel named Poki. One mean buggah, I tell you, even give Pang one scar on the nostril. But Iris, she give me the eye, so I said, 'How 'bout get rid of Poki then?' But he said, 'How can?' and said every time he come home from work at Moanalua Kaiser, Poki hop on his shoulder and chirp, 'Pangy! Pangy! Pangy!' And Iris could not answer. 'How can?'

"He neva did. Then after Iris wen pass away, and Poki too (Poki jes wen curl up under da food tray, li'dat, like he hiding), and the daughters went mainland, Pangy give all his birds Manoa Schoo. Was sad, but hard for take care, yuh?

"So afta work, maybe three, four times a week—for what? fifteen years?—he hang out with us single and divorced guys at Jimmy's shop for eat and drink and watch TV. An I tell you, ole Pangy could grind, jes like them sumo guys, Konishki and Akebono. And since that time, how many mo hearts he went fix? How many lives he save? Three hundred? Four hundred? One time afta work, have barbecue my place, and I wen fall down da driveway. Mel said Pang give me mout-to-mout and wen slap my chest. Afta, Pang tell me, 'Eh, Brah, gotta brush your teeth.' I say, 'Tanks, eh.' Then last month, Pangy wen save Kenji's life. . . .

"Seems that everyone, fo some reason, telling Pang, 'Tanks, eh.' That's why we all here, yuh? Fo show gratitude. Fo celebrate one special life."

So in our tribute we create an inspiring fiction, a flattering memory we can tuck in the billfold of our mind, grown thick, now, with the passing of so many contemporaries: a pleasing snapshot of a face at its best, shorn of barnacles and blemishes. But Pangy's portrait (and the Boss's, too, come to think of it) needed little touching up. You'd be hard pressed to find anyone who would talk meanly about him. Like flowers, he made breathing joyful.

I am almost at the front where Pangy's coffin is flanked by several huge wreaths propped on white tripods, the air thick with the scent of white carnations and the musk of white roses.

I think of my father as I stand before Pangy's open casket. I think of my mother. I think of the Boss.

I want to stick a panatella between the corpse's pale lips. But something is amiss. The color is wrong.

I think of mochi.

I think of flour.

I am sitting at the Charthouse bar, waiting for Willow, Pangy's daughter. I look at my watch; it is past eight, and I'm hungry. But cheery. My face hot and flushed from the vodka martini. I don't know why I'm here, why Willow wants to talk to me. I hadn't seen her in fifteen years, since she went to New York and never came back. The bar is noisy and crowded. One big, pulsing, gurgling hum, like a woolly mammoth. The big guy on my left brushes my arm and I squirm on my stool. I look at the entrance again. A bunch of loud, overweight tourists with plumeria leis lumber in, jostling each other like steer. Rolling rolling rolling rawhide. Perhaps from Texas. Ship 'em to Omaha to the slaughterhouses. Best steaks on the mainland. Like the day of my collapse: I am famished, hadn't eaten all day, hadn't drunk a thing. I push my empty glass forward and signal the bartender for another. *Howdy partner.* I wonder how many I had that night. Our table still wasn't ready. The women were waiting on chairs near the hostess stand, Mel, Taku, and Al were grumbling about construction equipment. Pang was making myth of the round we just played. I could barely hear. Finally, hoisting my drink, I wandered like a sleep walker, following the guys to our table, where Pang quickly ordered two bottles of wine. Sometime during dessert, I am lying on the floor. I am in a tranquil haze, feel no fear, no anxiety, no pain. Just a floating numbness. Just drifting, detached from the distant voices that I sometimes hear, detached from the vague shadows that appear at the edge of my vision, hovering shapes approximating familiar faces. Just detached, disconnected. Just floating, levitating on a gentle sea, nothing amiss. Just calm and peace and quiet, almost serene, suspended between wakefulness and sleep, familiar with the business of slipping away. Just peace. Just floating, when I hear my ex say, "Kenji, Kenji, Kenji!" Then I am floating in the air on a stretcher, noting my fleeting passage, at intermittent stages, past tables and chairs, through passageways, down stairs, from the restaurant to the ambulance to the hospital. Feeling cold, then freezing, then shivering from the two IV's, the cold coursing through my body, suffering from the resuscitation, resentful at the interruption. I'm in some kind of holding room. Jimmy is there. The IV needle pops from my arm and blood spurts everywhere. Jimmy runs out. Then, breakfast is crap. My ex, Christine, has sat with me through the night. Not another minute, impatient and angry at the late doctor, I check myself out, Christine upset. Couldn't I wait a little longer to hear the test results? And, what, endure lunch, too? Hahaha. So I walked out the hospital entrance, suddenly sixty years old.

"Kenji?" I turn.

She is wearing a dark blue dress with a high ruffled collar, a swath of long black hair falling across her left eye and cheek and modest breast. A large man in a black suit, his back to us, frames her like the night; her face is like the moon emerging from dark clouds. Like the line from Sappho: "Now rose the moon, full and argentine." I am reminded of Matisse's portrait of his daughter Marguerite, her pure white face, her features reduced to their pristine beauty through the fewest of brush strokes, the faintest colors. She wore no telltale jewelry; Willow was at once eight and fourteen and twenty-nine years old.

"Uncle?" she calls me, a common, local honorific suggesting family, though we are not blood-related.

"Hi, Willow," I say, sliding off my stool. I feel loose-limbed, like pudding. We hug. She smells of pikake blossoms. I step back and hold her at arm's length. "My god, you're beautiful. Haven't changed at all. Maybe a little taller. Come, they're still holding our table."

As the maitre d' leads us through the dining room to a table on the lanai that overlooks the night sea, people stare at us. I want to say, *No, she's not my daughter.*

She orders a cosmopolitan and I order another martini.

"Like something to eat?" I ask.

"No thanks. I picked on some funeral food." Hors d'oeuvre, I think.

For a moment, I imagine Willow with her hair up, and with her smooth white face, I picture her in a white kimono with cherry blossoms, a geisha dancing with a fan. "Are you still teaching?" she asks.

"That's right, I was teaching when you left for N.Y.U. Drama, acting, right? Washington Square, Greenwich Village."

"For a year anyway. I transferred to the School of Design in my sophomore year."

"So I see. Is that," I say, tilting my head, "one of your creations?"

"You noticed. I have a boutique on Madison Avenue now."

"So school, dress design, your own business, perhaps a boyfriend or two?" She smiles, an inscrutable smile, but does not blink (she hardly blinks at all). "How long have you been away?" I ask.

"Fifteen years."

"So, you became a New Yawker."

"Like you," she says with self-assurance, merely pointing out a fact.

"And you've been to Paris, Rome, Zurich, Tokyo, I imagine?"

That inscrutable smile again. Intimating the sea. She twirls the stem of her glass between her hands, her long white fingers, the long, mother-of-pearl nails reflecting her pink drink; I watch the carmine lipstick stain circle this way and that. Not a hair out of place, not a blemish on her skin, no gesture wasted, gratuitous, or false. Capturing all the light from the night around her, even the air aglow, like the moon.

"And now you're home again. Your father meant a lot to us. I'm sorry."

"I am sorry for my sister. I am sorry for my aunt. I am sorry for his many friends. But I am not sorry for myself," she says serenely, having taken possession of the table, the chairs, this lanai, the restaurant merely a backdrop, a painted set by van Gogh.

"I know you were close to Larry when you were in New York."

"The Boss?" I said, lifting my spine.

"He talked about you and Sully and Joe and Tony. And he seemed to talk more and more before he passed away. I met him when he had catered one of my client's cocktail parties, and I had him cater one of mine. We became good friends. He was like the godfather of your neighborhood, wasn't he? I never met a more generous spirit."

"He got Christine and me our first apartment. And hired me as a bartender when I was going to college. Neighbors, college kids, he helped everybody. He was also good at healing broken hearts."

"I know," Willow says, serenely.

"The Boss, in fact, reminds me of Pangy, your father." Willow turns her lovely face to the moonlit sea. "Both were big-hearted men." I study her profile. The night. The sea is sublime.

She turns to me again.

"Thanks," she says, locking me in her gaze. This muse.

"For what?"

"For showing me the obvious." This beauty who must inspire beauty. *Were I an artist!* She unlocks my gaze.

"By the way," I say with the feeling of having arrived, of being where I ought to be, feeling as placid as she, "why did you want to talk to me?" The waiter brings us another round. Willow lifts her face to him and he glows, intoxicated, temporarily inoculated against depression, grief, suffering of any sort, his tray now a silver shield, his duty, chivalry.

"Why did I want to talk to you?" she repeats my question meditatively. "Mostly because we have things in common. Besides, you're comfortable." *Yeah. Like a sofa.* "Being with family is painful right now, especially if one doesn't feel a similar sadness for my father's loss. And then there are those unspoken, petty resentments . . ." But Willow says this without rancor. "While being with old high school friends—I was with several the other evening at the Mandarin—it just felt very awkward. Like we were all trying too hard. We're all so different now. I mean, we were able to recapture, at times, the fun and funny moments we shared, recalling this or that classmate, but it was more like a parlor game of 'Do you remember?' with women who now have husbands and children and have dogs and yards and are consumed with family routines and idiosyncrasies and with relatively uninspiring jobs, pointing to futures I cannot share with them. I even felt a certain futility driving past familiar landmarks and old buildings and the places we used to haunt as teenagers. I guess geography, too, has a way of making us strangers." But Willow says all this without regret.

We are quiet for a while, hear the hum of the restaurant and the suspirations of the sea, which are hypnotic and calming and I feel at home.

"When are you heading back to New York?" I ask.

"Early tomorrow. And you? When are you going back home?"

"New York? —Hawaii is my home. Has been, I guess, for thirty years now. Maybe pretty soon I'll be a local."

She smiles and I think of quicksilver. I think of the moon. I think of white chrysanthemums. I think of Pang.

When Willow leaves ("Take good care of yourself, Uncle") it is nearly ten, and the general, mid-range reverberations of her voice dissipate, dissolve, and finally vanish with my last drink. I still haven't eaten and switch to beer, order some oyster shooters and calamari—lay the foundation for the night ahead at Pangy's favorite Korean bar in Mapunapuna. Al, Taku, Mel, and Jimmy will be waiting for me.

"Eh, where you been? You late, brah."

Joe Tsujimoto's most influential teachers were Joseph Heller, Donald Barthelme, and the Greek poet, Konstantinos Lardas—writers whose words had made an indelible impression on him during his undergraduate studies at City College of New York. Now more than forty years later he has put together a collection of his own writings, produced between various jobs and many years of teaching young people. He is perhaps best known for his teacher texts: *Teaching Poetry to Adolescents* and *Lighting Fires: How the Passionate Teacher Engages Adolescent Writers*.